Este

After everyone had left, Xavier said firmly, a lustful grin on his handsome face, "Come to me and give me a kiss, Estella."

At his suggestion, anger ran through her, but she thought of the child they were having and wrapped her arms around Xavier's neck, and kissed him.

Estella thought to herself, "*I guess I did come to him, one way or another, as he had predicted in the store, but he has married me.*" She smirked a little inwardly.

The foreplay ended with that kiss.

As usual, Xavier was in a rush, "I am sorry, I can't wait!" was his gruff explanation for his impatience.

He picked up his wife and dumped her on the bed, and then he bunched up her wedding dress around her waist...

Estella and Michael

They danced all night and had the best "date" he ever had. There was not a day that passed that Michael did not think of that night; Estella's girlish giggle, her smile, or how her body felt in his arms as they danced. Many onlookers smiled at them, their faces acknowledging the love they saw emanating from the beautiful couple on the dance floor.

He thought, "*If Xavier did not mistreat Estella, I would feel ashamed of the love I feel for her. But I just don't believe my love for her and wanting to give her a little peace and happiness is wrong. If she were my wife...*"

Memoirs
Of The
Senator's Wife

S. M. FORD

Disclaimer

IN DEDICATION

This book is dedicated to my husband — the love of my life
and my best friend. Our love is eternal.

Reviews for Memoirs of the Senator's Wife

Get ready for the ride! A delightful combination of romance, intrigue, mysticism, the occult, social consciousness and realpolitik. If any of these appeal to you, you're in for an enthralling, fascinating read. —Amazon Review

Sexy, funny and made me cry. The story is very compelling and well structured. A masterpiece. — Goodreads Review

Excellent book! I couldn't put it down! I had to know what was going to happen next!— Amazon Review

Can't wait for book two, if there is a sequel— Amazon Review

Now one of my favorite novels. Simply brilliant, an enjoyable and unforgettable read. — Amazon Review

A family saga *and* a chronicle of US history! Much much more than your average romance book. Buy it!
— Jacqueline T

Prologue

Tulsa, Oklahoma 1921

In a dream, a blue star can be seen in the darkness of space and a deep reverberating male voice announces itself, "I am Ausir. Wake up, Auset! This is your destiny."

Michelle Renee Lachapell has had the same recurring dream of a blue star and the accompanying, mysterious voice for her entire life. She awakens to the smell and sight of smoke billowing in her bedroom and is suddenly aware that her home is on fire, and she must rescue her family.

She begins coughing violently as she realizes the voice in her dream alerted her, and that her life is in danger. She rouses her sleeping husband, "Wake up! The house is on *fire!*"

She continues to shake him until he is up and awake, then picks up her youngest son, who had been sleeping between them, while her husband rushes to save their oldest boy who is sound asleep in his bedroom.

Grabbing her three-year-old, she holds him tight as she stumbles down the stairs and carries him out of the burning home. She collapses on the front lawn and waits anxiously for her husband and oldest son to join her.

In horror, she sees them exiting the flame-filled house; the flames consuming them from head to toe. She screams at them,

"Fall down!"

As they collapse on the lawn, she runs to a water pump, fills a bucket, and quickly douses both of them with water. Her young son is crying on the grass where she had carefully placed him out of the reach of the flames. She shrieks, "Oh my God!" as the flames seem to take forever to be vanquished.

Finally, she looks down and sees two smoking corpses staring grotesquely back at her. Nausea overwhelms her and vomit spews from her mouth, leaving her weak and trembling as she cries and moans in her anguish.

It is too late to save them.

She turns to see several men standing on the lawn, holding torches and staring ominously at her.

Her head spinning, Michelle Renee Lachapell succumbs to the blackness consuming her mind and passes out, collapsing next to her screaming son.

CHAPTER ONE

Estella's Childhood

1940's Texas

Two decades later, a frustrated mother was shouting at her young daughter to clean up for supper.

"Estellaaaaaa, get out of the sun! You look like a field hand and your hair is a mess! I told you a million times not to go swimming in the lake when the sun is high — and to always comb your hair back in a bun when you swim, so it does not get so frizzy. Get washed up and ready for dinner before your father gets home!"

Mama Renee waved her finger angrily at her daughter, raking her other hand through her curly dark reddish-brown hair.

"Yes, Mama," Estella stated coolly, wincing as she tugged harshly at her unruly locks.

Her mom was irritated, "It's always 'Yes, Mama!' but you still do whatever you please, and you say it with such a straight face. You should run for office."

Her daughter commented, "Yeah, then I could make pulling hair by mommies illegal!"

Mama chuckled, "Well, for now, I still have veto power,

young lady!"

She was always dreaming big things for her daughter, even though this was the 1940's in Texas and they were poor. So, the possibility of her dream becoming a reality for Estella was close to nil.

Mama's moods were like quicksilver, constantly changing. Estella's poker face was a learned behavior to cope with her mom's emotional swings. With Renee, one never knew if she was about to hug you or hit you. So, early on in life, Estella had adjusted herself to be agreeable at all times.

"Mama, are we going to be attacked like the people in Pearl Harbor? I'm afraid." Pearl Harbor had recently been attacked by the Japanese, and many were afraid and ready to go to war.

"Don't be afraid. I believe we will win this war and there won't be any attacks on the mainland," said Mama Renee, giving her daughter a reassuring hug. Mama Renee had premonitions that came true but, although the visions, dreams, and feelings that she received were accurate, not all important outcomes were shown to her.

Tragically, Estella's father did not make it safely home for dinner that day. Estella was back downstairs in thirty minutes, dressed and coifed, just in time to hear a knock at the door. The local sheriff explained that her father had died instantly when a drunk driver had run him off the road.

Renee became hysterical, more afraid of what would become of her and her daughter than of the actual death of her abusive husband.

Estella cried for months because even though he was abusive to her mom, as his only child, she had been a daddy's girl and was treated well by her father. Although she was happy that her mom

11

was now free from his abuse, the pain in her heart from missing her father and their quiet talks while fishing by the pond was unbearable. When he was alive, she would sometimes think that her mom should divorce him, but then she would pray that her mom would stay in the marriage so she could keep her daddy full time. This inner conflict made eleven-year-old Estella feel selfish.

There was only one girl, Sadie, that Estella was friends with from school whose parents were divorced. Divorce were extremely rare. At first the divorced dad spent time with her but then he moved away, remarried, had a new baby son and rarely saw her. Sadie's divorced mom had to work two menial jobs because her ex-husband was paying very little in alimony and child support — sometimes none at all. Due to not having a man around Sadie's broken home to protect it, they were seen as easy prey during those tough economic times and were even robbed a few times in their relatively safe town.

Richard Myrtle had been behind on the mortgage of their small farm, and the only field hand that worked there had not been paid in weeks. Suffice it to say, the Myrtles lost the family farm and had no relatives to live with. Mama had explained to Estella that she had grown up an orphan from Louisiana.

Richard's sole relative was an estranged brother, Jim, in upstate New York. He did not want anything to do with his poor family members since he had graduated from college and was now a teaching assistant at a prestigious university.

However, Renee was exceptionally beautiful, and the few times that she had met Estella's Uncle Jim he had appeared to be smitten by her beauty, charm, and grace.

Renee was 5'3," petite yet curvy, and wore her hair long, dark brown, and flat-ironed straight. There was a pale gold tint to her skin that gave her a sun-kissed glow at all times. Mama's golden-brown eyes had an exotic slant.

Many people in town could never understand why such an attractive and cultured woman as Renee Deneuve would end up married to Richard Myrtle, a poor dirt farmer from the backwoods.

Her husband was an average-looking man at best, with golden-brown hair, a short stature, and silver-grey eyes. He was decidedly rough around the edges.

But the fact that he spoke his mind in plain English had made Richard charming in a down-home way. He had gained some wealth several years before the Great Depression, even opening a small local bank, but had lost almost everything due to the stock market crash, along with the Dust Bowl. All he had left was the small Texas farm that had been in his family for generations.

When he lost his wealth, everyone thought Renee would leave Richard. But, as a religious woman, she had stayed in her marriage and had a daughter.

Uncle Jim was Richard's opposite; he was tall, handsome, and appeared cultured. He tried to distance himself from his family, and rarely returned home. But, to his credit, he came home for his brother's funeral.

Renee spent the last money that she had buying new dresses, hairdos, and groceries for Uncle Jim's dinner. Her reasoning was practical, "If Uncle Jim is going to take us back to upstate New York with him, we have to look the part!"

Estella was concerned, "But what if he doesn't take us back with him?" she stated sadly, concerned about her mama's small gamble that was all the money they had.

Renee suggested Plan B, "Well, the worst-case scenario is I

get a job waitressing or as a maid or laundress. Let's not worry about that. Let's think positively and pray," said Mama with a bright smile.

Estella bit her bottom lip when she was worried, and she was worried now. She knew her mother would not last three days as a waitress, maid, or laundress, so she was on her best behavior when Uncle Jim came into town.

At noon, Renee took Estella upstairs to the attic. There was a small, stained-glass skylight placed just precisely so that the noonday sun showed through. She pulled out her Bible and together they prayed that Uncle Jim would love her and help the two of them survive financially.

They read the Song of Solomon and Mama wrote Uncle Jim's name on a brown piece of paper next to her own with the word, "love" over his name, placing the paper into the Bible passage they had just read together.

She also wrote the same words on a mirror. She told Estella that her mother had taught her how to pray and manifest, and that this knowledge had been passed down through the generations.

Uncle Jim fell madly in love with the "heartbroken" Renee He was a sucker for women in distress. He packed Renee and her daughter up and took them back to upstate New York with him.

He was now working on his Ph.D. and had hopes of becoming a tenured professor. When that plan fell through, the resourceful mother decided it was best to marry another man who had a better chance of success.

Mama Renee was moody, beautiful, and practical; she did what was in her family's best interest to survive. No one could fault her for her ruthlessness when it came to marital relationships.

the counter along with Scott, Xavier's archenemy, all laughed.

This time, it was Xavier who was embarrassed. He was not used to being turned down and so quickly dismissed — not to mention being publicly embarrassed.

Estella thought that Xavier was accustomed to women falling at his feet and jumping at the chance to be alone with him. Despite her lack of financial wealth, she had been raised a little bit better than to accept an intimate study date with a man she didn't really know, no matter who he may have been.

CHAPTER THREE

The Gala

The Spring Ball was here, and Estella had finally blossomed into the Deneuve family beauty, just in time for the big dance. With a little help from Mama Renee, who had been mixing up for her the family "secret diet" drink, Estella had slimmed down from a pleasantly, plump cuteness into a curvy, classic beauty.

She was now a younger version of her stunningly attractive Mama. The previous year, Estella had attended the ball with her mother, who had been a chaperone, but this time it was special since she was attending as a student of the university and *with a date.*

Her mother had arranged for her to go with Josh Van Hoffen, the son of another faculty member, who was also a student attending the university and eighteen months older than her.

She had known Josh for the last nine years — they had even played games with each other growing up on campus together. She knew that he had always liked her. But, since she and Josh were both painfully shy, they never would have taken their friendship to the next level if it had not been for Mama arranging this date.

Although not wealthy, Josh's family was adequately well-off, and his father did not really have to work. Mama thought that

Josh would be a good and obtainable catch for her daughter, as he was already a family friend.

Estella wasn't really attracted to Josh's wide and short frame, but since she was only 5'3" — the same height as her mother— and curvy, she reasoned correctly that she and Josh would not look out of place together.

Mama asked her, "Are you okay going to the dance with Josh?"

Estella reasoned it out, "Well, he's stubby cute and we grew up together, so I guess we can handle one dance!" She laughed.

That evening, she wore a stunning, corseted white gown that her mother had selected with silver and rhinestone beading, just unique enough to stand out from the crowd; but not so flamboyant as to be gaudy or distasteful. Mama had excellent taste and was also an accomplished seamstress: not really good enough to make a living from it, but good enough to dress up a moderately-priced dress and make it look like an expensive and original designer piece.

While she was teaching her daughter how to spruce up her dress, Mama related that her grandmother had owned a dress boutique and had designed patterns for all of the most fashionable ladies of her time. She also stated proudly that all of the women in her family were excellent in pattern-making. She wished she had paid more attention to her dressmaking classes, which could have been a good side business for her.

Mama added: "the first mathematicians were seamstresses because to make a pattern and sew in three dimensions took mathematical skills." She elaborated on her family history, which she very rarely did, sharing that her grandfather had been a ship's captain who took his wife, the dressmaker, sailing.

In fact, her great-grandma had been told by her husband and others that she was a better navigator than he was and better than any other professional sailor they had ever met, for that matter.

On one occasion, they had been lost at sea. Her mother's grandma had guided them all safely to shore when no one else could, using the unique mathematical skills that had helped her become a popular pattern and dressmaker.

Estella had always bemoaned math class and asked her mother if she had been adopted since Mama had been a math major. Renee laughed and said she had learned geometry from making patterns with her grandmother in her dressmaker's boutique and that it helped her see mathematics in a unique way that her colleagues could not comprehend.

Many of her colleagues in the math department were in awe of her ability and probably a little jealous too. Renee also admitted that she had hated sewing as much as Estella, never becoming proficient enough to make dresses from scratch, but she was grateful that it honed her mathematical skills in a unique way since math was her major. Renee was a firm believer in individualized learning, telling her daughter that "not everyone can learn from books; some have a talent for a subject and don't know it because they are not taught in the way that would suit them in learning to master the subject."

So, with Estella's hatred of both geometry from books and sewing, Renee steered her daughter into her strengths of business and law.

In the meantime, it was time to dance!

When Josh and Estella made their appearance at the ball, even Xavier's girlfriend, Debra Van Ardwick, commented, "That's a lovely gown, Estella. I would love to know where you bought it!" Josh rolled his eyes while Estella blushed.

Renee had worked her magic on her daughter. She had highlighted her hair with dark gold against the backdrop of her dark reddish-brown hair so that her hair accented her cognac-colored eyes. The hairdressing cremes and treatments Mama had made her use religiously each week had paid off, giving Estella very thick, almost waist-length hair. So, although not fashionable as a "pageboy look" – which was the style of the day – Estella's hair was strikingly luscious. Renee laughed and said, "Rapunzel, let down your hair! Men are attracted to thick, long hair, not realizing it is a sign of health and fertility. They have no idea!"

Renee had sprayed her family's secret perfume *Oudh de Au* on Estella, which always attracted eligible men to the ladies of her family.

Xavier stared at Estella the entire night with those steely, cold blue eyes of his that succeeded in unnerving her.

Initially, she had thought that Xavier's piercing blue eyes were beautiful and dreamy. But now they just gave her chills of fright instead of chills of fascination. So, she just ignored Xavier's rude stare and continued to have a fabulous time with Josh.

The following night, Josh took Estella on a date to a Greek campus party as he was pledging the fraternity. She wore a pretty and conservative pink three-quarter length silk, full-skirted dress adorned with her mother's pink pearls.

Josh seemed more nervous than usual. Estella attributed to his nervousness to the pledge process.

When they arrived, the sorority sisters of Gamma Alpha were also in attendance. They were members of the premier sorority on campus and the sister organization to Gamma Omega, the premier fraternity on campus.

Aftermath

When Estella arrived home, her mother was anxiously waiting up for her. It was four in the morning.

When Renee saw her daughter in a compromised condition, with bruise marks on her arms and legs, a tattered dress and smeared makeup, she immediately guessed what had happened to her.

Mother and daughter sat and cried for over an hour, and then Renee asked, "Who hurt you?"

Estella said nothing.

Renee asked her again. "Was it Xavier or Josh or someone else who hurt you?" Her mother could not bring herself to say anything more than the word "hurt."

Estella whispered meekly, "No, Mama. It was not Josh... it was Xavier who raped me."

As she used the descriptive word of her assault, Mama began to cry uncontrollably.

"Where was Josh all that time?" Mama cried.

Estella just shook her head, "Drunk? Passed out? I don't know," she said.

"Tell me the whole story from beginning to end. Had you met

Xavier previously…and when?"

Mama continued crying. Then, Mama kept repeating over and over, "It was not supposed to turn out like this."

After Estella finished telling Mama her story, she asked her: "Should we go to the police?"

Renee's reaction was swift, "No, child. You did nothing wrong. But they will blame you because we are poor and they are rich. We will lose our jobs, your education, and your reputation if you tell anyone. All we can do is pray that Xavier does not brag about his conquest and that you are not pregnant or sick. Don't speak to Josh again, other than to say hello and goodbye."

Mama spoke tearfully and frankly, revealing the devastation she felt at that moment.

"Believe me, Xavier will suffer horribly in the end for what he has done to you, I promise!" Mama vowed.

Estella stared at her mom blankly for a while; dazed, hurt, and confused, then went to bed. When she awoke, she still could not believe what had happened to her and did her best to pretend that she was fine. But she would not be fine until many decades later.

Renee offered to find Estella a counselor, but she was not ready to talk.

For the first few weeks, Renee and Estella pretended that nothing had happened and told no one, not even Renee's stepfather, Nick.

This is, until Estella realized that she was pregnant.

Renee took charge. "We will have to put the baby up for adoption. Before you begin to show, you will go away for a little while, and then come back to school. I cannot stand the idea of you going to one of those doctors and bleeding to death in some

CHAPTER FIVE

Xavier's Reverse Courtship

Six weeks following the bathroom incident, Xavier Cyrus began to stalk Estella. Everywhere she went for about a week, he would show up.

She would make sure that she was never alone with him.

Instead of the cold stare, he would watch her with a fake, wistful look as if to say, "I am so sorry, let's start over."

Finally, Xavier was able to catch Estella alone.

Her second job was behind the counter at the student store. Xavier cleverly waited until everyone had left the establishment and approached her with his merchandise, pointedly stating, "I need to talk to you! Do you have a moment?"

Estella answered him quickly and firmly, "Do not speak to me; do not even look at me. Just take your purchases and go!" She mimicked one of his icy stares.

"I know that I hurt you, and I am so sorry. I will do anything to make it up to you. What can I do?"

Xavier looked at her with a fake puppy dog expression, eyes now warm and full of feigned sadness. Estella was sure he had melted the heart of many a naïve sorority girl or debutante with that pitiful look on his face, which was one hundred miles away from the hard, cold stare that she was sure was his true expression. He reminded her of a beautiful, calculating Venus flytrap.

"Well, this fly was smarter than to fall for his silly antics," Estella thought to herself. With disdain in her voice, she asked him, "Does the Monster Committee give all of you a manual on how to react to the women you hurt? That is basically the same thing that Josh said to me. You are all disgraceful. The only thing that you can do for me, madman, is to leave me alone."

Estella desperately wanted to walk out, but her shift relief had not reported yet, and she could not afford to get fired for leaving the register unattended. She really didn't think that Xavier would harm her, with students and faculty walking right outside the open double doors of the store.

But of course, Estella's unwavering statements and attitude angered him. Xavier didn't like being called out on his insane behavior. His face morphed into a ruddy mask of anger as he spewed his venom, "I can make your *future* and your family's lives very difficult, so do not think that you can address me however you please. I am trying to be nice to you and treat you like a person."

Estella corrected him, "Oh, I did not realize that I wasn't a person," she retorted, her voice full of bitterness and sarcasm.

"You know what I mean, Estella. I did not have to come to you and apologize at all, it's not like you can affect my life in any measurable way," seethed Xavier, his face now bright red with anger.

She tried to reason with him, "Obviously you want something from me, Xavier, or you would not be speaking to me. You are not apologizing to me out of the goodness of your heart. What is it that you want? You are right; I can't do anything to you, and I don't have anything that you have not already had. So why are you here?"

"I need you, Estella. I think about you all day and all night. I will give you whatever you want!"

He looked into her eyes as if trying to hypnotize her into agreeing with his bargain.

She softened her eyes and made them tear up and said in a pleading manner, "Please just leave me alone!" At that moment, Estella was thinking to herself *two can play at the fake face game!*

She did not want him to further harm her or her family; so, she felt it made more sense to come across as pitiful instead of sarcastic.

Xavier was relentless, "I can't leave you alone. Trust me, it isn't for lack of trying. I need you, and you will come to me one way or another. And no, I am not going to marry you!" He stated flatly.

Estella saw right through him, "I guess the devil does not pity anyone but himself!" She pointed out the flaw in his claims of "commitment" to her,

"I have noticed you with a brigade of women these last few weeks; can't you be satisfied with them?" she argued. That struck a nerve.

"Don't taunt me. I said what I came to say, now it is up to you to decide. I expect your answer by this time tomorrow!"

At that, Xavier turned and stormed out of the store, leaving Estella with a bemused look on her face.

like this!' on the night Xavier raped me. I thought it odd that the first name you asked about was Xavier's and said that he had 'hurt' me. Xavier *raped* me, mother!" Each time Estella said the word "rape," she saw her mother cringe in pain. But she was so angry, she felt nothing for Renee but disgust.

Her mom tried to explain. "No, I thought it would be a better marriage for you with Xavier than with Josh. Josh is only capable of becoming a professor or having a similar secondary position. Xavier's father is a mayor and almost a governor, and Xavier has the charisma to go to higher office himself one day. He will have political power and, as his wife, you will have power also."

Mama Renee, tears streaming down her face further explained, "This power also could help you in your community service work. Plus, you were attracted to Xavier, so I was trying to give your relationship a little push in the right direction. I never thought he would attack you, and the prayer did not make him attack you — it is already in his nature, he would have attacked you without the prayer."

"Don't you always tell me to be careful when requesting a specific outcome? 'Be careful what you pray for,' you always said! So, why weren't you careful with me? Why didn't you tell me what you were doing so I could make my own choices or, at the very least, watch my back, Mother? The problem is you didn't care as long as you got what you wanted. I am only a pawn to you."

Estella's anger suddenly turned cold. She felt emotionally dead inside and suddenly realized that she had no one watching over her.

She had never felt so hurt, alone, and defeated than she did at that moment. Mama was all that she had in the world. She was not just Estella's *best* friend, but now that Josh had betrayed her, she was her *only* friend. Mama had been her sole confidant, provider, and protector, and if Estella could not trust her, there was no one she could trust. She was now completely alone in this horrible world, except for God. Estella voiced that sentiment directly to her mother's face. "When my father and mother forsake me, I have God."

Renee tried to emotionally hold on to her daughter. "Please don't feel that way, my precious child. I love you more than myself; more than anything, or anyone. If I could go back in time and save you, I would. If I could have taken your pain onto myself, I would. I took a risk that I should not have, and I would undo it if I could. I was thinking of your security and happiness, as well as the future of our family. Someday, you will try to make social change with your volunteering, but if Xavier does marry you, you will be able to make a real impact. Do you remember the story of Esther from the Bible?"

Estella had lost respect for anything Renee had to say at that point. "I don't believe your contention that 'the ends justify the means'… at least to your way of thinking. If Xavier marries me and I have the power that you crave, you would put me in harm's way again."

It was an epiphany for Estella. She saw Mama clearly for the first time, and at that moment she was afraid of her; she no longer had parental feelings for the woman she had always called mother. Then and there, she decided to stop calling her Mama, only Renee.

Renee lashed out at her daughter, "You crave power too, you just don't know it yet. I would take any harm instead of you if I

The Priest

The university parish priest, Father Arden, had also been Xavier's priest for the last one and half years that he had been in attendance at the school. Although he did not attend church regularly, Xavier respected the good Father enough to meet with him. When summoned by Father Arden, he showed up dressed in a suit and tie.

"So, Father, what can I do for you?" Xavier said with his innocently contrived choir boy smile.

The priest was all business, "Son, I need two hours of your time. Can you give that to me?"

"Yes, Father. What can I do for you?" Xavier asked with a puzzled expression.

Father Arden got right to the point, "I am not going to beat around the bush. It appears that you have raped and impregnated an innocent parishioner of mine and you will have to marry her!"

As he delivered his ultimatum to Xavier, he was standing in front of his locked office door. There would be no easy escape for the young man. Father Arden was putting his position on the line to intervene on Estella's behalf.

Xavier could easily complain to his father and have the priest removed from his position at the university, even though that would be a difficult and scandalous approach to his problem. After all, Father Arden was not a Cardinal. But as a respected priest, his steadfast character reference of Estella and assessment of the case could turn public opinion against Xavier, no matter how he and his friends would try to disparage Estella if it came to that.

"Preg...pregnant? How do I know that it is mine?" Xavier stuttered coughing and turning beet red.

"Son, I have known Estella Myrtle since she was twelve years of age, and a more upstanding girl and family I have not met. You are an upstanding man, and I know that you will do the right thing by her and your child, and I am sure God will also put this mishap behind you."

For emphasis, Father Arden placed his arm around Xavier's shoulder and looked him in the eye firmly, trying to force an affirmative answer from him. But Xavier tried to stall him. "I need to think Father. I will meet with you tomorrow." Then, he turned and began swiftly walking towards the door. Father Arden blocked him.

"There is nothing to think about, Xavier. I can perform the ceremony right now, or I could go to the police and the school chancellor right now with the weight of my word and the power of the Church behind me."

Xavier tried to use logic to squirm out of it, "Wait! Don't you need blood tests and a license?"

The young man was now sweating and turning pale. This situation was spinning out of control on him. What had been unexpected when he had first entered the office was now feeling like a noose tightening around his neck.

His mind was racing. *Why was Father Arden intervening to*

this degree on behalf of a penniless girl with no connections? The priest was closing the deal. "I have friends downtown and have taken care of all of that. Also, you can call this divine intervention," Father Arden said as if he was reading Xavier's thoughts.

No more, Mr. Nice Guy. Xavier was getting desperate. "Step out of my way! I will not be marrying anyone until I think about this further," said a suddenly defiant Xavier on his way to the door.

Father Arden injected some common sense into the mix, "Have it your way, but you think about how difficult your *future* will be when you are expelled and have a police record. Isn't your father up for re-election?"

"You are bluffing," Xavier snarled as he tried to push his way through to the door.

Father Arden shot back, "Are you going to take that chance? Maybe this situation is more than just your hormones at work, son. Is it possible that you are very drawn to Estella because she is supposed to help you? Your father did not win the gubernatorial election in Texas because he was originally from New York, and in a statewide election outside of Dallas, voters saw your family as rich carpetbaggers.

"Estella was born and raised in Texas to poor Texas farmers whose ancestors fought at the Alamo. As your wife, she will have a wide appeal for a statewide election, and she will also be able to help you in a national election in bringing in more votes from the South. You will get the northern votes, being originally from New York, and Estella will help you with the southern states. It might be destiny, Xavier. Don't destroy the bright future I see for Estella and you, son." Father Arden stated this firmly, squeezing Xavier's arm one more time.

Xavier had been a passionate believer in destiny due to his high opinion of himself. He had always seen himself as God's chosen superior creation and that the world revolved around him. So, Father Arden was tapping into his mindset. Maybe the priest was right about him being "led" to Estella. It would explain his odd reaction to her. Xavier had never felt so strongly for anyone in his entire life, but he was conflicted. He was drawn to her, true. But, on the other hand, his vanity repelled him from her as well. His insatiable pride, when combined with his already unstable personality, created a violent reaction within him.

He had always envisioned marrying Debra Van Ardwick, the New York society debutante whom he had known all his life. It was not just because of the continuous harassment of his mother that he should pursue Debra, but it was also because of his vanity to have the most sought-after heiress in New York. Even though he wasn't physically attracted to Debra, it didn't matter because when she was on his arm, he was thought of as old New York money — at least that was his perception.

Debra's family belonged to the first Dutch land barons of New York, and they were also related to old Aristocratic European money as well. She had been a debutante in New York, Amsterdam, and England, which everyone thought was a little bit excessive.

During Debra's season in England, she had been proposed to by the Earl of Chadwick and could have been a countess but had turned him down and returned to college claiming her undying love for Xavier.

The Cyrus money had come from Texas oil money just two generations ago when Cyrus's poor grandfather had left New York in search of oil field riches back in the late 1870's.

Now, in Father Arden's office, Xavier mulled over Debra versus Estella and the situation that he was in for about an hour since the priest would not let him leave.

Xavier's logic told him that Father Arden was probably bluffing.

However, as time elapsed, the growing look of angry Papa on Father Arden's face convinced Xavier that the priest would go down in flames to protect "Estella the Good."

It was time for the young man to face the facts.

"Fine," Xavier finally decided with a look of resignation. Even though "Estella the Good" was angry with him, he still trusted her more than fake Debra who had a mean streak.

His trust and desire for Estella were more important to him than the fleeting feeling of pride he always felt when he walked into a high society banquet or ball with Debra. Honestly, at the end of the day, did he really want to lay in a sexless bed with Debra — the "rattlesnake' — every night?

Once Xavier had conceded, Father Arden moved swiftly, calling his assistant on the intercom. "There is no time like the present! Send Estella and her mother in please, Sister Rebecca."

A few minutes later, Estella, her mother and Sister Rebecca entered, and the ceremony began.

Estella took off the long coat that had hidden her three-quarter length antique white lace wedding gown; it had belonged to her grandmother and had an early 1900's cut.

The marriage documents were signed and everyone, except Xavier and Estella, left relieved. During the ceremony, all that Estella could think about was the archaic "Marry Your Rapist" laws. The laws that most countries still have, if not written then by tradition, even the United States, that Margaret had referenced in their last session. *"How could I have let Father Arden and my mother convince me to marry this evil smiling monster rapist, Xavier, even for the sake of my child? These laws have to be changed. Women and girls have to be given better choices so that this insane option of marrying a rapist is not needed and banned."* She vowed to work to change the laws and create real opportunities and protections for her daughter's generation. If Xavier's family connections could provide additional means to reach these goals, maybe there was a reason she had to go through this horror.

Father Arden was in full planning mode, "I have also taken the liberty of securing an apartment in the dorm for married couples, and we will escort you there!"

When they all arrived at the dorm in the priest's town car, it displayed a *Just Married!* sign on the back. Everyone in the dorm that day was there to throw rice on the couple due to Father Arden alerting the resident dorm assistant who had been called to surprise the happy couple. He had hastily organized a quick welcome from the other married residents.

"There is no going back now," a distraught Xavier thought to himself.

The dorm apartments came furnished and, unlike his dorm room at the Gamma Omega house, Xavier and Estella had a private bath and kitchen.

Xavier continued to mentally rationalize his new future, "Look on the bright side, it could be destiny!" as Father Arden had pointed out. Also, he would finally get some relief from the blue balls he had been experiencing ever since the morning after the bathroom incident. Since that night, he unsuccessfully tried to be with at least ten different women, but all he could do was think of Estella.

This just wasn't natural.

The unhappy couple had some wedding cake and champagne with their guests in their dorm apartment and accepted the surprised congratulations of their well-wishers, pretending everything was normal.

One catty wife named Karen, who was a close family friend of Debra's and married to an assistant professor named Roger, approached Xavier. Karen asked, smiling sarcastically, "I didn't even know the two of you were dating. Did you invite Josh and Debra over for some cake too?"

Xavier was up to the verbal joust, "Actually, it was love at first sight. I could not live without the beautiful, *sweet* Estella, and, could not wait to marry her since I don't believe in long engagements."

Then, he jabbed Karen, "How long were you dating Roger before you were wed?" Xavier smiled. Before the now flustered Karen could answer, the quick-witted Xavier bopped her again, by kissing Estella on the cheek while giving Karen a dressing down for dating Roger for nine years until he finally proposed.

Xavier ignored the woman's impertinent question regarding Debra and Josh.

Estella was proud that her husband had actually defended her marriage to him, and his verbal protection warmed her to him a little. She thought, "*Uh-oh. Is this the feeling of abuser-love starting?*"

Embarrassed by the veiled insult, the catty wife rejoined with "Well congratulations again; I hope you are blessed with many children very soon...I'm sure." She was "hinting" about the possibility of Xavier and Estella's shotgun wedding. Back came Xavier.

"And may you have your first child soon, as well!" Xavier smiled evilly. He was cruelly referring to the fact that Karen had no children, although she had been married for six years and was over forty years of age. It was a public secret that they wanted many children, and their parents had been pressuring the infertile couple for grandchildren.

Xavier could be mean, especially when provoked.

At that point, Karen turned an ashen blue and had nothing more to say.

Father Arden was watching Xavier closely during their impromptu reception. When all the guests had left the dorm room, the observant priest squeezed Xavier's arm once more and whispered, "Treat Estella with kindness and respect. I will be calling her in the morning to confirm that she fares well. Start your relationship afresh and court her gently."

After everyone had left, Xavier said firmly, a lustful grin on his handsome face, "Come to me and give me a kiss, Estella."

At his suggestion, anger ran through her, but she thought of the child they were having and wrapped her arms around Xavier's neck, and kissed him.

Estella thought to herself, *"I guess I did come to him, one way or another, as he had predicted in the store, but he has married me!"* She smirked a little inwardly.

The foreplay ended with that kiss.

As usual, Xavier was in a rush, "I am sorry, I can't wait!" was his gruff explanation for his impatience.

He picked up his wife and dumped her on the bed, then bunched up her wedding dress around her waist and thrust forcefully inside of her unprepared body.

He was gentler than he had been in the bathroom, but it was still a horrible and painful experience for her.

Thankfully, it was over quickly.

Xavier collapsed on top of Estella, moaning, and sweating. He then dozed off. While she was trying to roll him off of her, he awoke and began to undress his wife completely.

"I still haven't seen all of you naked. Would you mind getting up and turning around completely for me?"

Xavier was always so polite as long as people did as they were told.

Estella got up and let him inspect her.

She wanted to say, "Would you like me to open my mouth so you can look at my teeth also?" but decided to bite her tongue.

She had to find a way to let go of this bitterness that she felt for him because it would not do her — or her child — any good to continue to fight with him, But, on the other hand, she didn't want to be his slave either.

Xavier pulled Estella back down on the bed and began to kiss her all over, which she actually found quite pleasant.

Then, she felt his tongue between her legs. She had never felt anything like it before! As much as she hated Xavier, Estella couldn't suppress the flames of pleasure that began to shoot through her entire body. Then, his tongue wound its way deep inside of her body. She thought to herself, *"Can a human tongue really be that long?"*

She let out a small gasp at the unexpected pleasure and heard Xavier's deep chuckle as he realized what his wife was experiencing for the first time.

The vibration of his laughter, while his tongue was inside of her, caused the pleasurable feeling to intensify.

Estella tried to wiggle away, ashamed of what the man she hated made her feel, but he held Estella's hips firmly to his face. He tickled a place with his tongue that she had never known was within her and she exploded, moaning like an animal until she fell asleep.

Estella awoke a few minutes later to Xavier pumping inside of her, watching his wife climax had excited him again. He thrust his tongue into her mouth as he groaned his release. She tasted herself on his lips and could not help but find her own release once again.

They made lust all night.

Estella dared not think of it as love because she still did not love him and could not forgive or forget his previous abuse. But she had to make do for now, after all, there was their child's future to think of, or as Renee would say: "It is what it is."

CHAPTER EIGHT

The New Couple

The very next morning, Estella received a call from Renee and Father Arden. She quickly reassured them that all was well.

Xavier received a call from his parents who kept him on the phone for a few hours in a full-blown argument over his new wife and his marriage to her.

From what Estella had gathered from Xavier, the Cyrus's were flying down the last weekend of the month to meet her and to further berate their son.

*****

Debra Van Ardwick paid a visit without calling. Estella was expecting Mama when she answered the door, but instead, she was greeted by "Smiling Monster" Debra.

And she was literally smiling a fake smile with a champagne bottle in hand adorned with a ribbon wrapped around the top. "I hear congratulations are in order. So, where is the other half of the happy couple?"

Debra queried. Estella was perfunctory, "Xavier is out taking care of his business." And she commented to herself, "*And you should mind your own business too, Debra!*" Yet, she remained gracious to her archenemy. "Thank you for the gift!"

Estella took the bottle of champagne and thought to herself, "*I won't ever be drinking this because it is probably poison!*" She laughed inwardly.

"Do you mind if I come in?" Debra pointedly asked as she tried to press her way through the door.

Estella demurred, "I was just on my way out; maybe some other time. I will let Xavier know that you stopped by. Thanks again!" she said, attempting to close the door.

"I really would like to speak to you *now!*" said Debra, in a firm, angry voice.

"Let's plan for another time, give me a call, and we will do lunch," Estella said sarcastically.

"I will speak to you through this door if I have to!" Debra insisted, pressing the issue further with a raised voice.

"You do whatever it is you have to do Debra, but you will respect my time and my space. Why don't you keep your dignity and just leave? Also, show the class that you claim to have and call first before just stopping by. This is my home, and we do not have the type of relationship in which you can just stop by unannounced and demand entrance! Now, I suggest that you step back before this door crushes your foot and one of those new designer shoes you have on," Estella stated flatly as she aggressively attempted to close the door.

Debra moved her foot from the door jamb just in time. The monster was no longer smiling as she took Estella's advice and walked off in a huff.

Estella decided in her pregnant state that she wasn't going to let 5'11", big-boned angry Debra into her apartment while she was alone.

Xavier avoided Debra for several days. He finally wrote her a letter saying that it was best they did not see each other for a while. He wrote that he still cared for her as a friend but that their relationship would not have worked out. After all the time they spent together, it had never really blossomed into an exclusive relationship, that their relationship had always been more of a friendship than a fiery romance.

Estella personally thought that it was a little cowardly of Xavier not to meet with Debra in person. Then again, since they both belonged to the Smiling Monster Committee, she fully understood what treachery Debra was potentially planning to perpetrate on Xavier had he met her in person as retaliation for jilting her.

It was then Estella realized that that was the reason that Xavier had finally relented and married her. He had not trusted Debra for the same reasons that Estella had not trusted him. Xavier knew innately that Estella was not a ruthless backstabber out for her own self-interest, so he never had to constantly watch what he did or said around her. He had not had anyone like Estella in his life before, that he could truly relax around and trust that what he said would not be used against him at a later date. Debra was always a threat to him in that way.

Since his mother had not offered to give him his grandmother's ring as would have been the family tradition, Xavier took Estella ring shopping and on a honeymoon in Manhattan. They stayed at the Marlton Plaza Hotel, ate at the Golden Tea Room, saw *Ginian's Rainbow* on Broadway, and shopped on Fifth Avenue and the Diamond District.

He demonstrated through the weekend itinerary that he had planned that he was not very original. Xavier simply enjoyed watching his wife enjoy those famous New York experiences for the first time.

Estella had never been able to afford designer label clothes before, and it was fun for her to indulge herself at the exclusive "invitation-only" boutiques where Xavier had arranged fittings for her.

He presented his wife with a beautiful two carat, emerald-cut, diamond ring in a Victorian setting from the world-renowned jeweler Biphanti along with a carriage ride around Central Park in the romantic evening dusk. The New York City skyline was magnificent at night, but never more stunning to Estella Cyrus than on her romantic carriage ride with her new husband.

The last weekend of the month came too soon for the newly-weds. Xavier and Estella were actually getting along well, much better than either of them had expected. He complimented her home-cooked meals and homemaking skills. but at the same time, he encouraged his wife to go back to school when the semester started again.

Xavier said that they could either purchase the house they had found near campus, or his father may be able to arrange one of the vacant faculty houses for them. Besides, he would hire a maid to help Estella around the house and take care of the baby while she was in class. Estella no longer had to work, of course, and Xavier promised that he would see what could be done about getting Renee a better job at the university so that she would not have to work long hours.

He also assured her that when he received his trust fund at the age of 25, Renee could quit working and he would hire a nurse to care for Estella's stepfather.

Estella and Xavier made love every night and every morning. Just as Margret predicted, she began to love Xavier over their 23 days of marriage, which to Estella, was both sick and shocking considering all that he had put her through.

But, the combination of fabulous lovemaking, his charm, and the promises to help Renee had made Estella less fretful and caused her to forgive him and concentrate on their happy future with their upcoming baby.

But then, his parents came into town as promised for the weekend…and all hell broke loose.

CHAPTER NINE

The Cyrus Parents

If Estella had thought that Xavier was the newly elected President of the Smiling Monster Committee, then his parents were founding members and trustees.

Xavier thought it best if the two of them met at his mother's favorite restaurant in town and he made arrangements with his parents to do so.

However, an early knock on the door announced his parent's arrival ahead of schedule. His father, Xavier Sr., greeted him coldly, "Hello, son. We arrived early and thought to stop by here first. I hope that it is no inconvenience."

Despite his tone, Xavier responded graciously, "Mother and Father, may I introduce my new wife, Estella Cyrus."

His wife smiled nervously, as Xavier continued the introductions, "Estella, meet my parents, Mr. Xavier Cyrus Sr. and Mrs. Catherine Van Horne-Cyrus."

Their greeting to Estella seemed sincere: "How do you do?"

"How do you do?" she replied.

It was all very formal, cold, and odd to Estella, whose family had a relaxed manner of speech.

Cyrus Sr. had a suggestion for his son. "Xavier, let's step outside for a drive so we can leave the ladies to get acquainted." He placed his hand on his son's back attempting to steer him out the door, but Xavier wouldn't budge, "Father, I think we should all get acquainted together first. Please join us, Mother and Estella."

He was not enthused about leaving "Estella the Good" alone with his mother, "the shark."

But his father was insistent, "Nonsense, son. I need to speak to you man-to-man and face-to-face!"

Xavier recognized the look on his father's face and realized that Sr. would not take no for an answer. "Estella, Mother, we will be back shortly," Xavier assured them as he and his father walked out.

Once they were alone, Catherine clapped her hands over Estella's, smiled and said, "Alone at last! Tell me all about yourself, Estella. It is good to finally meet you!"

Estella kept it basic, "Well, I grew up in Texas, and I attend school here at the university where Xavier and I met. My mother, Renee, is a graduate of the school and my stepfather is a retired professor from there."

Estella had kept it short, positive, and simple on purpose. She was certain that Catherine already knew everything there was to know about her; Xavier's mother just wanted to know how her daughter-in-law would describe herself.

Catherine was not interested in small talk, "Let's cut to the chase, Estella. Xavier's father was a fool for love...so much so, that he broke off our engagement to marry a penniless, no-name when we were in college. I guess this is a little bit of history repeating itself." Xavier's mother gave a rueful shrug and continued. "Although *Sr.'s* pathetic lover pretended to have money and claimed to be from a wealthy Georgia family... at least you're honest — I will give you that much. She was using her stepfather's last name as her own — Emily Newport of the Georgia Newports — but she was really of no family in particular, and was borrowing clothes from her roommate. The bleach-blond, skinny little elf-like twit wasn't fooling me. I am really not sure what Sr. saw in her; she must have drugged him. Anyway, the pretender was quickly revealed and eventually, Xavier begged his way back into his betrothal with me. When Xavier Jr. gets tired of slumming it with you, he will return to Debra. Save yourself the heartache and leave now with this check for your troubles."

Catherine shared her story as if she were speaking to a confidante, but at the same time, she was insulting Estella and trying to buy her off.

Then, she handed Estella a check for fifty thousand dollars.

Catherine added, "Oh, and we will take care of your little situation; we know of a very reputable doctor in the area," And, with that, Catherine stood up and began to walk away, dismissing Estella as though it was a done deal.

It wasn't.

"I will be keeping my baby and my husband, Mrs. Cyrus," Estella stated angrily, as she ripped up the check.

With raised eyebrows and tension in her voice, Catherine responded, "Have it your way, but Xavier does not come into his grandfather's very modest trust fund for another four years. Four years is a long time to be penniless, at least for Xavier, and we will be restructuring the lucrative trust that his father set up so that he does not receive those funds any longer, either. Living off a moderate income for the rest of his life is not something that Xavier will be able to handle, mark my words. Move on with your life now, dear. If Xavier cannot stand to be without you, I am sure he can still visit you sometimes while he is married to Debra and you will forever be well compensated."

Of course, Catherine was right; Xavier could not handle being penniless for even a day much less for four years.

Estella was fed up. "I will not kill my baby, Mrs. Cyrus. You should be ashamed for even suggesting the murder of your grandchild to desperately protect your precious status in society and for superficial reasons of class that you have made up in your sick mind. I will pray for you. Even though I didn't come from wealth, I know that money cannot buy you true class, decency, or the love of a quality person. If Xavier wants to divorce me, that is fine. But I am keeping our child! Good day, Mrs. Cyrus!" She said, opening the door for Catherine.

Catherine Van Horne-Cyrus did not really consider herself a snob; she actually believed that what she was doing was in her family's best interest. She had come from old New York money which had been lost during the Great Depression. Catherine married Xavier Sr. because he had new money, but no family name, and she had a family name, but no money. This was a good and practical tradeoff that had served them both well — financially and socially.

As Xavier's parents saw it, Estella seemed like a nice, beautiful and intelligent girl, but she had nothing in trade that could benefit their family, so they had no use for her. However, *Debra's* family name blended with the Cyrus combined wealth would create a powerful family dynasty. Catherine knew how easily financial disaster could ruin even the most prestigious of families. She had been just a child during the Depression. But still, she suffered the ill-effects of being on the verge of poverty and being on the social fringes until she met and married Xavier Sr. Then, she was fully accepted back into the fold with his money. Being a part of that society was a triple-pronged proposition; it was not just a name or money. One had to possess name, money, and an honorable reputation to belong and remain there.

Individually, Catherine and Sr. were on the edge of their society, but together they were a power couple. A marriage into Debra's family would solidify their family position, place Catherine back into the inner circle of their society and create a financial insurance policy in case of another Great Depression scenario.

However, if Estella, combined with Father Arden, made a stink about the divorce, it could negatively impact the family's reputation. The scandal could also affect Cyrus's political career — especially if Estella had her child and it appeared that the family was abandoning a "good" Texas girl in an election year.

So, Catherine's strategy was to bluff until the child was born and then give Xavier back his trust fund. She knew there would be scandalous headlines put out by their political opponents if she did not give back his trust fund:

Rich Cyrus Family Abandons Grandchild Born to Texas Farmer's Daughter Living in Poverty!

That headline would probably be the death knell of the Cyrus family's tenuous political career in Texas and even the South.

Meanwhile, in a secluded area of University Park, Xavier Sr. and Jr. heatedly argued. The son was standing up to his father: "I am a man. It was my decision to make. I am in love with Estella, and I am not going to leave her and our child." Then, Xavier stated the reality of the situation. "Besides, if I leave 'Estella the Good Texas Girl' now, it is going to look bad on me and especially you in an election year. Have you thought of that, father?"

Xavier was tired of arguing about the situation with his dad and was ready to return to his apartment to rescue Estella from his mother. But Sr. wasn't quite finished yet.

"Of course I have, but your mother is really not going to allow this marriage, son. I am sorry, but we are going to cut you off until you come to your senses," Xavier Sr. stated sternly.

"I am a man and you are a man, so stand up to mom. You were in love once, too!" Xavier angrily challenged him.

"Marrying the girl that I almost did in college would have been the worst decision of my life. She was a lying, cheating gold-digging whore, who eventually married another classmate of mine and ruined his life. Reminding me of the mistake I made before I married your mother, does not help your case at all; it just proves mine," Like his son, Sr. was now turning red and angry too. His conclusion inflamed Xavier, "Don't compare my angelic wife to a cheating gold-digger."

Xavier seethed, balling up his fist angrily. "Well, you started the comparison," Sr. pointed out.

"I was merely comparing the feeling you felt the first time

that you were young and in love. Father, you know that we have a child on the way, your grandchild — in point of fact — and you would cut me off with a pregnant wife? Do you have any true feelings for me at all except as a tool for your own ambitions and to shamelessly promote your political agenda? Don't you care about your name being one of character?"

Xavier looked genuinely hurt.

Sr. was adamant, "We have made up our minds — there is nothing more to say. I *am* a man, and now you need to be a man and take care of your family on your own," Sr. said as he tried to end the argument.

But, Xavier had more to say, "How many Van 'whatevers' is this family going to have to marry to finally feel accepted in New York society? Why don't you just change your name to your wife's name and call it a day so that the rest of us can be set free? Grandpa told me of his first and only love who he jilted for Grandma Van Klieg when his oil money came in. Why is it so important that we are fully accepted by a bunch of assholes? What is full acceptance? How many clubs do you have to be initiated into? How many special handshakes must one know? Estella was right; you are all monsters." Xavier was still shaking with fury as he finished his angry tirade.

Sr. was bemused. "Yeah, and you are one of the Crown Princes of us monsters," he laughed cynically. "Don't fault your mother and me for trying to keep us on our throne and doing what is necessary to expand and fortify our small kingdom with marriage to a neighboring king's daughter. You decide to marry a peasant girl, setting us back with what we have been working towards for generations, and you think that we should be fine with that? You know what happened to small kingdoms that fell?

Their kings and children were either killed or made into peasant serfs themselves."

Senior paused to give his son more specific advice, "Life is a slippery slope, especially over several generations. I just want to do the best that I can do now for my progeny. I don't want our family to fall on my watch. Have I been ruthless? Yes. Am I going to hell if there is one? Probably. But being poor in this world is hell on earth right here and now; not in some other realm that may or may not exist. You ask Estella about what you did to her and her poor family that could not protect her. That was hell on earth to them. Think if that had been your daughter. You brought Estella into this situation when she could have married your frat brother and had a nice life. So, I think us 'monsters' will be in hell together."

Xavier looked guiltily down at his shoes and turned a brighter shade of red.

"I can see from the expression on your face that you didn't think I knew about that. I have my spies; the information may be delayed by a few weeks, but I know everything. I've known everything about you from the day you were born and I will do until I die. And, if there is an afterlife, I will watch you from there, too — to make sure you don't squander our hard work. Also, if Estella is your destiny, the two of you will rise to the occasion together. Enough said; goodbye son and good luck."

Sr. gave Xavier an icy stare, saluted him coldly, and walked away.

Xavier called out after his father, a little panicked: "We'll rise to the occasion if we are really destined for each other? Well, I guess so, if that demented logic helps you sleep at night. I just hope the monsters in this nightmare world don't prevent us from rising to the occasion, as you put it."

Sr. had the last word: "Yeah, when you had money in your pocket and our family power to back you up, the world was a sweet dream to you. Now you will have a taste of the reality that we have been working so hard to protect you and our family from," he rejoined as he kept walking.

CHAPTER TEN

Struggling

Xavier was very depressed when he returned to the apartment. His wife observed that he actually looked like he was on the verge of crying, which caused her to tear up, as well.

They lay down in bed for a half hour not saying anything, just holding each other. Then, Xavier told her in a choked-up voice, looking sad and sincerely vulnerable, "I need to know the truth. Do you still want to be with me now that I can't support you in the ways that I had promised you?"

Estella quickly reassured him: "Of course I want to be with you! I am your wife, and I will stand by you through anything, Xavier. It's going to be fine," trying to sound as positive as possible.

As she stroked his hair, he trembled a little as he held her tightly.

He asked her, "Do you love me, Estella? You have never told me that you loved me!"

Xavier said this as he searched her face honestly looking like a needy little boy. His wife tenderly said, "I love you and I forgive you, Xavier."

She kissed him gently at first and then began raining kisses all over him. It was the first time that Estella had ever initiated lovemaking with him.

Strangely, Xavier needed Estella to proclaim her love, but he had never told her that he loved her. Estella wisely realized this was not the time to bring up that argument.

Then, she did her best to pleasure him with her mouth for the first time. Xavier looked a little shocked at first. "Do you want me to stop," she murmured against his skin.

"I don't kno..-uh, know. I mean, don't stop!" He had always thought of Estella as an innocent angel, so Xavier was having difficulty seeing her in this light.

His wife wasn't sure if it was wise to try this sexual act since Xavier did have this strange Madonna-whore complex in his mind, but she wanted to give him a pleasurable experience after such a horrible day, so she soldiered on.

She was obviously doing a reasonably good job with her first attempt because after a couple of minutes, he began to thrust forward.

Then, suddenly moaning loudly, he grabbed his wife's hair and began to rock her head furiously back and forth, as he climaxed, choking her.

"I am sorry, Estella. I'll be gentle next time, I promise. I am just not used to a *lady* doing that for me!"

Then, as he realized what he had just said was offensive, he added, "I'm an asshole and a screw-up," said Xavier, looking really sad again.

Estella had never heard Xavier berate himself.

"Honey," she soothed him, "You are just going through a lot today. I was just trying to make you happy, but I shouldn't have pushed myself on you while you were so distressed!"

"You gave me a lot of pleasure, my sweet wife, and I loved it. I got carried away, and then the force of habit kicked in, and I messed things up for us again. I guess you were right about my being selfish, but honestly, women have always thrown themselves at me, and I have not really had to think about their pleasure or comfort if I didn't feel like it."

Xavier said this in a matter of fact manner, not trying to brag or make Estella jealous, but just trying to explain his actions. "Come up here, darling. Let me hold you. I really do love you, Estella!"

Xavier held her tightly like a security blanket all night long.

*****

The next morning, Xavier went to the bank and found out that on their way back to the airport his parents had withdrawn every dime of his money from the joint account he had with them.

His tuition was paid out of his grandfather's trust in yearly disbursements; but his books, room, and board had been covered by his father's trust fund.

Panicked, he realized that he only had $393 in cash. The apartment was $97 per month, and groceries cost $35 monthly.

Xavier would have to find a job quickly.

When he returned home, Xavier explained their financial situation to his wife, and she told him, "I am so sorry about your parent's wrong-minded decision, Xavier. But I will stand by you if you want to stay married. I checked with Renee, and we can move in with my parents. Now, it's my turn to ask you truthfully: do you want to divorce me?"

Xavier swiftly, almost too quickly, responded, "Of course, I want to stay married!"

Then, he stepped forward and put his wife in a bear hug, mainly because he did not want Estella to see his face.

She could always tell when he was being dishonest just by looking at him. But she accepted his answer for now and thought, "*I will have to ask again in a few months when he starts working.*"

"Why do you refer to your mother as Renee?" asked Xavier.

Estella explained her reason, "Because she pressured us to get married and I told her I would never refer to her as 'mother' again."

Technically, she was being honest, although she had left out some of the details.

"Do you still regret her pressuring us to get married?" he asked her almost shyly.

"No, I don't, even though I honestly don't think I can ever get over what you did to me. I forgave you because of our child and because I have grown to love you."

Even though Estella knew it was insane to love Xavier after the abuse she had suffered at his hands, she really had grown to love him. She wondered if evolution had created this coping mechanism inside of people to develop feelings for abusers. Margret did say this was a typical response in forced marriages when women are not able to escape. To at least make the abusive situation tolerable; some women's psyche makes them think they are in love with the abuser.

*****

Xavier found a position as a front desk clerk at a local hotel, but after a few days, he was "mysteriously" terminated. This setback put Xavier in a foul mood for a few weeks as he looked for another job. During that time, he wouldn't make love to Estella and was generally mean and grouchy around the house. He refused to work on campus to allow his "friends" and frat brothers to heckle him, so he continued to look for work in town.

He finally landed a job that he really wanted as a law clerk. He was so excited about this new position that he came home with flowers and champagne, and he and Estella made love all night.

But when he reported to work later that week, he had been "mysteriously" terminated after a few days.

Infuriated, Xavier called his father, "I know that you are having me terminated from my employment. Even if you do not want to help me, at least don't hinder me. What kind of person are you to do this to me when you know your grandchild is on the way?"

"I am sorry to hear things aren't going your way, son. But that is a ridiculous accusation. I suggest that you review your actions on the job and step up your work ethic," Sr. chuckled.

Xavier mimicked Estella's vow to Renee, "Even if I did divorce Estella tomorrow and I came back to you for my trust fund, I would never really see you as my father again. Goodbye, Mr. Cyrus!"

Then Xavier hung up on him.

Xavier kept searching for a suitable position for several more weeks but failed to find one. The bills were piling up so his wife made a suggestion, "My position at the cafeteria reopened I could go back to work there!"

That option was unacceptable to her husband. "Hell no, my

80

wife is not working in the lunchroom, especially not when she is pregnant!" Xavier yelled.

Estella didn't know what to do, so she called Renee for advice and her mom showed up the same day. Estella explained the scenario to her, "Xavier can't keep a job, probably because his father is retaliating against him and using his influence to get him fired. He yells and starts arguments with me all the time even though I don't fight back. We never sleep together anymore; he sleeps on the couch and he has been drinking a lot. He won't let me take my old job back to try to make ends meet."

Estella paused choking back tears, "As you know, I am six months pregnant and showing; so no one, except my old employer in the cafeteria, will hire me. And no, he will not move in with you and Stepdad. I just don't know what to do — and I don't think he loves me anymore."

Renee was the voice of reason, "*Mon petite*; don't let him make you upset while you are pregnant. If he does not want to live with us, then you come by yourself. You tell him that I need help for a little while taking care of your stepfather. Sometimes distance makes the heart grow fonder. Also, I will see if I can find Xavier a job," Renee counseled.

Mama inquired all around campus and in town, asking her friends for a job for Xavier. Some confirmed that Xavier was being blackballed by his father.

So, Renee confided to Father Arden that the senior Cyrus was impeding Xavier's ability to make a living. The good priest promised that he would try to find the young man a job.

True to his word, he called the next day with the only two possible jobs he could find that were in close proximity for Xavier to attend school. One position was a waiter at a five-star

Italian restaurant — Donatello's. The other was as a construction worker for Giovanni Contracting. Both companies were owned by parishioners of Father Arden's church in the city who also understood that Xavier was being blackballed by his father, and since his father had no influence over them, Xavier had a fair chance at keeping these jobs.

Xavier, who had never worked with his hands before, was having a difficult time with the jobs. He had a disdain for manual labor and was embarrassed to make a living in these establishments.

The icing on the cake was when Debra walked into the restaurant where he was working, accompanied by Scott, his childhood nemesis. Scott and Xavier had always competed against each other in any and everything they could think of: including girls, sports, and grades.

So, when Scott and Debra came to the restaurant and sat purposefully in his station, Xavier felt sick and disgusted. He asked a co-worker for a favor, "Hey, Luigi, can we please trade tables? My ex is in my station with her date?" Xavier explained.

Luigi was not sympathetic, "No, sorry. That table is too out of the way from my serving area, and it is too much trouble to trade stations," rejoined Luigi, who strongly disliked Xavier. He perceived Xavier as pretentious because of his style of speech and mannerisms. Luigi thought to himself, "*Who does this guy think he is, anyway? It will be fun to watch his ex-girlfriend humiliate him.*" Luigi smirked.

Xavier implored his manager, "I'm really not well and have to leave early."

The manager bluntly confronted him, "Do you want this job? If you leave now, don't bother to come back," At that, the manager turned away from a very irritated Xavier.

Xavier was out of options and did not want to face Estella after losing yet another job, so he walked over and waited on Debra and Scott. "Hello, here are your menus and can I bring you any drinks?"

Xavier tried to treat them like any other table.

"Why, hello Xavier. We haven't spoken in a while. How are you and your wife?" Debra smirked.

Xavier curtly responded, "We are both well and very happy together. Now I have other tables to attend to; so, I would like to take your drink orders."

His nemesis spoke up. "We will have a bottle of you finest champagne — C*rug Lonnay* — and a vanilla shake. Oh wait, I am sorry. Scratch the shake — that will be for your job next week."

Scott had initially ordered the most expensive champagne on the menu and then tried to make fun of the fact that Xavier could not hold a job. Scott gleefully pointed out that each job that Xavier did hold was progressively worse and that Xavier would soon end up working at a fast-food chain in the end, serving shakes.

He was being cruel to his former buddy.

As the personal insults piled up, Xavier snapped, "Just go to hell where you belong, Scott!" Xavier turned quickly away and went to get their drinks.

When he returned to take their order, his manager was standing at Debra's table. "Xavier, did you tell this customer to go to hell? It doesn't matter what the customer says to you, you cannot respond in that manner. Please leave our establishment."

The manager fired Xavier on the spot.

*****

Xavier came home late — drunk and angry — picked a fight with Estella and then fell asleep on the couch.

In the morning, he did not have the heart to tell his wife that he had lost another menial job. Even though he was not cut out for those positions and hated them, he still felt like a failure for losing them. He was beginning to wonder if his father was right and that he was losing all the jobs because of his poor performance.

Estella decided that for the sake of her health, she was not going to continue to argue with her husband. In the morning, she kissed him and said, "Renee needs me to help her take care of my stepdad, so I am going to live with her for a little while." Xavier angrily reacted,

"So, you are leaving me? What happened to the *stand by your man* malarkey that you tried to feed me when I threw away my trust fund for you? My family and friends were right — you are just a gold-digging bitch! Get out, *leave* and don't come back! And by the way, after the baby is born, I will be filing for divorce!"

Estella shot back, "You're insane, Xavier and I am even crazier for putting up with this mess. If that is the way that you want it, fine! Screw you. I am not going to fight with you every day while I am pregnant. I should have said that from the beginning instead of making an excuse."

She threw a few things into her bag and left.

When she related the argument to Renee, her mom calmly counseled her, "Don't worry about him for now; he will calm down and come back to apologize, soon I am sure. You just relax.

The baby will be here in two months and then you will really know the meaning of work and stress!"

She laughed as she ruefully recalled her first few months after Estella had been born.

After about six weeks, Xavier began to stalk Estella again, begging her to come home every chance he could get to speak to her, "I am so sorry, Estella. You were right! I must have been loony to say what I said to you. I love you and miss you. I know this sounds like a cliché, but I really can't sleep and can barely eat without you. Please come home!"

This time, his sad puppy dog look actually seemed sincere.

"After I have the baby, I will consider it, Xavier, if you will go to marriage counseling with me; I have asked Father Arden, and he is more than happy to work with us," she replied dryly.

Estella was so sick of Xavier's wrongdoing and apologies that she was tired of his antics and unwilling to trust him again. She did not want her heart broken again, and she did not want the stress to impact the health of her unborn baby. But conversely, Estella had to also consider reconciliation for the sake of her child's future.

Xavier was not enamored with the idea of counseling with Father Arden, "Oh, hell no! If you want us to see someone who is neutral and who does not think I am the Devil, well, I will consider counseling. But I am not going to see Father Arden," Xavier said with contempt.

"Have you considered that you just might be the Devil?" He stared at his wife and then Estella smirked at him. "Just kidding," she replied.

And then, they both laughed.

"So, you want to make deals with the Devil in counseling?"

He raised one eyebrow, laughing. "I miss you so much, Estella; even when you're making fun of me, the apartment is so lonely and empty without you," Xavier sighed and hugged her.

Then he began to kiss his wife and started trying to undress her, but Estella gently pushed him away, "Not here in Renee's apartment, please!"

She was surprised that he would be attracted to her with her pregnant belly so huge. "Okay. Come back to the apartment just for one night?" Xavier begged.

"I'll be there tonight, but you are just going to hold me, right?" She had missed Xavier too, so she gave in.

"Of course, I'll pick you up at 8:00!" he looked overjoyed that his Estella had forgiven him once again.

Promptly at 8 PM, Xavier pulled up in his expensive, Italian black convertible Omega *Someo* that had been in the repair shop for the past three months because he was unable to afford the repairs.

"How were you able to get your car fixed?" his wife inquired.

"I sold a few things. Here, put this on," Xavier replied, handing his wife a box. Inside was a beautiful maternity dress. Estella did not have any attractive clothes for her advanced condition, but this was a gorgeous royal blue three-quarter length silk dress with an Empire waist.

Xavier was outfitted to the nines with a navy-blue suit and a paisley silk tie. He had always owned a beautiful wardrobe, but Estella had never noticed this particularly expensive Italian suit.

"Where are we going?" she asked when she noticed that Xavier had already passed the entrance of their apartment.

Her husband beamed, "We are going to dinner!" Then he drove for about twenty minutes and pulled up to Donatello's.

"Oh, so you get an employee discount here or are employees allowed to eat here free sometimes?" she exulted.

His wife had not eaten in a five-star restaurant before those first 23 days of marriage or since. "Something like that," he said as he took Estella's arm and escorted her inside.

"Table for two, over there," Xavier motioned to a quiet area in Luigi's station. The snarky waiter looked stunned at Xavier's attire, never having known Father Arden's arrangement with the owner and mistakenly thinking that Xavier was a career waiter having, only seeing him in a waiter's uniform.

Hence, Luigi complained to his manager. "Is this some kinda joke? I do not want to serve this guy if he's gonna run out on the bill and along with my tip," he said, dropping his fake Italian accent since he had been born and raised in Brooklyn.

The manager whispered to his employee, "He drove up in this year's *Omega Someo*. Plus look at that rock on his wife's finger and the way they are dressed. He must have come across some money from somewhere. Be nice to them and listen to their conversation. See if you can figure out what racket he is into now then let me know!"

Luigi could see the wisdom in his manager's suggestion and promised to himself, "*Whatever Xavier can do, I can do better. I need to pal around with him,*" thought the competitive employee.

Armed with a fake smile, Luigi greeted his former co-worker, "Hey Xavier, it's good to see you again, man! Here, take this table by the window. It's our best one."

Luigi proceeded to kiss their tails all night long. By the end of the night, when Luigi still could not figure out what Xavier was doing to make all of that money, he finally asked as Xavier and Estella were stepping out the door, "Hey, can you let me in on what you're doing these days?"

Xavier shot him a smug smile, "I am in the oil business. I see one of your customers beckoning you, so you need to get back to your pathetic station…in life. Good evening, Luigi."

Xavier and Estella got into the car as Luigi and the manager looked on in envy. The fired waiter just wanted a little revenge for their disrespect of him. However, Estella thought that putting the man down for his "pathetic station in life" was obnoxious. She did not know at that time that Debra had gone to the restaurant and Luigi had refused a simple favor to exchange stations out of spite that had led to Xavier being humiliated and fired.

"Xavier, how could you disrespect the waiter like that? I have waited tables in the cafeteria and don't come from wealth. In your heart, do you have the same disdain for me? Is that how you would treat me if you were not attracted to me?"

She was taking up for Luigi because she had felt hurt confused seeing her husband disrespect a hard-working, "innocent" man.

"I will always love you. Luigi had disrespected me while I worked at the restaurant," Xavier said, squeezing her hand reassuringly and still grinning from the encounter with the slimy waiter, and having had the opportunity to get his little revenge.

But Estella was not mollified. "Why would you include me in that unpleasantness? We were having such a nice night. Must you really seek revenge on every soul who disrespects you? I mean honestly, if I were to have to find a way to get back at every person who said an unkind thing to me, I would spend my entire life plotting vengeance!"

Estella was exasperated with Xavier. She turned her head

away from him and looked out the window. Only then did she notice that they were driving in the wrong direction. "Now, where are we going?" she asked quizzically.

Xavier smiled slyly, "It's a surprise!"

Maybe it was the hormones that made Estella feel paranoid, but she had heard of men killing unwanted pregnant women. She quickly dismissed her strange thought as being too "out there."

After living with Xavier for several months, she always believed he was a little nutty, but he wasn't that crazy. Plus, she kind of loved his quirkiness. It was, at times, an endearing quality that made him unique.

A half-hour later, Xavier pulled up to the house they had decided to purchase before the falling out with his parents. It was a beautiful four-bedroom, three-bath Tudor home with two fireplaces, located on five acres with a circular driveway.

From a realtor's description, it was an upper-middle-class starter home, definitely not the mansion that his parents lived in nor that Debra would have demanded, but a home that Estella would be perfectly happy with for the rest of her life. Estella thought to herself, "*I have no problems with this home being my starter and my ender home.*"

She absolutely loved this house!

"Why are you getting out, Xavier?" she said with nervous excitement; hoping this might really be her dream home.

Xavier's answer sent shock waves through her, "I got the key from the realtor. Let's go in."

He grabbed his stunned wife by the hand and pulled her inside. The house was ready to be lived in with the furnishings that they had picked out together, and Estella recognized some of their pictures on the mantel!

It was beginning to dawn on her that this really could be her new home. Her heart was afraid to soar, but she had to ask him, "How is this house possible? You could not have just sold a few things for all of this!" Estella gasped in shocked amazement.

Xavier looked at his wife with those sexy blue eyes of his and announced, "It is ours now; my parents had a change of heart." Her husband hugged and kissed her and led his love to the master bedroom, which was on the first floor.

Estella was so excited, she dragged him to the nursery, which was down the hall from the master bedroom, and of course, all of the baby things that she had picked out were in there too! The color of the room was a neutral medium lilac, set against the medium-grained wood of the crib and accessories.

Estella felt silly for even thinking that Xavier could ever wish her or their baby any harm, even for a second. "Come, sexy. Let's go into the bedroom," Xavier announced as he led his wife into the master bedroom and pulled her blue dress over her head. He then knelt down and placed his head up against Estella's stomach to listen for any signs of Marie.

She took his hand and placed it where he could clearly feel some movement from his daughter. She had never seen Xavier so genuinely happy. He picked his wife up and carried her to their four-poster Louis XV mahogany bed and gently placed her down on it. He sexily kissed her all over her body. From the back of her neck, to around her ears, he was making love to her mouth, down her upper chest, over her nipples, conquering her full breasts, seducing her hips, rolling over her stomach and sliding down her inner thighs where he parted her trembling thighs and used his long tongue to pleasure her to the height of ecstasy.

He took his time making love to her with his mouth, causing

her to uncontrollably climax several times. Following her final climax, Xavier teasingly suggested, "Can you return the favor?"

Estella was more than happy to do just that.

She made love to him with her mouth, swirling, sucking and enveloping his manhood as he lay still and gently bucked against groaning and grunting with wild abandonment.

Xavier pulled her mouth upward as he spilled himself on the sheets. Then he sang the "I Love You" song to her as he often did when he was happy.

The lyrics consisted of Xavier singing, "I love you" in different octaves, over and over and over again. Then, the lovers dozed off in each other's arms.

The following week, as he had promised, Xavier moved Renee and her ailing husband into the house with them and hired a nurse to medically assist both Nick and the baby's arrival.

Estella beamed with joy.

Xavier asked Renee to quit her jobs and she partially acquiesced, leaving all of her odd jobs, but keeping her main teaching assistant job at the university.

The following week Estella went into labor on-time and her beautiful daughter Marie was born perfect. She looked exactly like her father except for her dark reddish brown curly hair. Xavier would hold her and stare at her for hours, once he laughed and said that we should have named her "Perfection" instead of Marie.

CHAPTER ELEVEN

The Breakdown

After two weeks I overheard Xavier talking in heated tones to his father over the phone in the study. "I will get her to sign it today ok just transfer the money into my account TODAY," was Xavier's angry whisper.

When Xavier hung up Estella asked in a confused voice," Who are you going to get to sign what?"

"Stop eavesdropping it is none of your concern. I need to be alone," he pushed Estella through the study door and locked it.

When he emerged from his study an hour later, he acted like everything was fine, but Estella knew that was a lie. She could clearly see that Xavier had on his fake happy face again.

Over the following few weeks, the couple tried to pretend that everything was well, and that pretense began to feel like reality.

But then, two months later, that pretense was shattered when Estella received a phone call from Catherine.

"Hello dear, I just wanted to say that I am so sorry to hear about your divorce."

Estella was stunned, "What are you talking about?"

"Didn't you know that your divorce was finalized a few days ago?" Catherine asked quizzically.

Estella hung up the phone.

She understandably felt a sick sense of dread.

The first move she made was to break the lock on the door to Xavier's study and start searching through his files.

He had told her that he always kept the study locked because he did not want the nurse or any of the other servants such as the gardener, pool boy, the weekly maid server, or any other staff to have access to his personal documents. But now, Estella knew for a fact that he had locked the door to keep her out as well.

She discovered a lot of unpaid bills in his files, including the mortgage that was thirty days late, and bank deposit slips for $5,000 per month which was a little bit more than what the couple had spent per month.

The $5,000 deposits were from his father's account in Texas, but there had not been a deposit in over a month. Then, she opened the mail and saw that Xavier had just received a check for fifty-five thousand dollars from his father with a note attached, "*a little something extra for her troubles.*"

That reminded Estella of the day that Catherine had to tried to buy her off with a $50 thousand check "for your troubles."

Estella guessed that Xavier got his normal five thousand dollars, plus a bonus check — for her troubles — in payment for a divorce. What Estella could not understand was how Xavier could have divorced her without her signature! And, an even bigger question for her was, "Why am I even trying to hold onto this marriage?"

The whole relationship with Xavier had just been a hellish rollercoaster ride from the very start.

As she numbly stood there, she heard Marie crying and Estella thought to herself, "*I guess she must have heard my thoughts. I could almost hear her cry: 'I want my mommy and daddy together!' as all young children wanted their parents to stay together."*

Catherine had clearly said that the divorce was finalized and Estella had a sinking feeling here; even though she couldn't find the papers, that she was right.

What could Estella do?

Was she really going to call the police and complain that the divorce documents were forged? If Xavier wanted out of the marriage that badly that he had to forge her signature, then so be it.

Estella was tired of fighting the inevitable.

When Xavier returned home with flowers and a happy smile on his face, he wasn't wearing his fake smile. Estella reasoned that he had pretended his way to happiness and was in denial. In his mind, there were no forged divorce papers so that he could convincingly hold onto this joyful moment in which they were still together as a family.

He called Estella's name, and she answered, "I am in your study!" She heard Xavier's footsteps, half walking and half running towards his office.

Xavier was in attack mode, "How dare you invade my privacy!" he thundered, half in fear and the other half in fury.

Estella matched him in anger, "How dare you forge my signature! If you wanted a divorce, all you had to do was ask me. I would have signed the papers. When you said that you had sold a few 'things' to fix your car, you should have told me it was us that you had sold!"

Estella was resigned to her fate. She refused to ever cry over Xavier again.

Suddenly contrite, the man of many mood changes shifted once more, "I just wanted every moment that I could have with you and Marie before everything fell apart." Xavier came over to Estella and kneeled down in front of the chair she was sitting in and put his head in her lap. "Please stay with me!"

His wife was dumbfounded, "How can I stay with *you*? You are the one divorcing me!"

Xavier outlined his plan, "I will be moving back on campus tomorrow, at my mother's insistence. But I will still come and visit you and the baby on the weekends and continue to pay all the bills. Everything will be as it was; the nurse stays, you and your mother do not have to work, and will be given the same allowance. The only difference is that I will be living on campus during the week."

He was working hard to put a positive spin on his selfishness. Estella had a plan for him as well, "And, let me add, that the only difference is that you will never touch me again, Xavier! You will stay in the guest bedroom for your weekly visits." She stood up and retreated into the master bedroom and locked the door behind her.

For the next six weeks, Xavier visited every weekend and played with Marie; took her to the playground, bought her toys and clothes, and only spoke to Estella to discuss her bills.

Then, he showed up one day in the middle of the week when Estella's mother was gone. He surprised her while she was showering in the bathroom and locked her in his arms, imploring her, "Please, Estella, I need you. I can't be without you. "

"No, Xavier! Let me go or I am going to scream!"

She yelled as he pressed kisses all over her face, neck, and breasts. Then, he dropped down on his knees in the shower, grabbed her hips, and drove his tongue deep into her water drenched crevice.

At first, Estella tried to grab his dark brown curls to pull his head away, but then his incredibly long tongue did that tickling motion that he did so well deep inside of her almost touching her womb. She exploded all over his face, collapsing in a heap.

He spread Estella out on the floor of the super-sized shower and entered her with a groan. It was over very quickly, his usual time frame for a first encounter after a long hiatus.

After a few minutes, Xavier wanted her again and he pulled her on top of him, harnessing her shoulders in his embrace as he pressed Estella's body hard and fast down onto his manhood, thrusting wildly up to meet her.

They climaxed together in guttural grunts as the water from the shower head beat down on her back and his chest.

Finally, Estella pulled away from him and confronted him.

"Must I change the locks on the door, Xavier? I can't do this with you any longer," she said, as she put on her robe.

Xavier was defiant, "This is my house, and I will come here as I please and I will have you as I please. I pay every bill in this house and I take care of your family, also. You will no longer deny me, Estella," Xavier stated firmly.

She laughed scornfully at him, "Ha, ha, ha — you must be mad. Or, did you forge my signature on some type of indentured servant document too? I will pack myself, Marie, my mother and my stepfather up and go back to living in our two-bedroom apartment rather than be your mistress. I always thought that you were like a Venus flytrap, but now, you have added this house and all its comforts to your insidious web, as well. I am going to get a good attorney — alimony for me and child support for Marie. If it wasn't for her, I would have just left you without asking for any money and never looked back. But I have to think of her well-being before my pride. Leave now, or I will call the police."

"You never called the police before, why would you now?" Xavier asked angrily.

"I never had a document stating that we were married before and a birth certificate that lists you as the father before — I had no rights before. But now, as the former Mrs. Cyrus, I have all the rights in the world. You cannot deny knowing me or our child, and now you have to pay child support. Now please go," Estella said with righteous anger.

Xavier stared blankly at Estella with a frozen, distant look and left.

Over the next several weeks, Xavier went back to seeing his daughter on the weekends and paying the bills, as he and Estella ignored one another.

After about two months, she noticed he had missed a couple of visits. She also noticed a disturbing physical change in Xavier's countenance; he began to look sickly and progressively depressed. She thought about the mother of her divorced friend Sadie and thought, "*Would Xavier emotionally divorce Marie as Sadie's dad had done to Sadie? Should I rethink my decision to end my relationship with Xavier; for Marie's sake?*" She asked him, "Are you feeling okay?"

He nodded, "I'm fine."

But she was not convinced and rightly so.

Soon after that, the hospital called and told Estella to come at once; Xavier had collapsed.

CHAPTER TWELVE

Magical Marie and Reconciliation

When Estella arrived at the hospital, the doctor informed her that Xavier had not been eating or taking care of himself and that a simple head cold had turned into pneumonia. The police had found him wandering the streets in close to zero-degree temperatures with no coat on and drunk. They had taken him to the hospital without filing a report, in deference to his family.

The doctors had also done a psychiatric evaluation and believed that Xavier was probably suffering from bipolar disorder, but they did not record that in his medical file, again in deference to his family.

Estella stayed with Xavier all night, and in the morning, she brought Marie to cheer him up. His mother, Catherine, was already there, and this would be her first meeting with her grandchild.

Catherine and Xavier Sr. were sitting by their son's bedside crying.

"I have never seen him this ill," his mother sobbed.

Then she saw Marie, and, through her tears, Catherine asked if she could hold her. So, Estella handed Marie over to Catherine, and she and Xavier Sr. took turns embracing her.

Over the next few weeks, as the two women nursed Xavier back to health Catherine and Estella came to an understanding and began to get along with one another.

Xavier's parents fell in love with Marie and began to feel guilty that they had been mainly responsible for breaking up Xavier and Estella.

By the time that Xavier had finally recovered, Catherine actually wanted to try to get her son and Estella back together.

She didn't have to try too hard, because when Estella thought that Xavier was actually going to die, she realized that she didn't want to be without him, either.

Xavier Sr. used his influence to get the divorce decree rescind-ed.

Estella, Xavier, and Marie lived happily in their Tudor home for the next three years while the couple both finished college and Xavier finished law school.

They then moved to Texas, so that Xavier could start pursuing his political career. He paid off their home in New York and put it in Estella and Renee's name.

Renee and her husband began living there because Renee had finally earned her Ph.D. in mathematics and became a tenured professor at the university.

It was time for Xavier to run for political office as the candidate for the House of Representatives in the congressional district representing northeast Dallas County. It would be one of the most outlandish races in Texas political history and, Xavier, Estella, and his mother, Catherine, would be the savvy architects of it.

CHAPTER THIRTEEN

The Congressman

As Xavier continued to respond positively to his bipolar medication, his doctors became more and more encouraged to adjust his dosages down.

But, the best tonic for Xavier was being at home with his lovely Estella and his beloved daughter, Marie. They not only gave him much needed emotional and psychological support, which leveled off his mood swings, but they also provided him the impetus to pursue a high visibility career.

A political one.

Political office had been Xavier's dream as a child, and now it was within his grasp to achieve it. After several meetings with Democratic leaders in Texas, Xavier had become convinced that he had a realistic chance to win a seat in the House of Representatives. More importantly, at least to him, he believed it was his destiny.

His venue would be the 30th congressional district, comprised of mostly white and black voters, with a significant percentage of Hispanics completing the racial mix. The seat had been held by the retiring Raybud "Bud" Bailey, aged 73, and a Lone Star "good ole boy." Everyone in the Party loved Bud; he was a back slapper and more colorful than a Christmas tree. He kissed more babies in Texas than all the store "Santas" combined.

When he rolled into a city or a town, he lit them up like the Fourth of July.

But Bailey had been diagnosed with terminal lung cancer due to his incessant smoking and drinking over the long years of his hard-charging life. His doctor had told him to kick back and enjoy what was left of it.

He told his voters that the man to replace him was his key campaign aide, Wallace Stevens, but Mr. Stevens did not possess the same flair as his boss and was a distant second in the polls to a hot-shot lawyer from Dallas named Jackson Dorn.

Dorn was a younger man than both Bailey and Wallace, being 34 years old. He had carefully been groomed by the Party to eventually run for the U.S. Senate, and the House seat would be his final stepping-stone to achieving that goal.

He had begun his career as a passionate defense attorney, but over the years, he had gotten tired of winning case after case for the criminal element who were really guilty and had deserved prison time or the electric chair. So, he took a major cut in pay and became a government prosecutor.

Dorn was an eloquent orator, a firebrand on the stump, and a championship debater. With those skills and a beautiful wife and family surrounding him, he seemed like a likely winner to move on to Washington D.C.

Especially since the voters were ready for a younger representative. In that case, the only real competition Dorn had was the equally vibrant Xavier Cyrus.

But Xavier, now twenty-eight years-old, lacked the experience of his opponent and Dorn was ready to take full advantage of that fact. He portrayed Xavier as a political wannabe with little depth and even less credibility.

In his campaign speeches, he loved to publicly berate Xavier as "the kid who failed the bar exam four times!"

The race between these two young men looked like a total mismatch on paper, but Xavier had a lot of assets on his behalf.

His greatest strength was himself. Xavier was a charismatic force to be reckoned with. He had not only stood out in college, he had dominated it. Everywhere he went, students had fallen over him. He had been the rock star of Bridgeham University.

Tall, handsome, charming, magnetic, confident, and able to equally impress both the men and women at school was a huge plus in Texas politics. *If* he could carry that prowess to an adult level, Xavier was confident in his abilities.

He had the family name and wealth behind him, too. Cyrus Sr. had become nationally known, not only for his run for Governor in Texas but with his political and social contacts up and down the East Coast. There was a deep reverence for the name, Cyrus, in America. Xavier was ready to press it to his advantage.

Then, there was Estella.

She was the ace in the hole; the wild card that gave Xavier a very special pull in the Lone Star State.

Father Arden had been prophetic that day in his study when he won over Xavier with the idea that Estella Myrtle needed to be at his side if he was serious about a political career in Texas.

Estella was a natural in politics, especially so in her home state. That whole, "Texas dirt farmer" reference resonated with hundreds of thousands of voters in the northeastern part of Dallas County. They had been hit hard by the Depression, and now one of their own was aligned with one of the candidates. By now, Estella had blossomed into one of the most beautiful women in America and her little girl was sensationally cute, too.

The Cyrus family was like royalty to these good folks in

Texas. Who needs depth and experience when you are youthful, dynamic, and attractive? If anything, politics has taught political historians that it's not unusual for the best-looking candidates to win an election from the Presidency on down. It is unfair that less physically appealing office seekers with more credentials often lose to the rich and famous, but that is a political fact of life.

And Xavier Cyrus, more than anyone, understood that. He had exploited this truism at every level of his life and won. Now, it was time to take his act nationally.

Estella had been the missing piece of his plan. Debra Van Ardwick would never have gone over big in Texas — hell, she wouldn't even have been effective in Xavier's family bed.

But, Estella?

That woman had it all: warmth, charm, personality, passion for causes, motherhood, savvy, morals, and a brain.

And Texas loved her.

As Election Day approached, Dorn had a comfortable lead over Wallace and a more sizable one over Xavier. The problem for Xavier was named experience – he simply lacked it. Xavier had only ever worked consistently as Vice President of his father's oil company. However, when he did speak at a rally or was on the stage with his two opponents, he more than held his own. But he was probably not ready to pull off a congressional victory so soon out of law school. He was two years away from being seriously considered.

Estella tried to encourage him one night as they lay in bed together.

"You need to stay positive. True, you are inexperienced and are running for office for the first time, but everybody has to start somewhere!"

106

Her husband was unresponsive, sulking in the dark.

Estella kept talking, "You will eventually make it to D.C., if not this year, then soon. You were made for a great political career. Sometimes, it is all about the timing. Your day will come."

He was not as optimistic, "Dorn is a whirlwind. Everyone in the district knows him. He has built a great name for himself. The election is his to lose. All he has to do is not make a mistake, and he wins. I need a miracle."

His wife cuddled against him and cooed, "Miracles happen!" Xavier disagreed.

"The numbers in this campaign don't suggest that, Estella. We are up against it. At this point, I just want it to be over. It's like feeling a noose tightening around my neck."

Estella knew it was no use trying to cheer Xavier up. He was emotionally crushed; perhaps it was his bipolar condition that was contributing to all his angst. "Goodnight, honey; I love you!"

He mumbled, "Yeah."

His final glimmer of hope was a debate the weekend before Election Day. It was there that he hoped to dispel all the qualms about his youth, lack of experience, and his ability to legislate for his district.

But, if he lost that debate or even performed as well as his fellow Democratic Party candidates, it was over. He would have to dominate them on stage or wait another two years to run and probably not win again since Texans did not like betting on a losing horse twice.

Enter Catherine Cyrus and her sorority sisters that had not only mastered an ancient Egyptian tradition of mesmerization but had seen its power working in Estella as well. Or, as these women had stated it, "Estella was one of our kind," meaning that she possessed the same power as Catherine and the sisters. They saw her as the key to critically affecting the debate and giving her husband a way to win.

The sorority sisters had a powerful sense of history on their side in Egyptian lore. It was called "Mesmerization." The first high priestesses and Queens of Egypt had taught this power to their daughters and spread the knowledge throughout the world to those who also had been born gifted.

Catherine and Renee both had the gift, but while Catherine's mother had taught her daughter, Renee's mother did not.

Renee's mother believed it morally wrong to influence the thoughts of others. Renee's grandfather had belonged to a secret society founded in Ancient Egypt called *The Circle of Ausir* and his wife belonged to the spouse's organization called *The Circle of Auset*. But their daughter, Renee's mother, had rebelled and refused to pass it on to Renee. So, it was left to Catherine and her sorority sisters to train Estella to help Xavier be victorious in his almost un-winnable congressional race.

Although there was a male and female aspect to these secret organizations, only women had the gift of mesmerization. Catherine had Estella initiated into her sorority and trained her to mesmerize and influence the thoughts of others, rendering them addled and discombobulated.

Xavier needed a miracle to neutralize his opponents and save his political career. Catherine sensed the strongest spiritual powers she had ever encountered emanating from Renee and Estella. She was confident that once Estella completed her preparation, she could effectively use her gifts to cause Xavier's debate opponents to verbally collapse on stage.

Mesmerization was a cross between hypnotism, spiritual

power, and mental influence. It was a manipulative enthralling which rendered a subject incapable of expressing a normal verbal pattern when under its unrelenting pressure. The influencer could also create a suggestion in the subjects' minds so they would think it was their own thoughts.

Estella had been a bit hesitant at first to use the method, but after sharing her reluctance with Renee, she was convinced that when it came to politics, everyone and everything was fair game.

Renee had set her daughter straight, "Politics is a shady business. Every mom wants her son to be President, but they don't want him to be a politician in the process. Try to make that omelet without breaking an egg, as they say!"

Estella asked her, "Is it immoral?"

Renee was brutally honest with her, "Of course it's immoral, but it is not outside the political rules. In elections, everything goes, including character, honesty, and reputation. This is a no-holds-barred competition, and the only rule is to win, except murdering someone. Although, I believe that has happened in the past too! This is survival of the fittest."

"So, I am being too naïve?"

"You are not being tough enough, yes. As you remain in the political arena, you will see that the lines of right and wrong are frequently blurred. So, if you want your husband to win, which could benefit you and your causes greatly, then lighten up a bit!"

Estella found herself nodding in agreement as she listened to Renee spell out the reality of running for office, "Okay, Renee. Thanks for your wisdom. Pray for us."

Estella returned to Catherine and announced, "I'm in." Her mother-in-law hugged her, "Let's go put our boy in office!"

If Estella could not mesmerize Xavier's opponents, then their ideas and experience would overwhelm him on the stage and, ultimately, on Election Day.

It was a risky strategy to be sure, but at this late stage in the campaign, the Cyrus team had nothing to lose and everything to gain.

It was time for the political wife to work her magic.

*****

The debate began normally enough with each candidate giving a brief opening of their view of politics and an overview of their agenda. Xavier's was the weakest of the three, by far.

In the audience, Catherine and Estella cringed.

Then, the interactive round of questions and answers began, and the first sign of Cyrus team success came when Steven Wallace was challenging Xavier on his lack of experience understanding the small farms in Texas.

"My predecessor, Representative Bailey and I are friends of the farmers in this vital agrarian district. That's why Bud passed so many key pieces of legislation to help the small farmer in fighting off the large combines that threatened his existence. I ask you, Mr. Cyrus, where do you exhibit the know-how of being capable of continuing that protection with our most valuable agricultural resource, sir?"

Estella intently stared at Wallace on the stage and remotely placed herself into Wallace's mind and kept repeating inside of his mind, "I don't know. I don't know. I don't know."

Within seconds, Wallace began verbally reeling, "So, I say to you, Mr. Cyrus, uh, so, I say to you. I say… to you that, as I was saying, I am not sure what we are talking about here and that, er, when I say that... I don't know..."

Wallace completely fell apart.

He stepped back from the dais and wiped his now sweating brow and was incoherent for the remainder of the debate.

Then, it was the dynamic Jackson Dorn's turn to respond.

He stepped up to the microphone and jumped into the vacuum created by the now babbling Wallace Stevens and smirked at Xavier as he began berating him for his four failed law school exams.

Estella just turned on the power as she stared at Dorn who suddenly lost all semblance of coherency, "Can we afford to send a representative to Washington D.C. who can't even send a, well, um, a representative? Can we? For in the final analysis, uh, sending such a man, or was it a rep, er, or a man in question that we send then, uh, I don't think so. In fact, I don't even know that..."

As his voice trailed off, the audience was so completely stunned by the complete breakdown of Dorn's usual high degree of eloquence, that they tittered with laughter. His wording was so nonsensical that it was funny, yet tragic, to hear. No one had ever seen the persuasive Jackson Dorn fumbling his words into gibberish before.

Observers of the debate, including the moderators, were looking at each other and muttering, "What is going on here?" How could two highly-educated men suddenly turn into illiterate fools; incapable of finishing a simple thought?

As Jackson Dorn was escorted off the stage by two of his staff members, Xavier took the microphone with feigned sympathy for his two opponents. "My heart goes out to these two fine men right now. It has been a long and arduous campaign which has taken a huge toll on all of us, emotionally and psychologically. The strain of speaking several times a day, the stress of constantly traveling from town to town, the overwhelming pressure to remember facts, figures, and platforms in order to represent you, the proud citizen of Texas, can be debilitating at times as we saw here tonight."

Then, he dramatically paused for effect as he powerfully and confidently addressed his audience knowing that with his secret weapon Estella, he would win the un-winnable race.

"I believe our district needs and deserves a man who can keep a clear mind and can lucidly articulate the hopes and dreams of all of you. To not only be the Democratic Party representative or the 30th district representative, but to be your personal advocate. I cannot afford to ever crack under the pressure of this job, for I need to be strong for you, and together we can make the American Dream come true, for *you*! You can always count on me to passionately fight for your rights and goals as we move forward to make our district, our dreams, and our destiny what God Almighty intended them to be!"

Then he delivered the knockout blow.

"My name is Xavier Cyrus, and I will light up the skies over Washington D.C. to let them know that the Lone Star State is alive and well. That we are *powerful* in our fight for doing *right,* in the world today. Thank you!"

By now, even his audience was mesmerized and hanging on his every word as Estella sent out a mental broadcast to the audience to believe in, vote for, and love her Xavier.

He got a standing ovation, and some people's eyes in the audience even teared up.

Estella's gift for mesmerization and speech writing,

combined with Xavier's good looks, charisma, and oratory skills had just jumpstarted his career in politics.

Amazing.

Xavier just had to wait until Election Day to make it fact. He not only had the momentum from the forum and the respect and support of all who had watched the debate, he now had the votes, too.

On the following Tuesday, Texans in his district made it official: Xavier had won 52% of the vote, with Dorn and Wallace totaling 33% and 15% respectively.

Estella was especially thrilled, not just because her husband had been elected to Congress; but that he would now be representing, as the Democratic candidate, a large percentage of minorities: Negro and Hispanic voters. She had been a women's and civil rights advocate for several years now. His victory had been a dream come true for her opportunity to empower the less fortunate. Estella would be able to help those in need in the areas of housing, unemployment, social services, racial equality, and education. With Xavier now in a power position in the nation's capital; she too was in her own power position.

There was only one problem with her excitement, and it came from close to home: Her husband.

Xavier wanted to cater to the white voter, the wealthy, the "better." Minorities were never even a fleeting priority to him. He just needed their votes, period. After that, he had an agenda that left them out in the cold.

Xavier Cyrus talked about civil rights; Estella Cyrus lived and breathed civil rights.

Estella clearly understood that her work with Black people and Hispanics would have to be out of earshot from her husband or there would be hell to pay. So, in essence, the district sent two representatives to Congress: Xavier and his lovely wife, Estella.

They had always disagreed with each other from that first meeting that day in the diner, and now they were going to disagree again; this time on a far bigger stage.

They were two different people from completely different levels of wealth, culture, social standing, political views, and gender. Now, they would be married, raising a family and working against each other to further the American Dream for all people; not just the rich ones.

If this dichotomy was ever discovered by Congressman Xavier Cyrus, there would be hell to pay in his marriage! Estella was willing to take that chance to help those who could not help themselves. If Xavier didn't like it; he would have to live with it or live without her. This was not an issue of "just politics" to Estella; it was a matter of her very soul.

CHAPTER FOURTEEN

The D.C. Social Scene

It was 1953, and a new class of congressman was being sworn in.

One of Xavier's fellow Democrats in the House was a young man from Massachusetts, John Fitzgerald Kennedy.

America also had a new President, the war hero of D-Day; Dwight D. Eisenhower.

It was a time of financial prosperity in the country as the soldiers from WWII settled in with their brides, bought new homes, and began to raise families.

It was also a personally healthy time for the freshman congressman from Texas — moving to Washington and starting a new life was a daunting challenge for the Congressman's wife. Estella was overwhelmed by the seat of power and the number of social engagements that she was now required to attend.

The young woman especially reveled in the power to help others, but also its rich political history; the White House, the monuments, the legendary Potomac River, its presence as a power base. And the fact it was the most significant capital city in the world.

As she and Xavier climbed the massive number of steps to the U.S. Capitol building, he chided her, "A long way from that little diner on campus, huh?"

Estella smiled, a little out of breath from the exertion; she was excited and nervous all at once.

The girl from the small town was definitely out of her element, but she was thrilled to be there at the same time.

Xavier saw her biting her bottom lip; he sensed her nervousness, and squeezed her hand to comfort her, then said, "You have me" which gave her immense confidence. She was used to dirt farms and down-home folks, little Bridgeham University, school dances, and studying at the library. But this? How do you prepare for majesty?

International leaders and their associates dominated the city.

One night, there was a dinner for the President of France; two mornings later, there was a National Prayer Breakfast, and the following week, the President of the United States was giving a speech on the economy from the Oval Office.

It was dizzying for the humble woman who grew up poor in rural Texas. The biggest event in her young life had been a county fair. Now, she was expected to engage governors, senators, heads of state, the intelligence agencies, powerful media outlets, and socialites.

This was *the big time*!

Estella had no idea what to wear, how to speak, who to trust, and where to fit in. Her only consolation was that her husband had little idea of what to do, either.

However, his overconfidence and bravado helped him through this new way of life, while Estella's nervousness at some social occasions made her prone to nausea and stammering.

At one luncheon where she was asked to speak on being a freshman congressman's wife, she felt so nervous she wanted to throw up. Xavier squeezed her hand "Don't get nervous, Babe.

Fake it until you make it. Laugh when you think of the ski trip we just had, and you will feel better."

Xavier reminded her of when they ran into Debra and her new spouse on vacation on the ski slopes right after winning the election. Debra had gotten so distracted watching them, that she had lost her balance and knocked down a whole row of other skiers! No one had been injured, but there were poles and ski equipment everywhere, and all involved had a crazy time standing back up. Debra had looked mortified and turned a weird shade of ruddy pink as she embarrassed easily. Xavier and Estella and all those not affected by the fall could not help but laugh at the scene.

Estella's laughter eased her nervousness every time, so Xavier kept the jokes flowing even if some of his puns were a little mean.

Xavier had fed his wife the anecdotes prior to her speech: "Sturdy Debra looked like a human bowling ball wiping out every pin in sight!" he guffawed. "She was rolling down that mountain like a snow-capped version of a Sherman tank! No one in her path had a *chance*!"

Estella was laughing so hard, she was a hit on the stage!

They found a quiet, brick home in the exclusive Georgetown neighborhood, an upper-class suburb along the Potomac River. It was elegant, sophisticated, private, and laden with historical tradition. But Estella quickly went to work, making it into a personal home for her family.

Little Marie, now five years old, quickly had her tricycle unpacked and began vigorously riding up and down the sidewalk while the movers dodged her constantly.

It was a highlight for Estella to join Sr. and Catherine for

Xavier's swearing-in ceremony as a new member of the House of Representatives. She was gratified to see the pride in his parents' eyes as he repeated the oath and was duly installed in his House seat.

Now, it was time for Xavier to get to work and for Estella to figure out the social and political intricacies of the D.C. maze. Xavier had a leg up on his wife. He had the advantage of a mentor who was showing him the ropes on how to succeed in the volatile clique of Washington politics: he was the Speaker of the House, the Honorable Samuel Burke, a powerful Democrat who also served as one of FDR's advisors. He had been in Congress for 24 years and was highly respected on both sides of the aisle. Burke saw a lot of potential in Xavier and began grooming him for a committee chairmanship upon first meeting him.

They had met personally several times a week, on the golf course, over drinks, at strategy lunches, and at the prestigious sports club, *The Razor*. Now, it was time for their wives to meet and become friends, also.

Accordingly, the two couples were having dinner at *Rouissant*, an exquisite French restaurant, in the heart of Georgetown. Sam Burke was in a happy mood, "A toast to the beautiful women in our lives, Estella Cyrus and Dolores Burke!"

Glasses were clinked together, and the champagne flowed to honor the wives of the notable Speaker and his protégé.

Dolores Burke commented, "Estella, I am looking forward to knowing you a lot better, beyond the political realm!" Estella echoed the sentiment,

"I would welcome that too!"

Burke chortled, "Well, it's all been settled; after dinner, let's go skinny-dipping in the Potomac!" Everyone laughed, and they clinked glasses again.

At that point, the two wives retired to the ladies room to freshen up, leaving Sam and Xavier alone at the table.

The congressman said to his mentor, "I have to say, Sam, your comment about skinny-dipping was shockingly imaginative. Have you and your wife ever done something like that?"

Burke laughed, "Not exactly that, no. But Dolores and I have had our randy moments!'

Xavier pushed for a little more information, "Is there a forum for something like that in this town?" Burke paused before continuing the conversation as if he were being discreet about what he was about to say, "Let me put it this way, Xavier; D.C. is a power town, it's not about what you know, it's more about who you know."

Xavier nodded knowingly. "One of my favorite maxims, but what does that have to do with skinny-dipping?"

Burke looked around the restaurant before delving deeper into that part of the conversation, "Well, I have discovered there is a powerful line to the top through a very erotic experience that connects me to instant credibility."

Xavier was leaning in and listening intently now, "Such as?"

"You're not ready to hear all this yet; but someday I will introduce you to an extraordinary group of people, some senators, congressmen, diplomats, presidential advisors, billionaires, who partake in a powerful ritual that is beyond the pale of reality."

Representative Cyrus was champing at the bit now, "Sam, I have to learn about all this, please!"

Burke demurred, "Not yet, Xavier; but when I set you up in

this, uh, experience, it will automatically put you on the fast track to power."

"Can you give me a hint...something?" Cyrus begged his mentor.

The Speaker winked and said, "Think skinny-dipping, but far more intense!"

They looked up and their wives had returned to the table, ending the enigmatic conversation. Xavier was as intrigued as he was frustrated. He could not wait to hear more from Samuel Burke regarding this exciting concept that could jumpstart his reputation in politics. For the moment, he could only imagine what Samuel Burke was alluding to, and the always impatient Xavier Cyrus found that to be maddening.

CHAPTER FIFTEEN

Refining Estella

As Estella was taking Marie for a walk along the Potomac River, she saw a familiar face jogging toward them. It was one of her new neighbors, Linda Simmons. They had met at a barbecue a week earlier and had hit it off.

As her friend neared, Estella greeted her, "Nice day for a run!"

Linda smiled, "Keeps the stress away, yes."

She leaned down and greeted Estella's little girl, "And, you must be Marie!"

"Yes, I am!"

"Nice to see you're not shy," Linda laughed. Marie beamed.

"That's because I'm gonna be President someday!"

Estella dryly commented, "She takes after her father."

Her new friend laughed, "My daughter wants to be a veterinarian!"

Estella felt comfortable enough with her new friend to share a bit of frustration, "I'm a bit overwhelmed these days; this town is a big, fat puzzle to me. I feel like a rat trying to find the cheese in a maze, and I keep hitting dead ends!"

Linda agreed, "It's the most social of cities with all these tiers of influence, propriety, and social standing. You have to know how to play the game!"

"I'm pretty naïve about that…" Linda laughed and bade farewell. "It's good seeing you; let's have coffee later in the week and talk about this, okay?"

Estella nodded, "I'd like that!" Linda jogged off, and Estella rejoined Marie as they walked back to their car.

At dinner that night, Xavier was unusually quiet. Estella brought him more coffee and asked him, "Are you alright?"

Her husband did not answer right away and then looked up and blurted out, "Yeah, I'm fine!"

Estella frowned at him, "You don't seem fine. You've been working a lot of late nights. This is the first time you've been home for dinner in over a week!"

"Freshman congressmen don't set their own schedules, Estella; they set themselves. I'm swamped trying to keep up."

"Well, don't forget, you have a family."

Xavier laughed, "I don't think you will ever allow that to happen!"

Estella went into the kitchen to get dessert. While she was gone, she overheard her husband ask Marie, "Do you like your new school?"

Marie answered, "Oh, yes! We're learning about the planets."

Xavier asked her, "What's your favorite one?"

His daughter replied, "Earth, Daddy; don't be silly!"

Estella laughed at that exchange.

The following evening, she and Xavier, accompanied by

their Secret Service agent, attended a formal dinner honoring all the new congressmen at the Dayflower Hotel, which housed one of the largest ballrooms in the city.

It was a spectacular ballroom, traditional and lit with gorgeous crystal chandeliers.

Always lauded for her impeccable taste, Estella wore a flowing Chanel chiffon gown that accentuated her sensual gracefulness.

As the chiffon flowed in waves around her, it almost appeared as she was walking on water; the crystals on the gown shimmered like droplets as she glided across the ballroom. Her dark red hair was a beautiful contrast against the navy of the gown.

Xavier and Estella were having a fabulous time at first and were the most strikingly attractive "it" couple at the ball during the cocktail reception.

However, when it was time to sit in their seats for dinner, Estella was assigned to sit next to and across from two senior congressmen's' wives who were notorious for their cattiness. They tag-team grilled her with odd questions for an hour until Estella became so nervous, she picked up the wrong fork to eat her shrimp cocktail.

As she looked around, she saw several women, obviously high-society types, looking in her direction and smirking at one another.

Immediately, Estella felt ashamed. She just wasn't used to this level of scrutiny. Her face turned beet red, and she fumbled with her fork when Xavier leaned in and whispered, "You're making a fool of yourself; that's your salad fork!"

"Oh, sorry. I got distracted and nervous," Estella whispered back and immediately picked up the correct fork, but in her nervousness, she dropped it and winced as it clanged loudly against the Laterford crystal that was part of her place setting.

Estella quickly excused herself, amid titters of laughter, and disappeared into the bathroom. She looked into the mirror and scolded her image exasperated: *"These people aren't for you! I am so sick and tired of smiling monsters!"*

She wrote a note and asked the attendant at the ballroom door to pass it to the waiter assigned to Xavier's table. In the missive, Estella let Xavier know she was unwell and had to return home and to please give her excuses and apologies to the people at the table.

Estella left through a side door to the street, hailed a cab and went home rather than return to the event and face another two hours of the Catty Wives Club inquisition.

When Xavier arrived home, he pointedly commented, "Well, that was rude!"

Estella apologized, "I'm sorry; I'm having trouble fitting in here. You know I was feeling nervous again."

"Well, walking out on me is not the solution, Estella! Perhaps you should see a doctor about your nerves and get some medication."

"I didn't walk out on you; I walked out on *them*! I don't want to be one of those blank-eyed pill-popping puppet wives. I am trying meditation and natural remedies to deal with my nerves first."

"I want you to go upstairs and call my mother right now!" barked Xavier.

She fired back at him, "You are not helping with your judgment of me, yelling, and your lack of support. At first, you

126

made me laugh and held my hand when I was nervous: you have changed. You're letting these people inflate your head if that is even possible for your head to be any bigger than it already is! I wouldn't be surprised if it just floated off your head into oblivion!"

Xavier kept pounding her. "This is not just mild nervousness, Estella. You and your panic attacks are getting old! Get yourself under control or get meds. You can't be 'unwell' all the time in this job as a politician's wife; I have to be on almost 24/7, and so do you if we want to rise high in this career."

Xavier calmed his voice.

He still had an annoyed look on his face deciding, to hurtfully use the medical term, "panic attacks" for her nervousness, to make his wife feel even more inadequate.

As Estella sat on her bed, she felt completely alone. She felt she was not only losing her husband; she was losing her own life, as well. Instead of moaning to Renee; she decided to be proactive and get some social help.

She dialed her mother-in-law.

The next evening around dusk, Estella was sitting on her front lawn when she saw a limousine pull up in front of her home. Out stepped Catherine Cyrus with a big smile and several packages. She addressed Estella, "I was in the neighborhood, so I thought I would swing by and bring Marie some toys!" Estella smiled,

"Thanks for coming, Mother."

Catherine hugged Estella who returned the embrace, and they went inside. Estella made some coffee, and the two of them caught up on each other's lives.

After Estella updated her about Xavier's work in the

House of Representatives, Marie's pronouncement that she was going to be President and her frustration with fitting in with the high society crowd, Catherine responded to her.

"I am going to help you fit in with the social mavens of Washington D.C. You have to learn how they think, how they plan, and how they behave. You are now a politician's wife. You have to look and play the part!"

Estella helplessly stared at her with pleading eyes, "I have no idea how to do all those things, Catherine. It's like they are from another planet!"

Her mother-in-law smiled, "They are from another planet — the planet 'Imagenera'.'"

Estella laughed, "That's a good one, Catherine!"

"Okay, so let's get organized," Catherine summarized. "We need to break all this down by categories. Think of this as military training, basic, medium, advanced, and all-out War!"

Estella was impressed with Catherine's approach to her problem. "Becoming accepted in D.C.'s social circles is not random?"

"Oh, not at all. You must learn the main players, the calendar events, which ones to attend and which ones to avoid, who the accepted dress designers are, how to play the media, building your image and the people you will need in order to flourish and those you need to keep in check."

"It all sounds so complicated, Catherine. It's not like throwing on a dress and going to a gala!"

"A gala is just a spoke in your social wheel. Your wheel has many spokes. You have to refine all of them."

"What's the hub?"

"Social status of the highest accord! Let's begin."

And they did begin. Catherine taught Estella how to navigate DC society like a pro.

CHAPTER SIXTEEN

The Mistress

Is the marriage good?" Catherine asked her daughter-in-law on a follow-up phone call upon returning home.

"I couldn't be happier; everything is fine," Estella lied.

Catherine smiled, "It truly is a modern-day miracle. My son has finally grown up and accepted the role of a responsible husband and father."

*****

In a hotel room not far from his Georgetown residence, Xavier was enjoying a compliment, "I can see why Estella married you. You're the best lover I've ever had!"

He smiled down at her, "I have no doubt you are being honest. I have heard that on multiple occasions."

The voice in the dark giggled, "Speaking of multiple, I believe I am due for at least one more, maybe two!"

Xavier looked at his watch, "And, I believe I have time to take care of that for you! But then I need to hurry home, Estella is making my favorite pot roast tonight."

"Mmmm, mustn't miss that; I want you, my man, to be healthy and strong at all times."

Xavier smiled at her knowingly, "I believe you mean men, as in plural."

"Absolutely, I never put all my eggs into one basket, too dangerous."

Xavier began kissing her neck and moved down her body with seamless ease as he parted her supple thighs and began to pleasure them. The voice was gasping and moaning now, "Oooh, ahhh, oh my god, yes, yes, yes…oh, *yes*!"

Xavier asked her, "You like that?"

"Oh, you are such a naughty boy; don't stop. Don't ever stop!"

After a few minutes of complete sexual abandonment, the woman with the sexy voice finally let out a final sigh. Xavier stood up and quickly put on his pants. Within seconds, he was moving towards the door.

"When will I see you again?" she asked him.

"I told my wife I have a late caucus to attend tomorrow night. Meet me here in the room at 7:00 PM."

She purred, "Drive safely!"

"Always," he promised, as he disappeared into the hallway.

At dinner that night, as Xavier was happily wolfing down his pot roast, Estella sensed an unusual coldness from her husband. She asked him, "Do you still love me?"

Xavier looked up from his gorging and frowned at her, "What kind of question is that?"

Estella returned the sour look and said, "Then, answer it!"

"Yeah, I do," Xavier mumbled as he dove back into his

beloved beef.

"You do what?" she insisted.

"What you said!"

"I didn't say anything, Xavier. I asked a question: 'Do you love me?'"

Xavier was not into this conversation. In fact, he wanted to change it and talk about something else; anything else.

He nodded at Marie who was carefully listening to the repartee, "Not here, Estella; for God's sake!"

His wife was not appeased, "Telling your wife you love her in front of your child should not be off-limits!" Marie chimed in,

"Yeah, Daddy! Tell mommy you love her!"

Suddenly, Xavier stood up and pounded the table knocking over his glass spilling water everywhere.

Then, he shouted, "Yes, I *love* you! Now, are you happy?"

Estella was stunned and little Marie broke into tears sobbing, "Why is Daddy so angry about loving you, Mommy?"

Xavier stormed out of the dining room and up the stairs to his bedroom as he slammed the door for effect. Estella and Marie were both crying now as they sat at the table in shock.

She was now convinced that something was eating at her husband, and she was part of that something.

But what was it?

Or, more scarily, *who* was it?

That night, as she turned out the lights and slid into bed next to him, she whispered, "If I did something wrong to upset you; I am sorry. You can talk to me, Xavier; I'm your wife."

There was no response.

Estella lay there for almost two hours before she finally drifted off to sleep.

The next day, two significant phone calls were made; Xavier called his mistress and canceled their tryst for the evening, and Estella phoned Renee to ask for advice.

"Renee, have you ever dated or married a man who cheated on you?"

Her mother's antennae immediately went up, "Is Xavier having an affair?"

"I don't know, that's why I am calling you."

Mama was honest, "Yes, I have had a couple of my ex-boyfriends engage in unfaithfulness."

Estella had another question, "Can you tell me if there were any tell-tale signs that gave their affair away to you?"

Renee thought for a moment and then answered, "There are a few things all cheating men have in common, yes."

"Such as?"

"Well, the obvious one is a decreased desire in sex with his spouse. If he is carrying on a torrid affair with another woman, she is taking all his ardor. That's a dead giveaway there."

Estella made a mental note, "What else?"

"He will constantly bring up his suspicions that you may be cheating on him, which is a projection of his own guilt. Another manifestation of his guilt could be abrupt outbursts of anger or violence."

"Oh my god!" Estella exclaimed.

Then, she related Xavier's behavior at dinner when she had asked him if he loved her, which had led to the culmination of the dish hurling explosion.

Renee was concerned, "That is one of the main signs; he was not throwing that dish at you but at himself. He has been a bad boy and he knows it. Furthermore, he hates it."

"And himself," chimed in her daughter.

"Could very well be. How has your sex life been lately?"

"It has been below average, just about on life support really; but I attributed it to his work schedule, being out late several nights a week with meetings and…"

Estella suddenly stopped in mid-sentence.

Renee knew why: "About those frequent late-night 'meetings,' I am wondering if they were in a committee room or a hotel room!"

Her daughter was on the same page, "That's another sign, Renee. What has he been doing all those evenings?"

"Well, you could ask him, Estella. But I seriously doubt he would be happy about your prying."

"Xavier has always been secretive about his women. I remember that from college. He never let anyone know how many women were in his harem or their names. He always acted like there was only one, but we all knew better."

Renee sadly summarized, "Sounds like he is continuing his sexual ways."

"I honestly don't want to know, Renee. I would rather keep my life, shield my daughter, pursue my passionate causes, enjoy my growing power to enable them, and stay married."

"Ultimately, staying married may not be an option down the road. It all depends on how much this other woman — and we don't know for sure there is another woman — means to him."

"Thanks, Renee. But as his secret weapon, I don't think Xavier will be divorcing me anytime soon, at least not while he is still trying to advance politically. Losing me when he may need me would be foolish on his part!"

"Some loose women will do things a wife would never do in bed. Men are foolish when they are full of themselves, and they are thinking with the wrong head. Hubris may make him think he can win without you. Always stay prepared to live life comfortably without him, harden your heart and never give Xavier enough of your heart that it will hurt you if he leaves," Renee advised.

"Thank you for the advice, Renee."

"You're welcome. Bye."

Estella hung up the phone and numbly sat down in the kitchen waiting for Xavier to come home. Part of her never wanted him to ever come home again.

But, that would not have been healthy for Marie.

Estella was in a funk about this scenario, mainly because she wasn't completely certain there was even an affair going on.

Should she seriously try to find out the truth?

At dinner that night, as Xavier was eating, Estella examined his every response and reaction trying to discover any clue to his faithfulness to her.

She was gratified to hear him sincerely apologize to Marie, "Daddy was wrong last night, baby. I do love mommy very much and I should never have thrown my plate like that!"

Marie's response was precious, "That's alright, Daddy. We all get angry, sometimes. I get mad at my dolls and hit them with my pillow. Nobody's perfect!"

Daddy and daughter hugged and as Marie went up to her bedroom, Xavier made Estella a promise, "I'll make it up to you tonight, Darling!"

His wife suddenly felt sick to her stomach. The last thing she wanted during this emotionally-wrenching time was sex with her husband. For the rest of the evening, she dreaded going to bed.

At 2:30 PM, her groggy husband came down to the den and found her reading a novel, "Aren't you coming to bed, Estella?"

She perkily replied, "I'm not really tired and this book is really good!"

Xavier saw the title and frowned, "You've already read that book a dozen times!"

"Oh, but I learn something new every time I read it!" she cheerily exclaimed.

Xavier yawned and stumbled back up the stairs, while Estella fretted about how much longer she could avoid the inevitable.

Over the next several days, the absurd pattern continued; Xavier begging Estella to come to bed and she averaging two hours of sleep a night.

One morning, as Estella was pulling her car out of the garage to run some errands, she saw Xavier pull in behind her, blocking her exit. He jumped out of his vehicle and opened her car door shouting, "Stop!"

She quickly put her gear into park and looked quizzically at him, "What's up?"

"Why are you avoiding me every night, Estella? I know those damn books you are reading are retreaded material. You're using them to avoid coming to bed with me. I want to know why?"

Estella could not believe her ears as she calmly confronted him, "Ask your mistress."

Xavier's face went beet red. At first, he had trouble comprehending her statement. Then, he realized he had to respond and do so quickly to avoid detection, "I don't have a mistress, you're being paranoid, Estella."

"I don't think so, Xavier. You are not attending late-night political meetings; you are lying in the arms of a woman who is not your wife. Now, do you want to discuss it or should I just file for divorce and take our daughter with me," she bluffed.

Rather than admit to an affair, he switched topics and tactics. "You won't win in a divorce, Estella; you will be giving up too much money and this beautiful home, not to mention Marie."

"I'll take that chance, Xavier. I am not going to sit back and let you embarrass and disrespect me. Who is she?"

Her husband stood there silently; a sure indicator of guilt. He really didn't know what to say to Estella at that point. So, he put on a brave face and announced, "We will discuss this ridiculous accusation at a later date. I need to get back to work."

He walked quickly to his car and peeled backward out of the driveway, almost obliterating Marie's tricycle in the process. In a moment he was gone and Estella was now more confused than ever. Was he telling the truth? Should she pursue her instincts?

Or, should she drop it and hope he would get tired of the wench and come back to her on his own.

Xavier never stayed with one girl very long, except for Debra and he had only done that for social and financial reasons,.

For the time being, Estella decided to stop confronting her husband and let it be. She had bigger fish to fry; women's rights, civil rights, and the space exploration fish. Those were her three loves and since Xavier was paving the way for her power to make those goals realities, maybe the best revenge was for her to cram them down his throat. He hated minorities; he thought women should stay in bed or the kitchen, and he thought space

138

exploration was a big waste of time and money. So, she was going to make him miserable. He could have all the sex he wanted; she would use him to get all the power she needed.

She also knew that divorce wasn't her only option. Two could play this game. What's sauce for the goose was sauce for the gander, right?

Maybe, just maybe, there was another man in her future. Estella stood in the driveway and smirked to herself at the thought of an enraged Xavier Cyrus discovering his sweet innocent wife was having an affair and enjoying another man more than him. She was not sure her high morals would ever permit that, but it was a fun thought for sure.

That night, the thought became a very live reality. Xavier was assigned a Secret Service agent because of the numerous death threats he had been receiving prompting a need for protecting him.

At a military banquet for veterans, Xavier and Estella were summoned by the Deputy Director of the Secret Service and introduced to his new agent.

His name was Michael Hagar. He was a few years older than Xavier, taller and as good-looking. He was also African American.

Xavier was taken aback at first meeting Michael, but he hid his racist instincts well. Estella had a completely opposite response.

She was immediately enthralled with this new agent to the point she couldn't speak. Michael was the most gorgeous man she had ever seen in her life.

"And your name is Estella?" he politely asked her.

She smiled like a schoolgirl, "Estella, yes. Uh, that is my

name," she stammered.

The last time she had a goofy reaction like that was that day at the diner when Xavier had introduced himself.

It was *déjà vu*!

"That is a beautiful name. Are you Spanish?"

Estella began to explain her nationality. "No, I am actually, uh, not Spanish, I am, er, from Texas! The name Estella is French . I am named after my great-grandmother."

She couldn't take her eyes off him. His gaze upon her seemed to go right through to her soul. Her entire essence was suddenly bared to those piercing warm brown eyes of his. It was as if her soul recognized his and his soul recognized hers. "*Is this how love at first sight feels?*" Estella thought.

Finally, the Deputy suggested, "Xavier, I need to meet privately with you and Michael and go over the protocol for how all this works. Excuse us, Mrs. Cyrus!"

As the three of them walked away, Estella headed directly to the bar and downed a double whiskey neat. After a few minutes, she was finally able to breathe normally again. She whispered to herself, "This is going to be very interesting."

Indeed.

CHAPTER SEVENTEEN

The House of Dionysius

One day at lunch, Xavier looked across at his mentor and brought up the conversation they had concerning the fast track to political power. He asked his influential friend, "Can we discuss the extraordinary association you were telling me about the night our wives met?"

Burke smiled coyly. "Oh, that?

"Do you think joining said association could help me to be named to the Appropriations Committee?" Xavier said reverently as he leaned forward. "*I would really appreciate it, my friend.*"

The man who had taken Xavier to the pinnacle of political success was now ready to place him there. He began to explain the successful process. "Well, I am talking about a secret society of some of the most influential leaders in D.C., so yes; I think if you were initiated and all went well, you could be appointed to Appropriations next year."

Xavier was rapt now. "What kind of secret society, Sam?"

"If you share a word about this — even with your wife — without my permission, I will have to cut you loose and let you be on your own. Do you understand, Xavier?"

"It's in the vault," his protégé assured him, "under lock and key eternally."

Burke nodded, "Basically, it's a secret society of ritualistic sex. I can't divulge the actual name of the group until you are voted in and initiated."

Xavier let out an audible gasp.

His mentor continued in a whisper, "You name it — we sexually do it. The pleasures we enjoy here are without limits. Everything you can imagine human beings enjoying hedonistically is on the table."

Xavier uttered in awe, "My god!"

The revered leader laughed, "That's exactly what I said the first time I went to one of their meetings. It is a powerful ritual; replete with role-playing, costumes, characters, mystery and sex of all kinds — including orgies and sadism if that's your preference."

Xavier quickly gulped down his glass of ice water, "Go on!" he urged his leader.

"It begins with a secret handshake at the large steel-gated entrance to gain admittance."

Xavier asked him, "How will I know this handshake?"

Sam smiled, "I will happily teach it to you!" then continued: "I will never forget my first night there; Dolores and I were,"

Xavier interrupted him, "Wait, Dolores went with you?"

Burke nodded, "Wives always attend; except on rare exceptions. At first, she was nervous, with a lot of reluctance. But, after she began sexually engaging with both men and women…"

Another interruption by Xavier, "Your beautiful wife was sexually enjoying both genders?"

His mentor laughed, "Yeah, crazy, huh?"

Burke pointedly asked him, "You want to have sex with my wife?"

"Excuse me?"

"Do you want to have your way with Dolores?

Xavier was dumbfounded at the possibility. He modestly responded, "Well, your wife is very attractive, Sam… but, in all honesty, I couldn't…"

Burke cut him off, "*You* are *her* sexual fantasy!"

Xavier dropped all pretense and exclaimed, "I'm all over Dolores, *yes!*"

His mentor laughed, "I will make it happen for you."

Xavier nervously coughed and quickly poured more water into his glass and chugged it all the way down. Burke whispered to Xavier, "Watching my beautiful Dolores being kissed and fondled by several men and women for hours was a huge turn on for me. Of course, I was quite busy, as well! It was a night to remember, my friend."

Xavier couldn't wait to blurt out, "Where do I sign up?"

The Speaker laughed, "You don't sign up; this isn't like joining a club. You have to be invited by a sponsor who takes you there."

"Any chance of you being my sponsor, Sam?"

"Yes, a very good chance. Our next event is in June; it will be a night you could only imagine, and an evening you will never forget!" Sam Burke asked Xavier, as he refilled his water glass, "Will you and Estella be able to join my wife and me?"

Xavier almost had a heart attack. "Estella?"

His enthusiasm for being involved in this society

immediately cooled. His wife would never go for this idea and he did not want her to; she was his sweet innocent wife, "Estella the Good," never to be shared with anyone.

"Well, Xavier?" Burke pressed him.

"I'm not sure I can convince my conservative, moral wife that she should have sex with strangers in the next few months, Sam."

Burke tried to assure his protégé, "She will be wearing a mask. Everyone's anonymity is intensely guarded from the public. Only the members of our society will ever know that you belong. No one will ever be able to verify it's her. We take our sacred oaths seriously."

Xavier explained in more depth, "Yeah, but she will know it's her. Estella is very spiritual, and a Christian, well.. you know!"

Sam nodded, "When do you see her joining us then?"

Estella's husband laughed, "The Twelfth of *never*!"

"If you're serious, that's too bad, my friend. Both Dolores and I are very attracted to Estella. My wife is pretty hot for you, as well."

"Dolores is a looker, Sam. You're a very lucky guy!"

Burke summarized, "So, that's the deal: you figure out a way to get Estella to assent and your career path will take off like a sky-rocket. The sky's the limit. It will also be the sexiest pleasure you will ever experience in your life."

Xavier lobbied for an another option, "There's no way I can come alone or bring a girlfriend?"

His mentor shook his head, "No, sorry. Even with all the swinging and sex, this is a member's only sacred ritual. We have to unanimously vote you into the organization. It is for life, and only married couples can join."

The two men stood up and shook hands. As he watched his political leader walk away, Xavier's mind was spinning. He didn't want his wife involved, but he craved the increase in political power and career opportunities potentially open to him.

Could he be President one day with their help?

His mind was going wild with different scenarios and lies he could tell to join the club and not have his wife passed around like a sexual party favor for his own ambition.

Estella was the best-looking wife of all the congressional wives and everyone would want their turn with her if he joined their secret sex club. In one wild scenario, the bigoted Xavier thought, "*I could join the sex club and then say I contracted some atypical strain of Asian herpes on a diplomatic trip to Korea that I had passed on to my wife so that no one would want to touch her? Hmmm… it's far-fetched; but who would take the risk? Then again since we never had sex in the sex ritual they may annul our membership like one would an unconsummated marriage. Hmm…very possible.*"

His mind was going down a dark and twisted rabbit hole as he considered all the various scenarios and possible horrible and grandiose outcomes of joining the ritual sex society without his sacred Estella.

He went back and forth about joining the secret society in his mind; even the possibility of pressuring Estella to join with him, although the idea of seeing her with another man disgusted him.

Finally, he tried to no avail to put the nameless ritualistic society out of his head and focus on his career without their help, but the temptation of that powerful and pleasurable society membership kept popping into his head. Nevertheless, as the

146

months passed his political influence and credibility continued to climb without the secret ritual society backing him.

Xavier was gaining a lot of respect for his work on the House Finance Committee, much to Estella's chagrin.

With each passing day — as she observed her husband's political star shining brighter and brighter — she became more concerned that his light would result in the snuffing out of her dreams.

365 days after he was sworn in, Xavier's poll numbers among his constituents in North Texas were phenomenal, hovering in the 80% range.

As he thought about the upcoming ritual on Saturday night he was frustrated in his inability to have Estella accompany him. He only had a few days to take advantage of the society's invitation and its powerful impact on his future career. As he laid in Mily's arms, she cooed, "I'm so proud of you, honey. It would be an honor to be your wife."

Xavier laughed, "Except, we're both currently married!"

"Oh, don't remind me! My husband is no match for you. He pales in black and white compared to your magnificent rainbow. You are everything a woman wants and more."

Her lover smugly smiled, "Yes, I know."

She threw a pillow at him, "Oh, you're so full of yourself!"

He grinned with a heavy dose of cockiness, "You can always leave me!"

She mounted him and began aggressively used her hips to grind against him, "Leave you? *Never!*"

"My sentiments exactly!" he roared. "It's about time for another one of your violent orgasms, sweetness."

Within seconds, she passed out on his chest. Xavier smiled to himself, "Yep, absolutely violent…"

As Mily dozed contentedly next to him, Xavier suddenly figured out how he could pull off his initiation. It suddenly dawned on him how he could break his own glass ceiling without Estella joining the sex ritual society.

He looked down at her slumbering stand-in. Now, he had to sell his mistress on the idea.

Xavier smacked Mily on her small butt and woke her up with an offer, "Mily, I have a masquerade ball for you to attend with me, but you have to pretend you are my wife and dye your hair Estella's color."

Mily, seeing this opportunity to be Xavier's surrogate wife, mistakenly believed that he was auditioning her for the actual role of Mrs. Xavier Cyrus and squealed excitedly, "Yes, Xavier! What should I wear? When is the ball?"

"Not now. Time for Round Two, Babe."

He flipped her over and thrust into Mily's rear, taking her into a taboo place that he would never even attempt on his wife.

CHAPTER EIGHTEEN

The Initiation

As the car pulled up to the front entrance of Xavier's home to take him to the Dionysius House, Estella was surprised to see Michael open the door for her husband and stand there while he entered the vehicle and it drove away.

As he re-entered the home, she questioned him, "Aren't you supposed to be with my husband at all times?" Michael smiled, "This is not one of those times, Mrs. Cyrus."

Estella was confused, "Where is my husband going that you are not able to accompany him?"

"It's a private matter, Ma'am. He doesn't need me tonight!"

"Oh, is he going somewhere where his safety is guaranteed?"

"In a sense, yes. He will be with people that pose no threat to his life."

Estella frowned, "So, I guess you will be watching Marie and I, huh?"

The agent smiled at her, "With pleasure, yes."

"Do you like popcorn and Doris Day movies?"

Michael laughed, "I prefer action movies and pork rinds, but I'll be in the next room!"

Estella nodded, "Well, I will feel safe with you around, Michael."

He looked her right in the eye, "I will always make you feel safe."

That comment and the way he delivered it sent an emotional jolt through her. As she walked into the living room to join Marie, she said inwardly, *"What is this feeling he keeps giving me?"*

*****

Several miles out of Georgetown, Xavier and Mily, pretending to be Estella, pulled up to the gated entrance of the mansion in a black limousine with tinted windows and were greeted by a physically impressive security man, well over six feet tall and muscular.

As he stood within the compound, he opened a panel on the gate and extended his arm with the question, "Give me the proper handshake?" Xavier clasped the guard's hand and manipulated his own in the acceptable twist required for acceptance explained to him by Sam Burke.

The massive gatekeeper smiled at him. "Welcome." The armed man opened the gate and allowed Xavier and his companion inside.

As Xavier and "Estella" walked slowly clad in their grotesque animal masks up the long driveway to the forbidding Gothic edifice, they had the sense they were in Transylvania during the 1400's, not a short distance away from Washington D.C.

Xavier protectively put his hand around his woman and felt her body trembling. It filled him with a sense of danger and excited him at the same time.

His blood began pumping furiously.

"It will be all right, Mily. These are powerful people; they are here to pleasure you, not put you in harm's way."

At the front door, it mysteriously opened without Xavier even ringing a bell.

They entered the forbidding estate and immediately smelled in-cense and the erotic odors of a sexual aphrodisiac which overpowered them with sensual desire.

Xavier whispered to her, "This will be an incredible and unforgettable sexual experience. Don't be nervous."

As Xavier and Mily approached the end of a long hall, they were greeted by two servants that led them into a private dressing area where they were instructed to don red togas and sandals with no undergarments.

Having changed their clothing, they came into a hallway and taken to the great room with stunning baroque décor and suddenly they were in front of several hundred people, all wearing masks and red robes.

Xavier surmised correctly they were all naked underneath their red satin garments.

A voice boomed out, "Are you ready for your initiation?"

Xavier nervously nodded.

"Kneel down at the altar!"

Xavier and Mily walked to a small area with a few steps and a long pew. They knelt down and waited for further instructions. The society leader came forward and stood above them. He was dressed in a black toga and wearing the mask of a satyr. He picked up a chalice off the small table and announced, "We are now ready to consecrate you as husband and wife to join us in a mass marriage where our bodies all become one and belong to each other."

Xavier thought, *"This is exhilarating!"*

"I will now ask you to open each other's togas so you may show yourselves to our society."

Xavier and his now shaking mistress stood and followed the Satyr's instructions as the rest of the members surveyed the bodies of their new members.

The Satyr commented, "You are both worthy of our standards of excellence."

He handed the chalice filled with red wine to Xavier who drank lustily of it; then, he gave it to Mily who swallowed shyly and elegantly.

"It is now time for acclamation!"

The powerful Satyr asked the large mass gathered there, "Do you take this couple into your love?"

In unison, they cried, "We do!"

"Do you pledge your ultimate loyalty to them inside and outside of this House?"

"We do!"

"Will you treat both of them with the utmost respect and honor in any request they make of you?"

"We will!"

"Will this couple's sponsor, please step forward!" ordered the voice.

Samuel Burke, unrecognizable to his friends due to his outfit and mask covering, walked up and stood next to Xavier and his mistress masquerading as Estella.

The booming voice asked thunderously, "Do you endorse these applicants?"

Burke answered firmly, "I do!"

"Are they worthy of our statutes and standards?"

"They are!"

"Are they discreet and obedient to our secrecy code?"

Burke averred, "Completely and fully!"

"Do you stand by these novitiates with complete approval?"

"Absolutely, unequivocally, and without any reservation!"

The Satyr summarized, "By the order of The House of Dionysus constitution, I hereby declare these applicants fully-approved members for life with all privileges and powers. They are to be honored in every request they make in body and spirit that is in our power and does not conflict! Your names are now Apollo 11 and Diana 11 within our House, sign your names." Xavier and Mily's middle fingers were pricked by the Satyrs ceremonial knife and they signed their names in the blood that oozed from their fingers in a huge book on the black alter. Mily forged Estella's name without reservation.

Xavier began to feel woozy from something in the wine the Satyr had given him. He began to panic and sweat, thinking, *"Perhaps this was not a good idea. I should just get up and run the hell out of here. This ceremony is crazy."* Xavier looked at Mily's masked face and into her eyes which mirrored his concern.

Mily thought, trembling, *"What is this book about? Have I sold my soul? Is Xavier a devil are all these people devils?"* Although Mily had been involved in wife swapping, key parties, and swinger clubs with her first husband, she had never encountered anything like what she was now witnessing. This scene terrified and excited her at the same time.

At that point, Xavier and Mily were suddenly enveloped by over five hundred members welcoming them into the secret society. There was a lot of hugging, touching, sexual groping and cheering as the Dionysians made him and his sexually stunned companion one of their own.

The couple was led by the two servants amid the celebratory chanting and exclamations of the members out the back door of the mansion and into a beautiful floral area dubbed *The Dionysus Garden*.

In Latin, the Satyr shouted, "With the power of water, fire, air, and earth I invoke Dionysus the bringer of all our desires, and we offer Dionysus our energy in the form of sexual release."

The Satyr commanded the members, "Exclaim your Solstice desires!" then with a torch, he lit a bonfire at the top of which was a wooden statue of a bull as the members shouted a multitude of different desires mostly for greater wealth or power.

Mily, still trembling, thought, *"Is it my imagination or is that a muffled scream from the vicinity of the bonfire?"*

The drugged wine from the chalice began to calm her, and Mily was thankful for the drug as she reassured herself, *"No, it can't be a scream. It is just the shouting of the crowd."*

The Satyr exclaimed, "Commence the ritual!" Within seconds togas were flying everywhere as partygoers stripped and began "pairing off" in threesomes, foursomes and every numerical option possible, as the sex ritual began.

The only thing that remained on their bodies were their masks defined in dozens of ways from sexy satyrs to forest beasts and in every conceivable face-covering imaginable.

As Xavier gleefully looked around lustily, his concerns soon faded; he saw women with beautiful bodies being laid down on the grass with one, two or three men pleasuring them from head to toe. There were men of all ages with multiple women using their mouths in a variety of sexual ways to fulfill their fantasies.

Male and female, heterosexual, homosexual, and bisexual — they found each other, and the devouring of flesh was rampant.

As he entered the Garden, Xavier looked up and saw his mentor standing with the beautiful Dolores. She walked quickly over to him, got on her knees and began pleasure him with her mouth while her husband made his way to who he thought was Estella.

Before Sam could get to her, two men — one young and handsome, the other unattractive and old enough to be her grandfather — picked her up and carried her off to a grove of trees. As they had their way with her, Sam waited his turn patiently.

Within a few minutes, Xavier could hear her gasping, moaning, and screaming with delight under the moon of the June Solstice. Xavier smiled to himself, *"she would never get this kind of pleasure from her dull husband!"* He laughed.

His mistress had succumbed to her first taste of pleasure. Now, it was time for him to take care of himself! Dolores Burke had made him more than horny; he was ready for more. He saw a curvaceous young woman, probably in her early 20's, and motioned to her. She skipped over to him and he began to fondle her huge breasts.

Within seconds, another girl just as physically endowed knelt down in front of him and did her best Dolores Burke imitation. Now, Xavier was occupied with kissing the first girl and being tongued by the other one.

This was the tone for the entire evening.

As soon as one woman finished off Xavier; there were two more to bring him to a new level of sensual pleasure. It was an unending buffet of sexual delights that he never thought possible. Even the older women had sexy techniques that wowed him. He exclaimed gleefully to himself, "*All this and a new level of political influence and power that will enable me to soar in the House of Representatives and beyond.*"

As the evening wore down, Mily whispered to Xavier, "Can we go soon? My lower body is on fire! I have never been this sore!"

Finally, the two of them limped back to the front gate, where their limousine was waiting to take them home.

Xavier smiled, "Sam was right; it will be an evening I will remember forever!"

He gratefully kissed Mily on the cheek and said, "Thank you."

She moaned with pain, "It's gonna be a week before I can walk normally again!" Xavier laughed, handing Mily a gift box with a diamond necklace.

*****

The following evening, after soaring high among the clouds of fantasy, reality quickly brought Xavier plummeting to earth.

Estella was livid. "Xavier, what the hell is going on here, did you set me up? You said that I needed to go to represent us at Congressman Raines' reception at the Billard Hotel without you because you were too busy with work."

Xavier nodded, "Yeah, so?"

She was steaming mad, "Well, some congressman's wife that I had never seen before stroked my hand in the bathroom when we were alone and called me by my first name! When I looked appalled, she calmly apologized and said, 'Sorry, please forgive me. I know that behavior is only for The House, but I really enjoyed our time together and I thought you had, also!'"

As Estella was relating the incident, Xavier suddenly felt a sinking feeling in his stomach.

Estella wasn't finished, by any means, "At the same event I was asked to go to Happy Hour twice by a Congressman and a Senator both of whom I had never met, and they were acting sexually familiar with me and calling me by my first name!"

Estella screamed at Xavier in their bedroom as she endured the painful flashbacks to the night Josh had set her up to be attacked by Xavier. The panic attacks that she had thought she had recently overcome with therapy, meditation, and herbs were now back with full effect.

Xavier tried to neutralize her accusations, "Estella you are being paranoid; they were probably just being friendly. They probably met you at another event and you forgot the encounters. I forget half the people I meet. Calm down, baby," He tried to hug and comfort her with his fake concerned face.

It didn't work; she knew him too well. "You are a dammed *liar*, Xavier. I will never trust you ever again. If you do not tell me the complete truth right now, we are done forever and I am taking Marie this minute — out the door, to the airport — and we are never coming back. I'm not even going to pack! You can keep all that shit. You have one minute to explain!" Estella screamed the last bit as she began counting down the seconds on her *Soleq* watch.

She turned and caught a glimpse of herself in the mirror and saw a crazed wild banshee. The trauma and stress of being with

Xavier all these years had changed her persona from the calm, reasonable lady that she was raised to be into this snarling angry loon in the mirror. After seeing herself in this state in her bedroom's wall of mirrors, Estella shrugged her shoulders and gave up. "You know what? I don't even want to hear your explanation. I can't do this anymore. I am so gone..."

She turned to walk away.

Xavier grabbed her arm looking panicked because he saw she was really serious this time and he still loved her too much, at least as much as he was capable of, to let her leave without a fight. "I really am so sorry; I will tell you everything. But first, I have sworn a sacred oath of secrecy so you can never tell anyone ever about any of this. I must have your sworn word, Estella."

And, for once, Estella saw that Xavier was sincerely sorry. Also for once, he really was willing to tell her everything, even more than she wanted to know.

Her face softened towards him, "Yes, Xavier. I swear. You know I am a person of my word." Estella looked seriously into Xavier's eyes as she swore to keep the information he was presenting to herself.

He began with trepidation anticipating her reaction, "There is a secret worldwide society called The House of Dionysius, that many of the Congressmen, Senators, Governors, millionaire donors, high-level government officials and all their spouses, belong to; and we have rituals that involve sex of all kinds. I did not want to tell you about it because I knew you would not approve or join," he explained.

He paused to take a breath giving Estella an opening to go on another rant.

"What is the rest of the story? How do they know my name?"

159

Estella began to look angry again, concerned that he was still stalling and hiding the story from her.

"I am just trying to figure out the best way to explain all of this, Estella..."

Xavier had never been at a loss for words in his life as he was now. "They would only let me join The House if I brought my wife. Everyone must be married, and everyone's wife must join and participate in the sex rituals with other men. However, we all must wear masks when we meet. I brought someone who looks similar to you who pretended to be you. I took her to the rituals to have sex with the other husbands. In exchange, I receive powerful career help which will enable me to be named on the Appropriations Committee next year."

Estella asked disgustedly, "Who is she and how much does she look like me?" Xavier's wife could not help her curiosity even though she no longer cared enough to be jealous. After Xavier had broken her heart so many times, it now felt cold and as hard as a stone in her chest, where it had once held warmth for the father of her child.

"Jeffery's wife, Emily. You know...we call her Mily." Xavier referred to one of his office assistants that he and Estella had met at a meet and greet party at his office that Xavier had held for his new staff and their families.

Mily, the wife in question, did have a striking resemblance to Estella except for her bleached-blonde hair and smaller butt, unlike Estella's round and curvy one.

Xavier went into more detail, "The vow of secrecy extends to individual favors, including sexual or career opportunities and situations involving basically any type of favor. For example, if you feel that someone is sexually harassing you from The D

160

House, all you have to say to them is, 'By oath of The House; be silent. You are my sister,' — or if a male, 'My brother' — and, they will stop. Or, let's say you would like funds earmarked for a space telescope; you could meet with Congressman Carothers, who is the Chair of the Appropriations Committee, by calling his office and putting your name on his schedule for lunch or dinner and meet with him in a public restaurant. Of course, you would make pleasantries and small talk, but maybe halfway through the meal, you can say, 'Brother, I really need your help for money for the space telescope. I need $1 million earmarked for my project. Can you please help me?' If it is in his power and your request does not conflict with other interests, he will say 'yes.'"

Xavier gave further detail. "If you do not want anyone to know, even members of The D House, that he earmarked you this money or that you even asked just say, 'By the Oath of the House, be silent on this matter.' It will forever be your secret. I have a list of members and the list you were supposed to be given is locked in my study. If you ever need a favor outside of D.C., there is a coordinator on the list that can connect you with any D House members around the world."

Xavier was explaining and trying to bribe Estella at the same time, by dangling her need for a new telescope. He knew Estella needed money to purchase a new high-powered space telescope for the research purposes of the scientific organizations that were working on her space initiatives. As Xavier finished his long and drawn-out explanation, Estella focused on what mattered to her the most, her research for space exploration.

The telescope.

As Xavier unburdened his conscience in far too much detail about his infidelities in the House of Dionysus, Estella coldly asked him. "Does this room look like a church confessional to you? I am not a Catholic priest or your psychiatrist. You can keep this nasty mess to yourself or go to a professional that is forced to listen to all your dirty details."

Then, she dropped a bomb on him with her conclusion, "Xavier, please go now and take your things to the guest room. You disgust me." She shuddered with contempt for him.

CHAPTER NINETEEN

Estella and Her Political Causes

For the next several weeks, there were more late "meetings" for the "busy" congressman, but there was no protest from his wife concerning them.

Estella was too immersed working on three main issues: civil rights, women's equality, and space exploration.

All three causes still enthralled her.

Estella loved the possibility of one day seeing all mankind being treated with respect, dignity, and equality; if not in her lifetime, at least in Marie's. She would do all that was in her limited power to protect Marie and make a better and safer world for her daughter. For mankind to survive the catastrophes that many scientists predict colonization of other planets in the future would be necessary. Estella was taught by her mother as all the generations of her family were, that everyone should do their part no matter how small, to the best of their abilities to improve the world and help mankind.

Voter registration was specifically critical.

The more women and minorities that registered to vote, the more they could elect leaders that would positively impact their lives.

And then there was space exploration.

Renee had always watched the stars with her daughter, pointing out the constellations, especially Orion's Belt and the Sirius star systems, as her mother and grandmothers had done.

Estella fueled that same passion into her daughter, Marie Cyrus, who was captivated by the universe and its entities, particularly the stars. Estella's daughter had not only memorized the nine orbs and the major constellations throughout the galaxy, but she knew hundreds of facts and figures concerning them.

They were now a grandmother, mother, and daughter team to advance the education, research, and potential of space travel, not just to the moon, but to the planets and beyond.

Furthermore, Estella had met with Senator Carothers, as per her husband's explanation, and had attained her valuable telescope which enabled the scientists to move ahead with their research.

She hated the slimy process of the sex society, but all was fair in love and war. If her husband was going to assist her in pursuing her dreams in a sick, sexual way, so be it.

She needed that telescope!

Estella was going to play the game and keep quiet while allowing Mily to be her body double. But, when it came to space, she had internal ethical and safety questions.

"What if there were other beings or lower life forms on other planets; should they be disturbed by Earth's future colonists?"

"What if other beings had superior technology? Could reaching out to them jeopardize Earth? What if they decided to colonize Earth?"

"If we could not treat people fairly on Earth, could we get along with beings on other worlds?"

"Was it right to infect other worlds with the hatred and self-serving greed that we could not overcome on Earth?"

Of course, Xavier treated "their little project," as he referred to it, with amusement. Had he become aware of Estella's liberal passions as she lobbied for women's rights, racial justice, and voter enhancement for minorities, especially Negroes, he would have been livid.

The thought of her husband going ballistic over these causes made his wife work even harder to bring them to fruition.

Hundreds of times, Estella had asked herself the question that had always baffled her, *"Why is gender or a person's color of skin a determinant factor in equality?"*

Racism based upon color was absurd in Estella's eyes. And as an abuse survivor having to raise a daughter in this man's world was heartrending, even though Marie was growing up in a privileged family. Estella vowed to do what she could to improve the world, not just for Marie but for the future of all children.

A human being should never be judged by his or her exterior hue or gender; only by their character, self-respect, and contributions to society.

Estella realized that Xavier and men like him wanted to economically control and subjugate woman so that they could use them as servants, trophies, toys, and pawns. Estella would let Xavier think she was the dutiful controlled "wifey" while she used his position to further her agendas.

The main difference between the four main races — Negro, Hispanic, Asian and Caucasian — in Estella's eyes was that Caucasians men had power and they saw any other culture or race as a threat to that power. Civil rights and voter registration were direct threats to the bullying ignorance of racists like Xavier.

166

What Xavier did know was that his association with Sam Burke was paying political dividends. He had become the Speaker's righthand man in the House and had been named a Vice-Chair of the powerful Finance Committee, responsible for budgets and spending.

This enabled Xavier to have a key voice on what programs would move forward to laws or die in committee. But, the golden ticket that he really desired was to be named the Chair of the most powerful committee, Appropriations.

All congressmen wanted to be assigned the Appropriations Committee, which gave one the power to be in charge of writing spending bills and earmarking funds they could use as leverage with their colleagues.

Only very senior and well-connected congressmen even had a chance of being assigned there, much less becoming the chairman.

Xavier's appointment of Vice-Chair to the Finance Committee had not been good news for Estella. She realized her husband could be a major killer of her causes, just as her using his power and connections could help her causes. She decided to pursue her agendas with all the energy and passion she possessed while trying to sway Xavier to her side on important political issues. Xavier's admission of infidelity and his feelings of guilt could be used to her advantage now that he was trying to make up with her for his horrible behavior.

As Estella lay in bed alone and rehashed her latest confrontation with her hedonistic husband, she shook her head at all his rationalistic drivel concerning the ritual sex group and their supposed power of helping each other move to the top of the political heap. *"Xavier can justify any action he wants to take — moral or immoral — and he likes the power. Well, I will like it,*

167

too!"

Renee had been right long ago she thought to herself, *"You crave power, Estella; you just don't know it yet!"*

Yes, she did crave power. She hated that her mother had been right about her.

But, sex society or not, it was time for Estella to step up her passion for the people and causes in which she believed.

If her perverted husband and his pathetic mistress were going to pave the way for her to help minorities, women, and explore space, then so be it.

She realized that night that her husband had been both an influence and an impediment in her potential to affect the world in a positive way. Yes; his growing political power to national prominence had given her the inside track for her own programs; but his inconsistent and destructive behaviors had thrown her off course dozens of times, as well.

Xavier Cyrus had been the best of worlds and the worst of worlds in her life and in her potential as a human being. She was finally getting a grip on what she had to start doing if she wanted to spend the rest of her life fulfilling her dreams.

Estella had to mentally separate herself from Xavier and stop getting caught in his web of dysfunction.

There were so many people out there that she could help now! From poor women, Negroes, Hispanics, Asians, and Native Americans, to the homeless, the hungry, the helpless and all the millions who Estella saw clearly, as she mused in her bedroom, that she was called to help. She decided to help create a women's rights organization and align herself with the people of color and their courageous leadership. Simply put:

The NAACP.

Established in 1909, the National Association for the

Advancement of Colored People would be the go-to organization for Estella's commitment to racial equality.

The organization had stability, great leadership, and an undying passion to announce to the world that all men were created equal. All Estella had to do was plug into their movement and be part of something wonderful; something she truly believed in with all her heart. She would become intimately involved with those five letters in her lifetime.

In order to do that, she needed to go solo without Xavier's bigotry and move forward with a clear head to take charge on her own. She needed to become Estella Cyrus without so much of the Cyrus part.

She shook her head at all the moments that Xavier had stepped in and made her life miserable, abusive, or paralyzing.

She went all the way back to her childhood as she recalled the good and bad aspects of growing up with Mama Renee. There was no question as she laid there with tears streaming down her face, that she had been used way too many times by the two individuals she had trusted the most.

At times, they may have had noble intentions, but there had been too many moments when she had been devoured by their manipulations instead of standing up for herself.

If Estella was going to be a political and social force in America, the time was now for her to not only believe in the future of those she wanted to help, but to finally believe in herself.

That went for her passion for space exploration, as well.

Marie would join her in that latter project.

She would work with the agencies that governed these causes and help them succeed to make a better equal world and space travel realities one day.

As Estella drifted off, she could not wait for the morning. She was ready for the major changes that would define her new life.

And she smiled.

The dim morning light brought an unpleasant reality.

"I need some loving from my woman," an impatient Xavier grunted as he groped his wife's breasts under her nightshirt.

Estella was still waking up and tried to focus her eyes on the dawn of the new day while doing her best to stave off her horny husband. "Xavier, stop pawing me! I'm still asleep and I'm *not* in the mood!" Hearing him breathing heavily, she knew she had to get out of her bed as soon as humanly possible and negate his sexually ravenous attempts. Somehow, she tumbled over the edge of her bed unto the floor and before her husband could collect her; she was in the bathroom with the door locked and temporarily safe from his clutches.

"Estella!" he yelled as he pounded on the door, "Get back in bed, now!"

"My period just started!" she lied.

She was greeted with silence as he tried to do the math in his head to corroborate her physiological claim.

"That can't be!" he shouted, "This is the middle of the month!"

She yelled back through the door, "Stress has got my body all fouled up; I'm taking a shower now!"

She turned on the water just in time to hear him cursing loudly in the bedroom. By the time, she made it downstairs, he had finished eating his English muffin with coffee and with a newspaper in hand. He glared at her and left the house.

Estella was free to sit down and begin outlining her new

identity and purpose for life. As she sat down and began listing her thoughts on paper, she sipped her coffee with a new-found excitement.

Just as Catherine had taught her how to organize her social priorities, Estella used the same system for her political agenda. Her first topic was civil rights. It was time to make sense of her entry into it. She needed to find like-minded allies in the political arena that could begin to promote her new agenda without her name being involved. She couldn't wait to go to the library and soak up all she could about this remarkable organization.

After Marie was off to school, Estella took out her notebook again and wrote down the space agency she would contact as a volunteer to assist them in any way she could to promote the space program. The National Advisory Committee for Aeronautics (NACA). Estella knew the director of the agency and made plans to contact his office that week. She was pleased with her progress of the day.

She spent the evening hours following her day in the library, absorbing all the notes and books she had checked out, on both topics. She studiously familiarized herself with all of their goals, resources, programs, and personnel regarding civil rights and space exploration. She also organized a list of individuals on the Hill that could help her advocate for women's rights and made appointments with them.

Finally, an exhausted Estella turned out the light. It was time for sleep.

In the dawn's early hours, Estella dreamed of Xavier's large hand gently palming her breast.

"So, you got your telescope!"

This was *not* a dream!

Estella abruptly sat up in bed to find her nightshirt

171

unbuttoned and Xavier caressing her. "What in the hell are you doing, Xavier? How did you get in here?"

Her husband smirked and nodded at the open door with the lock lying on the floor.

Estella was not happy, "What's wrong? Did your work wife not do her job last night?"

She pushed his hand away and quickly closed her shirt while he laughed, "Hold me, love. The title wife only belongs to you. Don't refer to her as a work wife."

"How about ladder-climbing, enabling whore? More definitive?" Estella shot back.

Xavier smiled smugly, "Every career needs a boost now and then. Mily is simply doing what she can to promote mine. It's a mutual admiration society; she helps with the ritualistic people and I rescue her from her boring, impotent husband."

Estella was disgusted, "Okay, time for you to go. I have things to do…"

As she tried to scramble out of his grasp and head for the bathroom, Xavier threw her back down on the bed and ripped open her nightshirt. No more gentle touching now; he began to manhandle her roughly; first one nipple and then the other.

Despite her attempts to not be sexually affected, it wasn't long before her body betrayed her. His ace in the hole was that long tongue of his relentlessly sliding deep inside her. She had no power to stop its effect on her. In seconds, he had her moaning for mercy. Her brain was screaming at him to stop. Her body was begging for him to finish what he had started.

After several thrusts with his manhood, he was satisfied. He lay in bed like a conquering hero.

As her resentment grew in intensity; he tried to sound

172

interested in her causes and queried, "Tell me about this space deal with you and Marie!"

"What do you want to know, Xavier?"

"Is this going to stay in our family, or do you plan to take it national?"

Estella was quizzical, "What do you mean?"

"A little birdie told me that he was asked to include you in the NACA research studies."

Estella smiled. "I assume you are talking about Congressman Daley?"

Xavier nodded. "None other, Estella. Cool it with the causes!"

She was getting angry now, "The exploration of outer space is critical to our survival as a nation. The more we understand the untapped resources of the universe, the more we can advance our technology to improve the planet and if necessary, colonize another planet as backup plan far in the future. Why are you opposed to that?"

He had an edge in his voice now, "I'm not opposed to it; I am opposed to my wife playing a major part in it."

Estella was now ready to smack him, "You are disrespecting me?"

"No, you just need to know your place!"

"And, what place is that, Xavier?"

"Wife and mother, cook and cleaner, staying at home and being sexy for her husband!" With all the force she could muster, Estella kicked Xavier in the stomach with such force she drove him off the bed and onto the floor.

Before he could recover; she was into the bathroom and

173

shaking so violently with anger, she was happy she lacked a sharp weapon of any kind. She drew a bath and stayed there for over two hours before she finally calmed down. She never realized she had the potential to hate someone so intensely until that moment.

*****

It happened at the NAACP fundraiser over the Christmas holidays in Washington D.C. Estella was there representing her husband, accompanied by Renee. As the evening wound down, a woman approached Renee and addressed her. "Hi, Michelle!" she said to a startled Renee; "I am Cynthia; we were roommates in college!"

Renee shook her head, "I think you have me mistaken for someone else!"

As she turned to walk away, the woman blurted out, "I know you! Your name in college was Michelle Lachapell form New Orleans, and you got married to Don LeBlanc and moved to Tulsa where you lost your husband and your son in a terrible fire. Oh, I am so sorry you went through that, dear!"

Estella gave a funny look to Renee in disbelief as her mom again denied the woman's tale, "Ma'am, I believe you are thinking of someone else. I never lived in Tulsa, nor was I in a house fire. Have a nice day."

With that, she quickly walked away.

A man in his early 30's observed the conversation and said to the stunned woman who was also his godmother, "That woman was my mother!" Renee's former friend and roommate turned to face him,

"Yes, she is, Adrien. She most certainly is! She came and left

174

with Estella Cyrus."

Looking around frantically, Adrien noticed that the two ladies had left the event. He quickly grabbed his topcoat and ran outside to find Renee.

He saw their car driving off into the dark and jumped into his vehicle and followed them to Estella's residence in Georgetown where the Cyrus family and Renee were celebrating the holidays.

Heart pounding, the young man saw a security guard up ahead and thinking on his feet, he grabbed some papers and rushed to the front entrance of the house.

The guard stopped him. "What is your business, sir?"

Well dressed and well spoken Adrian strode up to the guard. Waving his sheet of papers at the sentry, he said in a desperate voice, "I'm in big trouble if I don't get these papers signed by Mr. Cyrus tonight, sir! Please help me!"

The security man waved him through. At the front door, the man took a deep breath and summoned the courage to ring the bell.

Fortunately for him, Renee was the one who opened the door. She took one look at the man and almost fainted, "Adrien! Oh, my god!"

Suddenly calm, he responded, "Hello, Michelle."

She stood and stared at him for several minutes looking him over from top to bottom as not believing her eyes.

It had been over 30 years since she had last seen him.

He was so handsome now, so grown up. He was an attractive brown-skinned black man in his late 30's, about six feet tall, with kinky black hair and a slender build.

Her little boy had grown up. He was gorgeous.

He was also very angry. She objected to his presence. "You shouldn't have come here, Adrien."

He bristled at her, "So, you're going to abandon me twice, Mother?"

Renee felt a chilling jolt go through her body. "He looks just like his father!" She was at a loss for words. The young man had tears in his eyes, "Why did you give me up, Mama?"

The stunned mother reached out to hug him, but he pulled away and continued glaring at her. "You gave me away when I was three-years-old. I will never forgive you for that!"

"I didn't have a choice, son; I was poor. I had no way to take care of you. You needed to be in a family that could provide food for you and a roof over your head. Plus, we were Negro; they could have killed you, just like they murdered your father and brother. Please understand."

He shook his head defiantly, "I don't understand. I will never understand. I was your *son*!"

At that point, Catherine poked her head through the opened door and asked the two of them, "What is going on here?"

Renee had no intention of bringing Xavier's mother into this, "Everything is fine, Catherine; please go back inside." Catherine nodded and exited as Adrien added a probing question on her appearance, "I take it that lady is a major person in your life, Renee?"

Renee did not answer him but asked, "Can we meet to talk tomorrow?" Adrien's eyebrows shot up,

"Is Cyrus of the wealthy oil well family?"

Renee ignored that question also and pleaded with Adrien, "Please let's meet tomorrow. I can meet you in front of the

Coffee House at Hains Point at 8pm."

"Of course, they are the wealthy Cyrus Clan! So, are they aware that their daughter-in-law is a Negro woman? I don't believe rich, white folk from the South would take too kindly to having a Negro for a daughter!"

Shocked at his statement, Renee's knees sagged, "It would be a major problem for them. Please, don't make trouble here, Adrien!"

"Oh, this is poetic justice, isn't it, Mother? You got rid of me because I was Colored to protect your fake racial identity and now, because of me, your secret is suddenly in jeopardy!"

"*Adrien!*" Renee screamed, "Stop threatening me at once!"

"I no longer have to listen to you, Mother. You lost your authority over me a long time ago. I will decide what I wish to decide and there's not a damn thing you can do about it."

Renee was crying now, "I beg of you, Adrien; don't make trouble! Your sister and I have worked hard to provide for ourselves, help you, and others. I always sent money to help raise you and send you to college. Please respect that!"

Adrien snorted, "Respect? You must be joking! What kind of respect is it that a mother would ship her son off to his aunt so he would not be a racial embarrassment to her. You favor that bed wench sister over me, to enable both of you a life of riches and fame?"

Before Renee could answer he fired a final verbal shot, "Listen to me, Michelle, or whatever name you are using these days. I will be back and make you pay for the horrendous secret you have been carrying and abandoning me. And, you can count on one promise from me. I will bring you and Estella down!"

177

Then, he turned and walked quickly away as Renee grabbed the door frame to prevent herself from collapsing to the porch.

She was devastated, but thankful that Xavier was in his study so not in earshot of the altercation.

After several minutes, Renee was able to regain the emotional strength to enter the residence and climb the stairs to her daughter's room. She heard Catherine call out to her, "Everything all right?" She waved her off and didn't stop walking until she entered the bedroom and closed the door.

Estella was reading a magazine when she looked up and saw her mother in an emotionally distressed state. "Renee, what happened to you?" she asked.

"I just had a very disconcerting visit."

Estella looked at her quizzically. "From whom?"

It took several minutes for her mom to reply. Finally, she half spoke, half sobbed, "From Adrien, he is my son I had to give him up because I couldn't provide for him."

Estella's face collapsed in shock. She quickly jumped off the bed and embraced her mother, "Oh Renee, I am so sorry. Was he ugly to you?"

Renee nodded, "More than ugly; he threatened me with retaliation for the pain I caused him when I sent him away to my sister."

"You did that out of love, Renee! You had no way of taking care of him back then!"

Mama Renee nodded, "That is true, but that is not his truth."

Estella whispered, "He is bitter?"

"He wants revenge, Estella. He is going to do whatever he can to bring us down."

"How can he do that, Renee?"

"He knows the secret about our heritage."

Estella looked puzzled, "What secret, Renee?"

"Brace yourself. I am about to tell you the truth about who we are; a truth that I have kept from you to protect you from a narrow-minded and hateful society."

Estella commented nervously, "You are scaring me, Renee."

"I don't know any way to tell you, Estella, so, here it is; we are Negros."

Her daughter gasped audibly, "What did you just *say*?"

"You and I are Negroes, Estella. It was because of our race that we would be denied the opportunity to succeed in this world. I had to keep it from you so that you didn't bear the terrible burden of shielding the truth from a racist world all your life."

Her daughter just stared at her. She was speechless. She had no words for this unfathomable revelation.

"I am truly sorry, Estella; I did it to protect you, to protect us. Please understand."

Finally, her daughter spoke, "And, no one else knows...just you and now Adrien and your ex-roommate?"

Renee nodded, "Correct. Not Xavier or his family. And, now you know."

Estella reasoned, "This is Adrien 's vengeful way of destroying us now?"

Her mom nodded, "Yes, that's right. He will tell the world, beginning with your husband and the Cyrus family and all of Washington D.C. and, it will be the end of us."

Both women sat silent for the next several moments. The reality of what they were facing was too ponderous to discuss at that moment. Everything they had fought for was about to be destroyed by an intimate member of their own family.

They didn't have the power to stop him.

But, someone did.

And, she was standing outside the door listening to everything that was being said.

CHAPTER TWENTY

Targeted for Death

Renee stood up and walked to the bedroom door. As she opened it, she saw Catherine standing there. "Oh, there you are! I was looking for you to see if you wanted to join me in the kitchen for Christmas cookies and coffee!"

Renee, being a little flustered to see Catherine standing so close to Estella's bedroom door and stammered. "Uh, sure. I'll be down in a few minutes!"

Catherine nodded, "Your face is red. Maybe you need to freshen up?"

"Yes I do, excuse me." Estella's mother confirmed quickly retreating to her guest room.

The next morning, in a quiet corner of Rock Creek Park in Washington D.C., Catherine Cyrus was disguised in a scarf and glasses as she met with two men who worked for her.

She had flown both of them into the nation's capital over the Christmas holidays to dismantle an ugly situation involving the potential problem facing her son and his wife. She had a vested interest in the brewing scandal threatened by Adrien Lachapell in retaliation of his mother's putting him up for adoption several years earlier.

Catherine Cyrus was not going to let him taint her family name. It was time for her to put a stop to his threat; even if it meant putting a violent stop to him. She addressed the two men in their 30's, "I have a very important assignment for you, which I will pay handsomely beyond the work you normally do for us."

The taller and more muscular of the two men, responded, "Yes, Mrs. Cyrus, whatever you need."

Catherine handed over the paper with Adrien's license plate number that she received from the security guard. The guard let him ring Estella's and Xavier's doorbell, but also took proper notes of Adrien's car plates make and model. "His name is Adrien Lachapell; age unknown, address unknown. He is currently in the D.C. area. Your job is to find him and bring me any data that will enable us to discontinue him and his current business. I expect to have all these answers from you within the next 24 hours. Time is of the essence; lives and careers are at stake. Understand?"

The other man asked her, "How do we contact you when we have this information, Mrs. Cyrus?"

Catherine was explicit, "I need this expedited. I will meet you back here tomorrow same time, with your discovery and we will proceed to the next part of the plan. Under no circumstances is anyone else to know, including my husband. That's all."

The Cyrus' had used these and other men sent by a mob contact in the past to break up the forming of fledgling worker's unions in their businesses. Catherine's uncle had made mob ties to assist him with the muscle to stop union organizing in his factories. When Catherine had gone to her uncle crying about her husband's business problems due to the workers attempting to organize a union, he had shared these contacts with her and

Xavier Sr.

Catherine's uncle, unlike Xavier Sr. or most of the men of their class, believed that the women in the family should be taught everything about the business in case of an emergency that called a female relative to take over the family businesses.

She reached into her purse and handed each of them an envelope filled with a sizable amount of cash, "Don't let me down. Here are your retainers. Get to work!"

Then, she entered her vehicle and quickly drove away. Catherine thought to herself, *"Xavier Sr. or Jr. need never know that my beloved Marie is a quarter black. I can handle this situation by myself."* She was not sure how her racist husband and son would take the news and there was no reason to find out.

*****

The next day, as Renee continued to visit her daughter and granddaughter in Georgetown over the holidays, she received a postal letter which required her signature.

She opened it and trembled as she read the words:

What I want is simple, Michelle. If you want me to go away then call a family press conference in Washington D.C. with you, Estella, Xavier, and the Cyrus family and announce to the world that I am your son. It's pretty simple, really!

Renee stood in the foyer; burning with anger. At that moment, she hated her son with a passion. She looked up and saw Catherine peering at her, "You look really upset, Renee. Bad news in the letter?" Renee numbly shook her head and walked past her up the stairs. Catherine exited the home and walked to her rental car.

184

She had a very important meeting at Rock Creek Park.

"What information do you have for me?" Catherine coldly asked her agents. She was all business.

The taller one handed her a file folder which she opened as he explained their findings, "His name is Adrien Lachapell. He is the youngest son of Michelle Lachapell, who survived a devastating house fire in the 1921 Tulsa race riots. Apparently, because her family was black, the Klan saw fit to exterminate them by setting the fire. Her husband and older son died on the front lawn and her other son, Adrien, three-years-old at the time, survived. With no money and fearing for her son's safety, she sent him to live with her sister, who raised him."

Lady Cyrus, having confirmed the conversation she overheard between Renee and Estella, decided to remove the threat to her granddaughter and son's career. "What do you recommend to eliminate him?" The senior agent smiled,

"An unfortunate car accident causing him to leave the highway and perish off a cliff."

"The sooner the better," she ordered.

"Done, Mrs. Cyrus."

"This will be our last meeting and no one but the three of us will be privy to the plan."

She handed a second envelope to the two men. "I want you both to disappear for a year. I have added an extra $5,000 for both of you. The Caribbean is beautiful. Enjoy your vacation."

"I can't swim!" exclaimed the smaller man.

Catherine smiled at him, "Then, you'll drown."

Then, she was gone.

The following evening, the bane of Renee's existence and the target of Catherine's wrath sat in a gay bar drinking heavily with his date. As they kissed and caressed each other in a darkened booth, Adrien suddenly stood up and excused himself, "Sorry, I have to cut this short. I have something I need to do. Meet me here tomorrow, lover!"

As he walked away from his pouting partner and got into his car, a white Chrysler, he left the parking lot so quickly that he failed to see a black sedan fall in pursuit behind him.

As Adrien sped up towards Georgetown, he approached a small bridge which hovered over the Potomac River, over 100 feet below. In his alcoholic stupor, he was having trouble staying on the road and muttering to himself, "That bitch has no intention of calling a press conference. I need to send her a more serious warning tonight to let her know I mean *business*!"

Just as he got to the opening of the bridge on the right-hand side of the highway, the black sedan caught up to his vehicle and veered in his lane causing the drunk young man to swerve violently to the right jump the bridge to the river below.

Adrien experienced a dream-like sequence that seemed more surreal than perilous until his vehicle smashed into the water at 40 miles an hour, shattering the windshield and hurtling him out the closed driver-side window.

Covered in blood and half-conscious, the chilling water began to freeze and devour him as he slowly sank to the bottom with scattered bubbles appearing on the surface to mark the only evidence that he and his car even existed.

The two men ran to the side of the bridge and looked over as they observed no sign of life. They smiled at each other and drove quickly away, having successfully accomplished their directive.

CHAPTER TWENTY-ONE

Renee Reconciles with Adrien

The powerful current of the Potomac River was a double-edged sword. In the past, it either doomed the struggling victim in its waters or miraculously saved them.

In Adrien Lachapell's case, the great waterway of Washington D.C. spewed the young man out like Jonah's whale. One minute, he was unconscious and gasping his last breaths underwater, and the next moment, he was lying unconscious and barely alive on the life-saving banks of the water's edge.

A fisherman found him just after dawn following his crash the night before. He hurriedly contacted the authorities and within several minutes, Adrien was being whisked away by ambulance to a nearby hospital where he immediately slipped into an in and out coma upon his arrival there.

The police also found his soggy wallet that thankfully registered an i.d. that was legible enough for them to contact his godmother, Cynthia, who had spoken to Renee at the fundraiser. Adrien had previously confided in Cynthia that he had done to visit his mother, who was visiting her daughter in Georgetown.

Within the hour, Cynthia was at Estella's home relaying the sad news to Renee that Adrien was in the hospital and apologizing for outing Renee as a Black woman.

"There has been an accident involving Adrien . He is in a coma at Jefferson Hospital."

Renee gasped, "Oh my god! What happened?"

"He was found unconscious on the banks of the Potomac River. He had been in the water. That's all I know right now."

"I was also hurt and felt abandoned when you left you were my best friend and you made me Godmother of your child then I never heard from you again I thought you were dead. Your sister told me that she did not know what had become of you. So, when I saw you looking, well, 30 years later, I was angry. I am so sorry this is my fault." Cynthia sobbed as she hugged Renee in the guest room.

"I forgive you. This is also my fault. But I did the best I could with the hand that I was dealt. I have to see Adrien." Renee, also crying, disengaged from Cynthia and they rushed to the hospital together.

On the way out of the house, Renee ran into Estella and quickly explained what happened to Adrien to her. "What are you going to do, Renee?"

Renee now faced a dilemma.

Should she go see her son and passively hope that he would die putting a permanent end to his threat to expose her black heritage or should she be a loving mama and go to the soul she gave life to and sit at his bedside until the good Lord decided his fate?

Renee did not waste a lot of time in making her decision, she immediately responded she was going to the hospital, to stand by her son.

He may hate her with acrid bitterness, but she did not share the same sentiment for him. Renee loved Adrien; just as she had from the moment he was born. She remembered the little boy she protectively carried in her arms out of that burning house to safety.

She was not going to abandon him now.

Estella totally understood, "Do you want me to go with you, to Adrien's bedside, Renee?"

"For now, it's best I see him alone. Just pray for us. I will call you in, if the time comes."

Estella nodded, grabbed her mother's suitcase and drove her and Cynthia to the hospital.

Upon arrival, Renee and Cynthia met with Adrien's doctor while Estella stayed in the waiting room. Addressing Cynthia, Adrien's doctor stated, "Your godson is in and out of a coma. He had a traumatic experience in the river. He is lucky to be alive."

Cynthia asked him, "What is his prognosis?"

He shook his head, "It's too early to tell. We have stabilized him and now we have to wait and see if his body can do the rest."

"May we stay with him in the room, doctor?"

The specialist responded, "Only two can stay. Who is next of kin?"

Cynthia stated, "His aunt is out of state. I am his godmother and this is my friend and her daughter in the waiting room," motioning to Renee. Cynthia had decided to keep Renee's secret and if Adrien ever recovered enough to speak, she would try to convince him to do the same.

Renee joined Estella in the waiting room and filled her in, "I am going to his room and staying there until he lives or dies. You go home. I'll call you."

Her daughter agreed, gave her mom a hug, and left. Renee proceeded to Adrien's hospital room in the ICU and took a deep breath before entering, not knowing what to expect.

As she let herself into the darkened room; she paused to let her eyes adjust to the dim light. She grabbed a chair and moved it silently to his bedside and sat down. Then, for the first time; she looked at his face.

She shuddered at what she was seeing.

By not wearing a seatbelt, he had been badly beaten up by the impact of his face against the windshield of the car. His countenance was swollen and badly disfigured. The handsome young man was gone and replaced by someone who looked like he had been slammed with a giant mallet.

But, in the still quiet of that darkened room, she was given some hope.

Adrien was still breathing.

"This is a hopeful sign," she murmured to herself. As she took his limp hand and held it, her mind drifted back to the night of that terrible Tulsa fire in 1921.

She vividly remembered all the details of that night as though it were yesterday. It had been so traumatic with so many horrid details from the moment she had been awakened by the blue star and that voice; a voice she would never forget.

Her mind raced through the chain of events; waking her husband, coughing violently, grabbing Adrien, running down the stairs with him in her arms, feeling terrified, collapsing on the front lawn, making sure her baby boy was safe, waiting anxiously for her husband and her other son to emerge without harm from the fiery home. The horror of seeing them in flames, grabbing the water bucket in a futile attempt to save them, becoming nauseous at the sight of their charred bodies. Then seeing those men, coldly staring at her with their torches, those evil men, mocking her pain and suffering and, finally passing out to awaken to a new life, now defined by the horror of losing her husband and son.

All she had left was baby Adrien and no way to take care of him.

And now… he was fighting for his life, just as his father and brother had done on the last night of their lives.

She felt her eyes tear up with the same sickening pain she had felt in 1921. It was like those men in hoods were mocking her all over again.

Adrien's mission to expose her Negro heritage had put him in that hospital bed facing death because of the color of his skin.

Her stomach churned with anger towards racism and how unfair it was in society. Because she was black, she had suffered immeasurable pain and there was no good reason for it.

Being Black had inflamed the Klan that night and being Black had given her own son a weapon to use against her for his perceived abandonment. She had paid a high price for not possessing the Caucasian ethnicity.

Only time would tell if that price would cost her a son.

As the hours turned into nightfall, Renee began to feel drowsy. It had been an emotional day and there would be more heart-stopping moments to come.

As she and Cynthia began to doze off, she was interrupted by two nurses who were sympathetic to their commitment to their injured loved one. They brought cots and made them up with linens, blankets, and pillows.

Renee profusely thanked them and laid down and went to sleep, hoping the next morning would bring some closure one way or the other.

Her last thoughts were from Psalm 23:

The Lord is my shepherd; I shall not want. He maketh me to lie down in green pastures: He leadeth me beside the still waters. He restoreth my soul.

The following morning, she arose and made up her bed, took a shower, and resumed her place next to her son's bed.

Before she realized it, it was evening again and there was still no sign of activity from her son in the bed. Three more days and nights followed without a sign that Adrien would waken and join her.

Another week went by and Renee's sister, Sharon, had driven for days to be by Adrien's side also. Renee remained steadfast; as any loving mom would do. Renee was prepared to spend years in that room if she had to.

She was never leaving her son again.

Renee, Cynthia, and Sharon prayed, cried, and nursed Adrien back to health. In the course of several weeks, the bruises disappeared and his face regained its beauty. Renee unceasingly prayed for him and his doctor kept reminding her, "He could awaken at any time."

Another week went by.

Nothing.

Then, God moved in a subtle way.

Around 2:00 PM on a Sunday afternoon, Renee felt a twinge in Adrien's hand. She was immediately alerted that something might be happening!

She squeezed back and, again, she felt a twinge in response. Over the next several seconds, they kept squeezing back and forth and then Renee looked at Adrien and saw him staring at her with his eyes open.

Renee gasped. This had been so sudden after weeks of nothingness. Adrien was alive and seemingly alert. How long would she have before he slipped back into his coma?

She gently whispered, "Welcome back, Adrien."

He just kept staring at her, not saying a word. After a few minutes, Renee began to worry that he was brain-damaged and unable to speak.

The thought horrified her.

But she needn't have worried; he soon proved he was coherent.

"What in the hell are you doing here, Michelle?"

"You had an accident. A fisherman found you unconscious on the banks of the Potomac River. You've been out ever since. You're lucky to be alive, Adrien."

She could tell he was shocked by her story of his plight and she watched him as he tried to mentally piece together his experience.

"I don't remember anything about that. Where am I?"

"You are in the intensive care unit at Jefferson Hospital in Washington D.C."

He asked her, "How long have I been here?"

"Thirty-seven days," Renee informed him.

"How long have you been sitting there, Michelle?"

Renee smiled, "The whole time."

"Why?"

"Because I'm your mother and I love you," Renee whispered.

He frowned at her, "Why did you abandon me back then?"

"I never abandoned you, Adrien. I just couldn't afford to take care of you after Daddy and your older brother died in that horrible fire. I had no money and no place to live. My first priority was to put you in a safe place to protect you. Your aunt and her husband were gracious enough to raise you in a two-parent home. Not a day went by when I didn't think of you, Adrien. I loved you more than anyone or anything for years. As I told you before, I sent Aunt Sharon all the money I could to help you."

Her son absorbed all the things Renee had told him without a response. Then, he announced, "I feel so tired!"

And then he fell asleep.

In a panic, Renee jumped up and shook him, "No, Adrien! Stay awake; stay with me!"

But, to no avail.

She ran to the nurse's station and they immediately summoned a doctor who rushed into the room and checked Adrien's vitals.

"Did he fall asleep or did he slip back into his coma?" asked a terrified Renee.

His answer did not reassure her, "I don't know. He could have resumed his coma, or he could have just fallen asleep and he will be fine. We will just have to wait and see."

Then, he left the room leaving Renee in total confusion. She sat down and opened her Bible to a passage she prayed would be prophetic.

But they that wait upon the Lord shall renew their strength; they shall mount up with wings as eagles; they shall run, and not be weary, and they shall walk, and not faint. Isaiah 40:31

Renee wasn't quite sure if the verse was personally applied to

Adrien or herself, but, she was encouraged by it. Either way, it sounded optimistic and she hoped that eventually both she and her son would soar like eagles!

That night, as she tried to sleep, she heard a wonderful sound that jolted her soul, "Mama?"

Adrien was calling her!

She almost fell out of the cot and ran to his side. He reached out his arms and she enthusiastically dove into them!

They both began crying, sobbing really. Renee was wailing tears of joy.

She had her son back.

Over the next few days, they shared their lives since that night in Tulsa and filled in all the missing pieces, people, events, and stories that they had not known about each other.

Adrien had never married, and Renee asked him why. He got quiet all of a sudden and then admitted to her, "Mama, please don't be upset; I am gay!"

She smiled at him, "More importantly, you're my son and I love you."

The doctor told them both that Adrien could leave the hospital within a week. To Renee's excitement, Adrien asked her, "Can I meet Estella?"

The following day, his younger sister came to visit, and the five of them, including Sharon and Cynthia, celebrated a glorious family reunion. Renee prayed over her two beloved children and thanked the Lord over and over again for "the miracle of her life!"

Then, in a moment of clarity, Adrien remembered something about the night he almost died. He told Renee, "I remember driving a car and there was another car, a black car like a sedan, that suddenly veered in front of me and forced me off the road. I don't remember flying into the air and that's all I can recall."

Renee thought about his recounting of that specific incident and concluded that Adrien had been launched into the Potomac River by that errant vehicle. The question she had had only two possibilities: *"Was that car that caused Adrien to swerve doing it accidentally or intentionally?"*

The more she thought about it; the more she began to believe the latter which led to a chilling conclusion, *"Was someone deliberately trying to kill her son? If so, who and why?"*

As she logically pursued this line of reasoning, she added in the element of what had been going on with Adrien at the time of the accident. He had been on a mission to destroy her, Estella, and the Cyrus family.

One night, as Renee tossed and turned on her cot in the hospital room, she suddenly had an epiphany. She shot up in bed and screamed inwardly, *"Catherine!"*

As she thought back to the days leading up to his accident, Xavier's mother had been in the house and had acted strangely, giving Renee the sense at that time that she was a little too noisy and concerned about Renee and the stress she was experiencing.

Had Catherine overheard the threat that Adrien had posed to the family? If so, Catherine would never allow her son to follow through on his promise to ruin the futures of everyone involved by exposing Renee and Estella's racial heritage.

Renee realized as she lay in the dark shaking violently with this concept that Xavier's parents would do just about anything to stop Adrien from following through with his threat; even killing him.

Renee thought to herself, *"Dear God; please don't let this be true! Please reveal to me that Sr. and Catherine are good people and that they would never stoop to such depths to destroy a human life just to preserve their own goals of power, influence, and social standing.*"

It was time for her to talk to Catherine and see for herself if that horrid possibility was even remotely true.

Renee returned to Estella's home a day ahead of Adrien's release from the hospital. His Aunt was going to pick him up the following day.

As Estella drove to Georgetown; Renee had a question for her, "While I was at the hospital, did you notice anything odd about Catherine while she stayed with you?

Estella looked at her quizzically. "Odd?"

Renee clarified her wording, "Out of the ordinary; was her behavior or conversations with you revealing at all?"

Her daughter thought about Catherine during that time and responded, "Yes, she seemed nervous and was constantly making calls on my phone. I started to eavesdrop on her and think I heard her say something about a coma."

Renee looked out the window and stated laconically, "Yeah, I'll bet!"

Arriving at Estella's, Renee went upstairs to her guest bedroom and flopped down on the bed without hesitation. She fell fast asleep with her clothing still on succumbing to the exhaustion brought on by weeks on a cot with all the stress and tension of wondering if her son would survive.

She woke up in the middle of the night, brushed her teeth, put on her nightgown, and went right back to bed. She awoke in the late morning and went downstairs to have coffee with Estella.

"It was so nice sleeping on a bed instead of a cot!" She gushed as she breezed into the kitchen only to see a familiar face sitting at the table, staring at her.

"Catherine!" Renee exclaimed."What are you doing here?" Renee was flustered by the appearance of Xavier's mother, "Where's Estella?

"I was on my way back from the Caribbean with Sr. and we decided to hit D.C. on our way home. Estella will be back soon; she had to run over to Marie's school. Our granddaughter forgot to bring her homework."

Renee nodded and poured herself a cup of coffee. She sensed an eerie tension in the room. Something didn't feel right. Catherine asked her, "So, are you comfortable with Adrien now, Renee?"

It was an odd question, one intended to entice Renee into revealing something more personal in answering it. But Renee didn't take the bait, "I'm happy he is going to survive that terrible accident, if that's what you mean!"

"Interesting," Catherine mused.

Renee sat down across from her, "Is there something you want to say, Catherine?"

"Not really. I just had the sense that your son was out to get you in some way and…"

"And, that is none of your business, Catherine," interrupted Renee. "I have my life and you have yours! My Godson Adrien and I are on good terms."

"He is your biological son! Don't even try to deny it! I have my ways of gaining information. None of my business? That's not entirely true, Renee," countered Xavier's mother. "We are an interconnected family and if one of us is threatened in any way, it affects the futures of all of us!"

"Where did you get the idea that I was threatened in some way, Catherine?"

"Oh now, come; there is no need to lie to me. I have ears and a brain. I was around when your son showed up and said things that made you feel uncomfortable. Please don't insult my intelligence."

Renee looked at Catherine's face and saw a kind of evil there. Her suspicion that Xavier's mother may have had something to do with Adrien's accident was now becoming believable.

"Catherine, you should not be eavesdropping outside of closed doors. I'm going to ask you something and I want an honest answer."

"I'll do my best, Renee."

"Did you have anything to do with my son's accident, if it was an accident?"

Catherine's pause at that moment confirmed what Renee had been thinking about her. Had Catherine been innocent, she would have answered *no* right away. Instead, she was forming a response to explain her potential involvement.

"Let me just say this to you: if Sr. and I believed that your son was prepared to hurt our family's reputation in a significant way, then, my husband and I would do what was necessary to stop him. This is all hypothetical, by the way!"

Renee looked into Catherine's eyes, "Is it?"

"Of course it's hypothetical, since you insist that Adrien never threatened you!"

"I never said he didn't threaten me, Catherine; I just told you to mind your own business!"

Catherine's eyes squinted menacingly and in a cold voice, she sent chills down Renee's body, "Did he threaten you, and therefore all of us?"

Now, it was Renee's turn to pause and think about her response.

"My son believed that I had abandoned him many years ago, which made him understandably bitter. It also gave him crazy ideas on how to lash out and punish me. He was hurt and misguided, but in the end, he realized that I loved him and he was able to forgive me. He is no longer a danger to me or our family."

Catherine shot back, "And you believe that?"

"Why don't you get to the point, Catherine. Don't hold back!" Renee challenged her.

There was no response from Xavier's mom. She finished drinking her cup of coffee stood up and walked to the sink where she quickly washed it.

As she was leaving the kitchen, she turned and addressed Renee, "I don't share your optimism. Your son is not only a very disturbed individual, he is a consummate actor."

Hearing that, Renee stood up and rushed at Catherine and pushed her into the wall. Catherine fought back and the two of them grappled with each other into the living room where Renee slapped her and knocked her over the couch.

"I know you were involved in that accident, Catherine! You tried to kill my son!"

As Catherine struggled on the couch, she reached up and violently pulled Renee's hair, bringing her down on top of her. Back and forth they went with the slaps and punches becoming more violent.

"He had to be stopped, you stupid bitch!" Catherine shouted at Renee. "That little psycho would have destroyed us all with the secret about you and Estella!"

"So, you tried to *kill* him?" exclaimed Renee. What kind of monster are you?"

"He brought it on himself; I did what was best for all of us! And none of us would have been in this position if you had followed the rules and not passed for White in the first place."

Renee balled up her fist and drove it into Catherine's nose, which emanated a loud "pop" and exploded in blood.

Catherine retaliated by driving her leg into Renee's stomach, driving her backward into the fireplace, where she hit her head on the unyielding brick foundation, knocking her out cold.

Catherine ran to the kitchen and grabbed a towel to stem the gushing flow of blood from her broken nose. Then, she returned to the living room and looked down at an unconscious Renee, "I swear to you, if your son tries to follow through on exposing you as a Negro, he won't survive the next plan I have for him!"

Then, she went back into the kitchen, drew a glass of water, and calmed herself down from the violent shaking of anger that was wracking her body and spirit. After several minutes she had composed herself.

She picked up the phone and dialed a Georgetown hospital and gave them Estella's address, "We need an ambulance. There has been a serious accident and my good friend is unconscious. Please come immediately."

*****

At the hospital, the attending physician informed a distraught Estella: "Your mother has sustained a very serious injury to the back of her head. She hit that brick fireplace full force without breaking her fall. We are doing everything we can do to save her life, Mrs. Cyrus."

Estella numbly nodded and asked him, "When will we know more, doctor?"

"The next 24 hours are critical. If she can survive them, we can be optimistic."

Estella thanked him and entered her mother's room and, like Renee before her, took a chair and pulled it up next to her loved one's bed to begin the life and death vigil.

Thirty minutes later, Xavier appeared with a large bouquet of flowers and anxiously asked Estella, "Any news, darling?"

"The doctor doesn't know. Brain injuries are hard to figure. Now, we wait."

"My mother said that she had been upstairs and heard a commotion in the living room. By the time she came downstairs, she saw your mom lying in a pool of blood and some guy standing over her."

Estella frowned, "Some guy?"

"Yeah, my mom said he looked like a gardener or some kind of worker. He ran over to my mother and punched her violently in the face, breaking her nose and then ran out the door. My mom miraculously pulled herself up and called the hospital. She may have saved Renee's life!"

Estella whispered sarcastically to herself, "I'll bet!"

"I can't stay long; I have a committee meeting," he informed his wife.

She sneered at him, "Give my best to 'Congresswoman Mily.'"

Xavier shook his head, "No, this is an actual hearing this time!"

"Where's your mom right now, Xavier?"

"She's in the emergency room getting medication for her wounds. She has a lot of bruises."

"I thought all the guy did was punch her in the nose?" Estella asked.

"Evidently, she was too traumatized to remember the beating he gave her. Dad is with her now. Look, I gotta go. I will be back tonight. Hang in there, Baby!" He tried to kiss her, but Estella averted his attempt. Xavier just shrugged and exited. She murmured aloud, "You and your entire family are a bunch of liars!" Then, she put her face into her hands and sobbed.

*****

Renee's mind was taking on a life of its own. Even though she was unconscious; she was tracking past events in her life. As the day wore on into the night, she drifted back to 1921 and the night of the fire.

Michelle again heard the voice she would never forget, "Auset, it is your Ausir. I am with you right now. Stay close; do not forsake me."

Renee heard herself murmuring in her unconscious state, "I know you. I am your love. I will always be with you, Ausir."

She smiled as she psychically communicated with him through the ages. Michelle sensed a connection they once had and held tightly onto it.

Then, she suddenly saw flames: ferocious, relentless, burning beyond belief and she grabbed baby Adrien and somehow made it to the top of the stairs and held on to the rickety railing as smoke enveloped them all the way out the door.

She coughed and wheezed as she collapsed on the grass and saw her little boy struggling to breathe also. Then, Michelle waited against hope for the appearance of her beloved husband and son to emerge safely.

That dream never materialized. They staggered helplessly out of that raging inferno never having even a slim chance of surviving it.

Michelle remembered running, grabbing the water bucket and dousing them to have a chance of reviving their lives until she looked down and saw their blackened bodies.

They were long gone from this earth.

She heard the sounds of scornful laughter and saw several men in white hoods, enjoying her pain and horrific loss. Michelle knew their torches had done their work and destroyed two people that were her life, causing her to collapse and lose consciousness.

As she continued to dream, she was in a white and golden room with her beloved deceased grandfather, Julian Lachapell, who had been a vital influence in her life. Her Grandpa tried to comfort her, "Don't take anything that happens down there too seriously, life is just a learning game, so don't allow your soul to be scarred by even horrible experiences learn from them."

Julian had also belonged to The Circle of Ausir, the Black American extension of a global ancient secret society created to do the will of God.

Julian was a Christian pastor who had a strong belief in the Bible, as did everyone in The Circle. She recalled during a childhood conversation she asked him, "Can you tell me about this voice I keep hearing from someone who claims to be Ausir along with the blue star?"

Her grandfather smiled, "Based on the things he is telling you and how he has protected you; perhaps, he is your guardian angel watching over you? I know your grandmother, my departed wife, still watches over and protects me in dreams. From historical records, Ausir was the very first priest of God and Auset his wife. The blue star may be the star that your grandmother would show you on nights you two took her telescope up on the hill."

Renee tossed and turned in her bed as she grappled with a part of her dream. Watching her body language, Estella cried out to her, "Are you all right?"

Renee continued to dream about her life the memories being relived vividly.

Michelle wakes up in her sister's home, with her three-year-old son Adrien crying by her bed. Michelle stares in an almost comatose state and barely speaks or eats, but her sister will not send her to a mental institution because of the stigma attached and concern for how badly they will treat her in an institution. Her sister tries to help her by showing her scrapbooks of happier times, one of her college graduation, her sorority sisters who visit her, her coronation as a beauty queen, but nothing, and no one can get through to her. Not even her grandfather can help her to overcome the trauma.

As one of the "talented tenth" and "the privileged few," Michelle had lived a charmed life until the night of the Tulsa riots had proven to her that no Black person was free and safe until all were free and safe. She and her family had been living in a comfortable bubble; until that life was shattered by the harsh realities of institutional racism, that had planted the seeds of the riots. There were no repercussions to Whites for killing and robbing even connected well off Blacks. Some Whites armed with the knowledge that Blacks had no real protection under the law that would be enforced, harmed Blacks in any way they saw fit, for any reason or for no reason at all. Blacks were easy prey to the jealous, the greedy, vigilantes or even bullies looking for sadistic fun.

On the anniversary of her husband's death, Michelle walked out of her body, and Renee walked in. Renee packed her bags, leaving a note that she loved her family but couldn't live in the world as it is, and she had to try to change this world to protect her living son. Renee stated in the letter that she was never coming back and asked her sister Sharon to raise Adrien as her own son.

Renee relives meeting wealthy landowner Richard Myrtle on a train to Texas in a whites-only train car. She lies about not only her race, but also her name, calling herself Renee Deneuve.

Renee dreams of happier times with Richard Myrtle their beautiful garden wedding, and the birth of their daughter Estella. From this new vantage point as a White woman, Renee used Richard's wealth to help lend money to Blacks to purchase farms and equipment. Then, after Richard lost his wealth during the Great Depression and Dust Bowl, she hears his angry drunken yelling as if she were still on the farm in Texas. Then the dream flashes to the knock on the door from the police informing her of Richards car accident and death.

The dream progressively sped up to the present until she saw herself falling and felt the pain caused by the back of her head impacting against the hard surface of the fireplace. Then she was floating above her body floating in the same star-filled tunnel that she remembered coming through on her third birthday, her first memory.

Ausir's deep voice and the force of his will halted her, "Your earthly family still needs you, Auset. I need you to help them do what they were meant to do."

And then miraculously Saturday morning, Renee woke up healed with Estella and Marie holding her hands.

Renee opened her eyes and blurted out, "Why am I in a hospital room?"

"Because you fell backward into our fireplace and cracked your head. Remember?" Estella informed her.

Renee shook her head, "I don't remember that at all!"

Her daughter's heart sank. She was half hoping that her mother would be able to implicate Catherine in the incident, but she knew that even if her mother remembered she would not press charges. Pressing charges would cause a scandal that would negatively impact Xavier's career, therefore, his power to help their causes.

But the doctors were overjoyed and within a week, Renee left the hospital with her daughter and went to Georgetown to rest up a few days before returning to New York and her husband.

Nick's illness had kept him bedridden and unable to be at his wife's side during her time of hospitalization. Now, Renee could finally return home and take care of him.

CHAPTER TWENTY-TWO

Xavier Discovers Estella's Causes

Estella stayed busy at the Capitol to pursuing her passion for civil rights. The NAACP was working with legislators to pass three critical bills which would enable Negroes more power to make their lives more livable in the areas of education, social services, and economic opportunity.

The black leaders in Congress were relying on Estella to support their future laws by unofficially lobbying her network, including white congressmen on the Hill and fundraising.

These congressional minorities considered Estella as one of them and treated her like a member of their own family.

Xavier, of course, had no idea that his wife was heavily involved empowering the black races that he only paid token attention to it for his re-election purposes.

If you were not rich and Caucasian, then-Congressman Cyrus had little use for you. That was not the only secret Estella was hiding from him. There was another issue on her mind, as well:

Michael Hagar.

The Secret Service agent was now a regular fixture in her life.

One day at the house, when Xavier was upstairs preparing for his day at the office; she asked him, "What do you think of my husband, Michael?"

The agent looked quizzically at her and then responded, "Could you be more specific?"

Estella laughed. "You know; what is your take on him as a person?"

Michael was professionally succinct, "He's a great legislator and a good boss."

Estella tried again, "I don't want your formal answer; you can be honest with me. What do you really think of him personally?"

"He's a great legislator and a good boss."

She shook her head, "You're not going to be completely honest with me, are you?" The agent smiled,

"I am being completely honest. Beyond my professional assessment of him, what I believe is irrelevant."

She stared at him, "Really?"

He turned the tables on her, "What do you think of your husband, Mrs. Cyrus?"

"I think he is a racist asshole!" she exclaimed.

Michael laughed, "Not exactly a professional assessment, but a charmingly candid one from a wife!"

"I have to ask you, Michael; would you honestly give your life for a jerk like him?"

There was a long pause. Finally, the agent nodded, "It's not my job to like or respect the people I am assigned to; it's my job to protect them with my life."

"I don't hate my husband, I just despise his racist beliefs. They make my skin crawl."

Michael stood there, stone-faced.

"You are a Negro. How can you tolerate racism?"

He clarified, "As a Secret Service agent, I can tolerate just about anything. As a man, I feel tremendous pain inside when I see and experience the bigotry against my race."

"I sense you are a good man, Mr. Hagar."

"I believe you are an exceptional woman, Mrs. Cyrus."

For several long seconds, there was silence between them. They both sensed a connection to each other. It was all Estella could do not to reach out and run her fingers gently on his face. Her heart was pounding. She knew there was something going on between them.

She thought, "*Get a grip on yourself, Estella. You're a married woman and you need to stay within your vows.*"

But, the years and years of being subjected to Xavier's verbal and physical abuse had taken their toll on her. Estella was now more than a little emotionally vulnerable and hungry for true love with someone who honored and cherished her.

She gazed into Michael's eyes and he stared right back into hers. Finally, he said, "I know."

Estella asked him, "You know?"

"I know what you are feeling, Estella."

At that moment, it took everything in her to stop from collapsing in his arms and kissing him everywhere. He had been feeling the same emotions as her. This was no longer potential chemistry, this was real, "So, what do we do, Michael?"

He quietly shook his head and whispered, "Nothing."

Estella nodded. He was right. Acknowledging was one thing; acting upon it was another.

She expressed her sentiment at that moment, "You really

affect me, Michael."

He didn't hesitate, passion shining in his eyes. "I know and I want to show you how much you affect me."

At that point, Renee came down the stairs and saw the two of them standing and staring at each other. "Am I interrupting anything?"

Estella blushed and Michael let out a nervous laugh.

Renee angrily whispered, "Stop this now! I see the looks you have been giving one another and it must stop now. You will destroy each other if this continues. You, Michael, will lose your career and you, Estella will lose your daughter because Xavier will get full custody in any divorce on grounds of infidelity with a Negro. Or even easier than divorce, the Cyrus's may just arrange a car accident with you *both* in the car." Renee reminded them of Adrien's near-death experience.

Estella thought to herself, "*I am an undercover agent sleeping with the enemy and Michael is a secret service agent. My mother is right again, we are in a hopeless and dangerous love, at least for the moment.*"

As Xavier bounced down the steps with a happy wolfish grin looking at the unhappy trio. "Good morning, everyone. Why am I getting the sad face from all you guys? The world is a great place, and it's a beautiful morning."

"*Of course, just about every morning is great for you, jolly jerk,*" Estella thought to herself and by the looks in the eyes of Michael and Renee, they shared her sentiments.

Michael, in a firm voice, addressed the congressman, "We have twenty-seven minutes to get you to your committee meeting, sir. Let's move!"

Xavier laughed, "I'm ready, willing, and able!"

As Estella watched the two men in her life disappear out the front door, she had to hold on to the stair railing to keep standing. Estella was falling deeply in love with Michael.

The Black legislators won one out of three victories with their new agenda and the support of the additional votes Estella had garnered with her lobbying. They had succeeded in earmarking funds for needy minorities to be able to gain school vouchers and further their education.

As Estella saw it, one success at a time was alright with her. A civil rights program was a marathon, not a sprint; and patience was key. The Negro in America had been rising from the abyss in the area of opportunity and it would take years of courageous and creative legislation to help members of their race to finally achieve the American Dream.

Of course, there were no charges filed or even an investigation done against Catherine. She and her husband were back in Texas happily attending balls and fund-raisers and living the high life of society.

Xavier and Mily continued their quarterly rituals at The House of Dionysius as they experimented with various ways to enjoy their sexual pleasures.

Estella took full advantage of her husband's relationship with the society, using their contacts and power to her full advantage in aiding the Black caucus.

Marie and Renee were avidly pursuing the planets and space, and the young girl was full of questions that Estella was scrambling to answer. "Mom, do you think that someday I can go into outer space and see what is happening up there?"

Estella smiled, "I don't see why not; every day, NACA is making progress towards astronauts visiting the universe.

Someday, regular people will have the same opportunity. Or you could be an astronaut."

Marie beamed with excitement, "I think that would be so cool!"

Marie was preparing for that eventuality by studiously examining all nine planets and the moon, as well.

Marie had a lot of ambitious goals; in addition to becoming an astronaut, she was still convinced the Presidency would be within her grasp someday. She was an ardent supporter of civil and women's rights along with a million questions about dinosaurs, her favorite animals.

Her personal love was the gentle Brontosaurus and her most feared reptile was the Tyrannosaurus Rex. "They scare me, Mommy. I'm glad I don't have to worry about them when I ride my bike!"

"If an astroid had not made the dinosaurs extinct, we probably would not have bikes or civilization at all," mused Estella aloud. She realized as soon as she said this, she should not have, because it upset Marie.

"What if a big astroid came now, would that make us extinct?" Marie had fear in her eyes.

"Baby, do not worry. The chance of an astroid hitting the Earth in our lifetime is very slim. Before another comet comes, you will already have become President and colonized other planets so we will all go there and be safe." Estella jokingly reassured her daughter. This answer seemed to satisfy Marie because she smiled.

*****

And, speaking of monsters, Xavier was gaining more and

more power with each passing today. He was moving to the top of the Democratic leadership in the House.

His involvement with The House of Dionysius was paying powerful dividends everywhere he went.

At his current pace, Xavier was the odds-on favorite to one day be a Vice Presidential nominee on the Democratic national slate. After that, if he and his Presidential nominee won, there was no question he would have a valid shot at the top office, in the future.

Estella shuddered at that possibility; she did not want her dysfunctional husband anywhere near the Oval Office. In her mind, Xavier lacked the character, the compassion, and the concern for minorities, especially Blacks.

As the Chief Executive, he would undermine all the hard work she and the NAACP were doing to bring the Negro into equality with White people.

Another of her passions, women's rights, would also be in jeopardy with her misogynistic husband. Xavier didn't honor women; he used and abused them for his own pleasure.

To see him take the oath of office and become a leader of his country with the likes of Abraham Lincoln nauseated her.

No, he had to be stopped far short of that reality. Women were second-class citizens in America. The country was dominated by middle-aged upper-class White men. It was a closed society when it came to opportunity and power.

Estella was as avid in her passion for women's rights as she had been for minorities, since she was a woman who had suffered abuse. She knew that the relationship with her husband was like a runaway train heading for a cliff. It was only a matter of time before there would be a fatal crash of some kind.

Xavier's goals and her political involvement were going to

encounter a major head-on collision, and it would be ugly.

Estella knew she was on borrowed time and there were only a limited number of months until Xavier would not only discover her political involvement that was undercutting him but, there would be hell to pay when he blocked her.

In the meantime, she considered each passing day a gift of opportunity to fight for minorities, to uplift the rights of women and do all she could to advance space exploration.

*****

It was nice to have Renee in her home again.

As they sat at the kitchen table, Estella asked her, "So, your mind is a blank the day of your accident?"

Her mom nodded, "I have asked God over and over to give me clarity on what actually happened that day. Do you believe it's possible that an intruder came into your home and attacked me?"

Estella vehemently shook her head, "Not a chance. We have a security guard in the front and electric fences all around the backyard. Catherine claimed that he entered through the front door. Impossible."

"You think she's lying?"

"She's definitely lying. I think you confronted her about trying to kill your son and it led to a physical altercation. She undoubtedly pushed you backward and you slammed your head into the brick fireplace!"

Renee was frustrated. "I wish I could remember!"

"Brain injuries are tricky; you may wake up one day and recall everything."

"Or, I may never remember anything," her mother moaned.

At that point, Xavier, along with Michael, entered the kitchen and he greeted his mother-in-law. "Welcome back, Renee; nice to see you again!"

"I hear you are tearing up the Congress, young man!" She complimented him. He smiled confidently,

"It's all about knowing the right people; isn't that right, honey?" Estella sarcastically asked.

Renee looked puzzled, "What do you mean by that, Estella?"

Her daughter nodded at Xavier, "Ask him!"

Xavier gulped down his coffee and quickly changed the subject, "You remember my Secret Service agent, Michael?"

Renee politely smiled at him, "Nice to see you again! "

Michael smiled, "You too, Ma'am." Xavier grabbed a couple of pastries and shoved one into Michael's hand stating,

"Running late, gotta go!"

As they headed for the front door; Xavier stopped and addressed Renee, "Oh, my mom asked about you. She wanted to know if everything is okay!"

Renee nodded, "Far as I know."

"I'm so proud of her for saving your life!"

Estella's eyes widened, "You believe Catherine saved Renee's life?"

Xavier explained, "Well, if she hadn't thrown herself at that intruder, your mom would have bought the farm!"

His wife bristled, "And, you believe there was an intruder?"

"That's what my mom told me, and I have no reason to doubt her," Xavier smiled.

Estella looked at Michael and his eyes told her that he wasn't buying it either. That made her feel even closer to him.

Renee commented, "Maybe that's what happened; unless my memory comes back, I'll have to take her word for it!"

Estella thought, *"We suspect that Catherine had some-thing to do with Adrien's car accident and the next thing we know you are in the hospital with a brain injury along with Catherine's flimsy story about an intruder slamming your head against our fireplace. Something doesn't add up here."*

Mama Renee held her head in her hands and moaned, "I wish I could fill in the details of what happened that day, Estella."

Her daughter came over and gently patted her mom on the head, "I wish you could too, mother."

After Xavier and Michael had left to go to Xavier's office. Estella suggested, "Renee, I need to run over to the Capitol to meet with the NAACP leadership for a few hours. Why don't you take a nap and I'll pick up dinner for us?"

*****

While Renee slept, her daughter spent the next several hours with the Black lobbyists and as she packed her briefcase to leave, she stood up and ran right into her husband staring at her amidst all the Black leadership.

Estella had a sickening feeling in her stomach. This was not good.

"What in the hell are you doing here, Estella!" he demanded in a loud voice and a very irate expression on his red face.

She took his arm and led him out of the room before he could embarrass himself any further. Out of earshot, she calmly told him, "I was invited by the NAACP to attend their meeting so they could ask me to volunteer for some upcoming legislation, that's all."

Xavier was furious, "You're a *liar*! I have heard from a very reliable source that you have already been actively lobbying for the civil rights of these, uh, these animals!"

She wanted to slap the fire out of him, "They are not animals, Xavier; they are human beings who rely on their congressman to not only protect their rights but to empower them in a racist America that has held them back for over 100s of years! I don't understand how you can love your nanny Sarah so much but hate her people."

"Sarah is a decent Colored woman. Ninety percent of them act like animals and we should not be forced to do anything we don't want to do with them. We should not be forced to go to school or eat or do anything with them. You have no business telling me about my job. I order you to cease this crusade of yours or you will face the consequences!" Estella stood up to him,

"And if I don't?"

He slapped her hard across her face with the back of his hand. "That's a preview of what you can expect if you fail to heed my warning. Do you understand?"

Without hesitation, Estella tried to return the favor, but Xavier deftly deflected her slap and then pushed her forcefully into a nearby wall, causing his wife to lose her balance and slide inelegantly to the floor.

As Michael brushed quickly past Xavier and tried to help her up, Xavier shouted at him, "Back off! Let her get up on her own."

The agent glared at Xavier and took Estella's hand and brought her to her feet. As she shakily stood there, he asked her tenderly, "Are you all right, Estella?"

Xavier wasn't so magnanimous, "If you ever try to hit me, I will knock you through a wall instead of into it. Now, get your ass home and start cooking dinner!" he commanded.

As he walked away, Estella stared at him with more than a little hatred in her eyes. Michael remained for a moment and said, "If he ever strikes you again, I will be introducing him to that wall. Watch yourself, okay?"

He gently stroked her hair. She leaned in and hugged him briefly. Like he had promised, she suddenly felt safe again.

She returned home and related the ugly incident to Renee, who was beyond furious. After Estella calmed her down, the two of them had a civil conversation.

"What are you going to do, Estella?"

Her daughter quietly said, "I'm going to keep pursuing my lobbying goals. Damn him!"

"He has a propensity for violence; please remember that!"

"Xavier won't murder me; it would kill his hopes of being President!" she concluded.

"Estella, he is smart enough to hire someone to take you out and get away with it."

"He knows I am his secret weapon and if he is behind in the poles Xavier will need me to mesmerize his opponents. Also you know I write all of his speeches and let him take the credit," Estella reminded Renee.

An hour later, the object of their stressful conversation arrived and glared at the two of them sitting at the kitchen table, "I see the hens are cackling away; I can only imagine what they're saying about me!" Xavier walked up the stairs muttering to himself, like a madman.

Estella wondered if Xavier was taking his medication for his secret mental health issues. Every time she asked, he angrily replied that he was taking his meds, so she stopped asking to avoid his wrath.

A few minutes later, the telephone rang. It was Congressman Lauder, a key member of the NAACP and a political power in the House on behalf of minorities. "Mrs. Cyrus, I got your note and I wanted to thank you for all your work on behalf of the Black Caucus. I wanted to remind you of our prayer breakfast meeting in room 1710 in the Capitol at 7:30 in the morning to discuss a new bill that we are drafting.

Will you be able to join us?"

"I wouldn't miss it for the world, Mr. Lauder; I think it is a noble cause! See you then."

As she started to hand up the phone, Estella heard a click that indicated someone had been listening in. Her guess was that Xavier had overheard the conversation.

"Mama, I need to talk to my husband upstairs. Give me a few minutes!" When she arrived in her bedroom, she saw Xavier pacing furiously back and forth. It did not take long for the fireworks to begin.

"You're not going to that meeting in the morning, Estella. I forbid you!" She laughed.

"Oh, you forbid me? Go to hell, Xavier; you don't own me!"

Without warning, he crossed the room where she was standing and backhanded her knocking her onto the bed. She verbally lashed out at him, "If you hit me one more time, I will not only call the police, I will retain a lawyer and make sure you never see me or your daughter ever again. There are laws that protect wives and children from physical abuse in their own home!"

"Here's what I think of those laws! This is my house — bought and paid for. Get the hell out!" he sputtered in rage as he dragged her off the bed and shoved her towards the door intending to kick her out of the house.

"I will happily leave with Marie. Don't touch me!"

"And, by the way, I can feel all that weight you have gained when I pulled you off the bed you are letting yourself go! Time for a new model!" he yelled, trying to hurt her mentally.

She ignored his childish taunts and went to grab her suitcase out of the closet. In her haste, she tripped on a pillow. She fell on her stomach, causing Estella to feel more pain than she had ever felt in her life. She crumpled to the floor holding her midsection unable to breathe.

Estella was having trouble speaking with all the pain she was experiencing. But she was able to somehow blurt out a few words, "Xavier, I'm pregnant!"

Her husband abruptly stopped and stared at her. He had no words for this moment. Estella had hidden her condition from him and now he was stunned and even repentant.

"Preg…you're pregnant?" He choked out the words, not knowing what else to say. "Why didn't you tell me, Estella, my god! When is the baby due?"

Suddenly, his wife began feeling contractions and she moaned, "It was going to be in a couple of months but I believe that plan has suddenly changed. Get me to the hospital, Xavier. Now!"

As Xavier helped her down the stairs, Mama Renee met them on the bottom. When she saw Estella gripping her stomach, she exclaimed, "Are you having contractions?" Her daughter weakly nodded. Renee held her daughter upright while Michael raced out to bring the car around to the front door.

Xavier continued to hold on to Estella and kept whimpering, "I'm sorry; I'm so sorry." Estella just glared at him.

"When did you realize your wife was pregnant, Xavier?" Renee asked him.

"About three minutes ago!"

At the hospital, the doctors and the nurses rushed out to the emergency bay and wheeled Estella on a gurney into surgery while Xavier stood numbly by looking pale and helpless.

Michael was so disgusted with him that he stood several feet away in the lobby.

Over the next several hours, Estella and her baby's life hovered between life and death until they were both out of danger.

Xavier stayed at the hospital all night; he ordered a room full of flowers and had heartfelt repentance for a wife that no longer trusted or respected him.

"How are you feeling, sweetie?" asked a sorrowful Xavier.

Estella didn't hold back,"As good as any mother would feel after being slapped several times in the face and shoved into a wall."

"I am so sorry; I will make it up to you, Darling. I sincerely mean that! May I see our baby?"

Estella reluctantly nodded and announced, "I want you to meet your son, Charles Sumner; named after a great fighter for civil rights and the abolition of slavery!"

As she pulled back the blanket and Xavier saw the baby's face for the first time, he recoiled in horror, "This isn't my child! This is a little Negro!" he exclaimed in disgust. Then, with eyes that emanated hate, he spewed his angry racism at Estella, "Which scum of an NAACP black bastard spilled his seed inside you, Estella?"

His wife was horrified.

"This beautiful child came from you and me, Xavier; your seed and my egg. It is purely ours."

"Then, why is he Colored   ?"

"Because I am a Black woman, Xavier; and, proud of it!"

"I've been married to a Negro all this time?" he shouted. "*My god!*"

Xavier quickly poured himself a glass of water from the tray next to her bed and then threw the liquid into her face and soaked the baby in the process, then stormed out.

As the nurse met him at the door, he snarled at her, "Tell the doctor he will be hearing from my lawyer!" The nurse looked beyond him to a hysterical Estella and grabbed a towel to dry her and Charles off.

"Well, he was bound to find out sooner or later," whispered Renee to a distraught Estella as she lay in her hospital bed.

"I don't know who or what I hate more at this moment: Xavier or racism!" Renee smiled laconically,

"Sounds like they are one and the same."

"Xavier and I have overcome so many problems from the first time we met in the diner: his assault on me, my pregnancy, his reluctance to marry me, Debra, his parents, his forging my signature to obtain a divorce, our financial problems, my struggles with Washington society, his racism, and contempt for people of color, his mistress, his temper tantrums, his ultimatums and opposition regarding my career passions, his physical abuse, and now this... I can't stay with this man. There is no marriage left to cling to, Renee."

Renee tried to stay positive with her daughter, "One day at a time, Estella. You survived all those things; this too shall pass."

Her daughter wasn't so sure, "I think what he did to me and Charles last night and this morning was the last straw. I have no more emotion for him, good or bad. I honestly don't care if he lives or dies. I am numb."

With tears in her eyes, Renee felt the same pounding pain she had felt on that front lawn in Tulsa over thirty years earlier. It was so overwhelming all she could do was pat her daughter's head and pray for her.

Estella had married a monster. Xavier was no different in texture from those wicked men holding their torches on the night she had lost her husband and son to their evil machinations.

Reading Estella's mind, Renee sadly exclaimed, "You are right. Xavier is a narcissistic monster. I am sorry I ever agreed with my well-meaning priest's suggestion that you should marry him. Please forgive me. Tell me what you need, what I can do to try to heal your mind."

"Xavier will never accept a known Colored wife or a Black son, Mama. My husband is all about image, just like his bigoted parents. If you want further proof of that, remember they tried to kill Adrien because he was a Negro! No offense, regarding your choices, but I could never give Charles up for adoption so that I can keep pretending to be white. I need to figure out a way that I can leave Xavier and take Marie and my son to safety."

Renee nodded, "The good Lord protected me that night at the burning house and saved Adrien's life, too. He will see fit to keep you, Marie and Charles Sumner safe from harm too."

"Well, the good Lord is off to a rocky start today," Estella mused. "Nothing could be worse than his abuse and rejecting his wife and baby the first chance he got to absorb our skin color."

Renee offered her life savings, "I have a little money saved that may last us a year if we are frugal. When you recover, maybe we should take Charles and drive out to Marie's summer camp to pick her up then just keep driving, run away, start fresh?"

"Or maybe not. Are you using reverse psychology tactics on me, Renee?" Estella responded now thinking practically. Being on the run with a newborn and uprooting Marie from her life and school did not seem like a workable option at this point. Plus, the Cyrus's would have them hunted and brought back or worse.

Even if Estella survived the Cyrus' to make it to a divorce court, Xavier would get full custody of Marie in a divorce, if not due to just their wealth and power, then definitely due to Estella giving birth to a Black child. Because Charles was so dark in comparison to both her and Xavier, the judge would assume she had been unfaithful and rule in Xavier's favor, even though genes sometimes skipped generations, as in this case. Estella shuddered thinking of what the Cyrus' had done to Adrien. She had never allowed herself to acknowledge the amount of danger she was in being married to Xavier until recently.

"No, I am not using any tactics I am just open to any and all options to help you in this horrible predicament. You said you wanted to go to safety with the children, so I will help and go with you. You have to do what you think is best in your life," Renee normally in control had given up trying to control the situation feeling guilty for her part in this tragedy.

Renee thought, "*What if I had just supported Estella in any decision that she decided was best for her life instead of influencing her to my will? Would Estella be happy in the life she could have built without my influence instead of this mess we are in?*"

"Mama, I am not blaming you for how my life is turning out. You did the best you could for me, and you gave me the best advice you had to give. I love you and I am sorry for blaming you in the past for my choices. We both did the best we could to get through this crazy maze of life." Estella hugged Mama Renee. As Renee wrapped her arms around her daughter and grandson, she was overjoyed that Estella had called her Mama forgiving her for all that had transpired.

At that moment, to Estella's surprise, Michael walked into the room. "Xavier ordered me to guard your door and not let anyone in, only the new private nurses and doctor he hired." Michael's warm eyes showed concern. He could not keep his secret service agent poker face on in this situation as he stared at the brown-skinned, sleeping boy and his distressed mother. Michael's true emotions of love, worry, and tenderness combined and shone in his eyes, making Estella love him all the more.

"Well, now you know why Xavier wants you to guard my hospital room. He is ashamed of the color of his son and does not want anyone not on his payroll and sworn to secrecy to see his son," stated Estella sorrowfully.

Michael remembered the time he had taken Estella to the Negro part of town on her insistence. She had just come back from vacation with a tan and curly beach hair; he had laughed and told Estella that she could pass for Colored. Looking as she did after the beach, she could feel comfortable at the Jazz club she had requested to visit that Whites never visited. They danced all night and had the best "date" he ever had. There was not a day that passed that Michael did not think of that night; Estella's girlish giggle, her smile, or how her body felt in his arms as they danced. Many onlookers smiled at them, their faces acknowledging the love they saw emanating from the beautiful couple on the dance floor.

He thought, *"If Xavier did not mistreat Estella, I would feel ashamed of the love I feel for her. But I just don't believe my love and wanting to give her a little peace and happiness is wrong. If she were my wife I would devote my life to loving her."*

Now that he knew she was really passing for White, part of him felt she was more accessible to him because she was one of his women. However, logically, Michael knew the love he felt for Estella was still just as perilous, hopeless, and forbidden as before the knowledge of her heritage because of her marriage to Xavier.

He asked her, "May I hold your baby?"

She smiled sadly and gently passed her son to him. "His name is Charles Sumner." Michael involuntarily took her hand to comfort her, with his other large hand he held and cradled Charles safely in the crook of one arm gently rocking him.

Lying in her bed and looking up at Michael's handsome, kind face, Estella had the strong sense that the man holding her baby would be a great stepdad for him. Where his fingers touched her hand, her skin tingled. Estella's soul ached for him to cradle her in his strong muscled arms as he cradled her son. She wanted Michael to rock and comfort her also.

Embarrassed at the thought, she quickly put it out of her mind and scolded herself for the sentiment. She did not have a right to bring her loving protector Michael, into this mess between her and Xavier so that Xavier could jealously destroy

Michael's life, also. Estella thought, "*Thank God Michael had only just met her and Xavier five months ago when he was hired as Xavier's secret service agent, or Xavier would wrongly think their newborn son was really fathered by Michael.*"

Michael asked her, "Did you name him after Charles Sumner, the famous abolitionist and Senator?"

Estella nodded, "Sure did!"

He stared at her son for the longest time and then he stated, "He has your beautiful, sherry-amber eyes, Mrs. Cyrus."

Estella wanted to pull Michael's hand closer to her and whisper in his ear, "*Michael, you have beautiful warm eyes. I wish I could lay, held in your arms forever.*" But instead, she politely said, "Why thank you, Michael. That's very sweet!"

*****

In another part of town, the racist husband and Charles' birth father was taking the day off to pour out his venom in the arms of his mistress. "I can't believe my baby is a Negro!" He exclaimed again and again. "He can't be my child. He is as dark as a chocolate bar, that is impossible that Estella and I could have such a child."

The saying "*Mama's baby daddy's maybe*" kept popping into Xavier's spinning head, he felt dizzy and nauseous. This was definitely not a beautiful morning for him. He took some comfort from the fact Marie had his exact eye color, which was a unique shade of blue, so he knew for a fact he had fathered his daughter. Marie did not look Black at all. He clung to the thought, at least he still had his little girl.

He searched his soul and mind to discern if he felt any differently about Marie now that he knew she was a quarter Black. After searching his feelings, he knew his love for her had not changed; he still loved Marie more than anything and would protect his little girl. He vowed that Marie's secret would be kept, that her Black heritage would never become public knowledge and that she would never even be told. The idea that Marie would be mistreated if classified as Black made him even more physically ill.

"I still just can't believe my son is a Negro."

Mily fueled his racist fire. "So is that slut of a wife, Xavier. You need to end your marriage. First, she didn't tell you she was pregnant, then, she betrayed you in Congress with her involvement with those darkies and now, she is trying to convince you that the baby is yours, which is a lie that no one with half a brain would ever buy! She is not a loyal wife to you, Sweetie!"

"You're right; she is a lying slut when I always thought she was sweet and innocent!" he exclaimed.

Xavier angrily mused to himself," *I believed Estella was the one person I could trust, but I could not have been more wrong. If I had known what a cheating whore she is, I would have dragged her by her hair to the House of D instead of risking being caught at the initiation with Mily the impersonator. I risked it all — my career, my, personal safety — if found with an impersonator just to protect Estella's highly dubious innocence. What an idiot I was not to see through her lies.*"

"You want me to become the new Mrs. Cyrus?" She coyly smiled at him.

Xavier immediately regained his senses. It was one thing to bash his Colored wife but divorcing her was not a smart idea. A scandal like that would have dire political consequences. He could not let it be public knowledge that his wife was Black, so that meant he had to convince Estella to give up Charles for adoption. He was never going to let his secret weapon Estella go, she belonged to him and he may need her to win future elections.

Xavier laughed to himself, *"Marry Mily? Not in this lifetime."*

"Let's just say, I wish I had met you first," he lied.

This was not the validation Mily wanted to hear. She pulled away from him and buried herself under a pillow.

Xavier consoled her, "You and I have a good thing; let's not spoil it."

Mily lifted the pillow and pouted. "What if your wife and that bastard baby had an accident. Would you marry me then?"

Xavier's eyes narrowed disgusted and angry with Mily for making the suggestion. "I am warning you, don't ever think about harming my wife or the child."

Then he started getting dressed to leave. He thought, *"What a twisted whore. I have to find a new body double for the House of D. I am bored with Mily anyway."*

"Don't go, I'm sorry," Mily pleaded. But he jerked his arm away, got dressed and left.

CHAPTER TWENTY-THREE

Estella's Son

Estella awoke the following morning to see Xavier staring down at her as she lay in her hospital bed. "What are you doing here?" she yelled.

"You're still my wife, Estella; I may not always agree with you, but I will always support you."

"Please leave," she stated coldly.

He placed a tray of breakfast items on her lap; scrambled eggs, bacon, croissants, melon slices, orange juice, and coffee.

"A girl's gotta eat!" he laughed. Estella frowned,

"Get rid of the food, leave the juice. I am still nauseous!" she moaned.

Xavier poured her a cup of juice, placed the tray near him on the bed and began munching happily. "Mmm, these croissants are delicious!"

His wife alerted him, "Hurry up and eat; they will be bringing my baby to me soon. I doubt you will want to be around for that event!"

Xavier gave her a funny smile, "I don't hate our child. How can I not love anything that came out of you, Darling?"

Estella squinted her eyes at him. There was something

insincere about her husband's behavior that she mistrusted. She had seen this mood of his before and it made her wary in the moment. The indelible image of a poisonous snake flashed into her mind.

"I don't trust you, Xavier. I saw the real you last night. I don't believe the act you're putting on."

He feigned sadness, which almost caused Estella to burst out laughing. "*This guy is a terrible actor!*" she mused to herself.

After he had wolfed down most of the food on the tray, he stood up to leave just as the doctor entered the room.

"Mr. and Mrs. Cyrus, I'm afraid I have some very sad news. The premature birth of your child was too much for him to bear. Your baby passed away in the ICU a few minutes ago. There was nothing we could do. I am deeply sorry for your loss."

Estella screamed into her pillow. Xavier stood up and grabbed the physician by his collar and seethed, "What do you mean there was nothing you could do! Hospitals make people better; not make lame and unprofessional excuses!"

Two of the nurses that had been standing outside the door rushed in and pulled Xavier off their supervisor. One of them spoke up in a loud voice, "Mr. Cyrus; we are not God, and neither are you!"

Two male nurses quickly joined the group and escorted Xavier out of the room. Michael, who had been standing outside the door, accompanied the congressman and the nurses to a conference room.

The doctor sat on the edge of the bed and consoled Estella, "I am at a loss for words. Your son was a fighter. He did everything he could to try and breathe. In the end, he just didn't have the air.'

Estella lowered the pillow and sat up. Tears streaked her face as she fought for words, "This can't be happening. I can't take this…"

"The most difficult part of my profession is to tell a mother that we could not help her child live. Again, I am sorry."

He silently strode out of the room, leaving Estella sobbing hysterically.

The young mother curled up in a fetal position under the blankets and sobbed. She had never felt such pain that reached down into her soul in her life. The finality of her son's death left her feeling completely helpless.

Her physician returned to his office and slumped into his chair, his head in his hands. Moments later, one of his private nurses entered the room and asked him, "Are you okay, doctor?"

He paused at length before answering. Finally, he whispered, "I don't feel very professional right now."

She nodded sympathetically and said "I know the feeling. My heart goes out to that poor mother. Please prescribe her birth control. I don't want to upset her further, so I will slip it to her mother so she can decide later if she wants to use the diaphragm."

*****

As Xavier exited from his car, he turned to Michael, "I need to make a personal call. Give me a minute!" His agent nodded and waited as the congressman walked to a remote location in the parking garage, not wanting his bodyguard to know Estella's child was still alive.

He dialed a number and was greeted by a familiar voice, "I am not happy about this, Xavier!"

Her son-in-law laughed, "Would you rather lose your

grandson, Renee?"

"What you did to Estella was criminal. I hate you for it!"

Xavier bluffed, "Any more accusations like that and that baby will really be dead, do you understand?"

Renee responded her affirmation with silence. She was completely neutralized.

"Have you contacted your sister?" he asked her.

"Yes, she will be driving up the day after tomorrow and will take Charles home with her."

Xavier assured her, "If Estella knew what we were doing; she would rather have this arrangement than a lifeless son. We will never discuss this again, Renee. Give Sharon the money and remind her to keep her mouth shut or the consequences will be so horrific she will never recover from them."

Renee began to cry, "You are evil. One day — believe me — you will get what you deserve."

"You're entitled to your opinion, Renee. But, had we told Estella that her baby was merely missing, she would never give up looking for him. This way, she has no motivation to proceed with that option. Now, be a good mother and do all you can to help your darling daughter recover from the tragic loss of that Negro. Bye for now!"

Xavier disconnected the call and headed back to his car to collect his Secret Service agent and get on with business as usual just like nothing untoward had ever happened.

When Estella awoke from a long nap, the room was dark. She flipped on a bed light and as her head cleared; she remembered the horror of the morning. She vaguely remembered nurses coming into her room and checking her vitals. In time, Estella laid there for several minutes processing details of losing

238

her baby.

She rolled over in bed and began crying again. Her emotional strength was at an all-time low. She dozed off for several minutes and was awakened by the appearance of her mother.

"How is my sweet daughter?" Renee cooed.

Estella greeted her in silence. The last thing in the world she wanted to do was have a conversation.

Renee consoled her, "Dear, Charles is at peace and safe."

"I just want to be alone, okay?"

Renee nodded, "I can understand that. I will go. It will take you some time to recover."

Estella snapped at her, "I will never get over the loss of my child. If anyone should understand that, you should!"

Her mom stood up, nodded at her, and quickly left the room.

*****

"You're the bravest man I know!" Valerie Victor, a Hollywood star, purred as she stroking Xavier's hair as he lay next to her.

"Why do you say that?" he asked her.

"You lose your precious son, and yet here you are with me making me feel special. How many men do that?"

He smiled at her, "I've always believed in putting others first, I guess."

"You should be devastated in your grief, and instead you bring me roses and Chinese food with a big smile!"

"Well, you are only in town filming for one more night and I wanted to see you before you left," Xavier stated to Valerie, one of his mistresses that he rarely saw due to distance.

Valerie shook her head, "But, you lost your son!"

Her lover nodded, "He's in Heaven with the angels now. I have to accept that. My little boy is in a better place."

"You are a saint, Xavier. I don't deserve you."

He smiled and said, "Well, why don't you show your gratitude then?"

Valerie immediately moved down his body and positioned herself between his naked legs. Within seconds, her mouth was displaying the sensual appreciation he had suggested. Xavier laid back, closed his eyes, and began moaning with pleasure. It didn't take long for him to explode with passion as a result of her most effective mouth and lips.

As she cleaned him up with her swirling tongue and then cuddled against him, he sighed, "All my sorrows melted in your love. Thanks, I needed that."

Valerie smiled smugly. "It is the least I can do for my wonderful man." Aging actresses' careers did not last forever, and she thought she might be Xavier's second wife one day — divorces were becoming more common. With his wealth, Xavier was a very generous lover. The idea of having more access to his money prompted her into this performance even though inwardly, she felt it was disgusting that he was with her after his son just passed. *"Men are so gullible and suckers for compliments. He really believes I think he is a saint?"* she thought.

*****

As Estella was preparing to check out of the hospital, her

doctor came by to comfort her once again. "We will all be thinking and praying for you, Mrs. Cyrus. I personally hope I have the opportunity to be your delivery doctor again someday."

She demanded, "Doctor, I want to see my baby."

He hesitated as his mind raced to find a deterrent to her unexpected request, "Well, uh…that will not be possible, Mrs. Cyrus."

Estella was puzzled, "Why not? I'm his mother!"

"Because your husband signed the papers for cremation. He now has the urn with Charles's ashes. Didn't you know?"

Estella was dumbstruck, "I had no idea, doctor! I never approved that request. I wanted him buried not cremated!"

"I am afraid it is too late for that, Ma'am. I wish I had known that Mr. Cyrus was not representing your wishes. You will need to take it up with him."

The wife was adamant in her promise, "Oh, I assure you that I will. Yes, I will!"

When Xavier arrived at the hospital to pick her up, Estella was waiting for him and not in a good way. "Who gave you the right to cremate my baby, you son of a bitch!"

Calmly, her husband explained, "We agreed to have him cremated, Estella. Don't you remember?"

"I never agreed to any such thing!" she shouted.

"I came in with the cremation papers early this morning and woke you up. I explained that we needed to settle his memorial so we could get on with our lives. You said, 'Okay, Xavier,' and I handed you a pen, and you put your name on it."

Estella was beside herself with anger, "There was no such discussion and you know it, Xavier! I would never agree to

241

cremation because I don't believe in it!"

Her husband smiled, "Well, I was surprised myself that you had a change of heart on the issue but what's done is done, and now we can start over knowing that our child is in the arms of Jesus."

It took all the strength that Renee had to hold her daughter back from attacking her husband. When they arrived home wisely, Xavier thought it prudent to hasten up the stairs and lock his bedroom door until his "darling" could regain her composure.

*****

Early the next morning, Estella's doctor informed his head nurse, "Put the cremation paperwork in a private file so we can use it if we ever need it to protect ourselves. I have found an unwanted substitute baby who sadly died of pneumonia and cremated him. We will use those ashes for the Cyrus family. The matter is permanently closed."

She responded, "Yes, doctor."

He whispered, "May God have mercy on our souls."

******

Renee's sister, Sharon, arrived at Renee's hotel room in Georgetown later that morning and Renee was waiting for her along with Charles. Sharon was not pleased with the arrangement, "You realize what we are doing is criminal, Renee?"

Her sister shot back, "I am protecting my daughter and Marie. This is the ethical thing to do. When your husband is a racist; you are left with few options. Eventually, Xavier would have killed this child. We are saving his life and sparing Estella from a lifetime of suffering along with a certain divorce. Besides, you are receiving $25,000 for your effort and monthly payments of childcare of $1,000.00. That is money you can use, Sharon. Please help me, Sharon." Sharon had no comeback on her sister's logic here.

Renee finished packing the baby bag and gave her sister a hug, "Drive safely and thank you. You mean a lot to me, Sharon!"

It was time for Sharon to return to her hometown, New Orleans, with baby Charles. This wasn't a vacation or a family reunion; this was a very important mission to be accomplished. Everyone had done their part and Xavier had handsomely paid them off.

Life went on.

CHAPTER TWENTY-FOUR

The Vacation

For several weeks, Estella was suffering from clinical depression and agreed to take antidepressants.. The loss of her baby had brought her to a very dark place.

Several times during the day she would take her glass of iced tea out to her patio and sit for hours thinking about the life her little Charles never had the chance to experience.

Her emotional loss and Xavier's crassness amplified her passion for women's rights to a new level. Her husband had disrespected her feelings, wishes, and choices by rejecting her Black son, mandating that he was not welcome in their home, showing no empathy at his death and then cremating him against her wishes.

She was not just an advocate for women's rights; she was the poster girl for them. Estella understood that there were millions of women across the country that were being sublimated by husbands, boyfriends, fathers, and bosses, simply because of their gender. This abasement showed up in various forms from their second-class paychecks, to their lack of standing in the workplace, to not being privy to opportunities for advancement, to being sexually harassed and abused. When it came to political, social, and economic power, it was a man's world, more specifically, a White man's world.

Estella was going to do all she could to balance the injustice between the genders in every way possible beginning at home and ultimately to national prominence. This was not just a political set of programs for her; this was personal. The irony was that it was her own husband, who had given her a major platform to accomplish her goals and yet, he had been one of the greatest perpetrators of defining American women as second-class citizens.

By day, she privately mourned; by night, she worked long hours into the night to figure out ways to find openings in the walls of gender repression. She courted congressmen and Senators to help her craft legislation that would take the first steps to women's equality all behind her husband's back. He was furious when he discovered her activism in civil rights; he would have been livid beyond belief if he knew she had extended her cause to women's rights, as well.

And then there was Michael.

Her admiration for him grew by the day. He had her on a pedestal, too. They were no longer falling in love; they were in love. Estella knew the day would come when the two of them would be together forever. There was too much between them to not be; they had the same singleness of purpose and the passion to go with it. They both wanted to change the world, lift the rights of minorities, end racial injustice, and bring the social and economic status of men and women to equal status.

They had a physical, mental and spiritual passion for each other that was to the boiling point. It would just be a matter of time before the sparks of their love for each other would explode in a fireball of intimate and complete abandonment.

Xavier was upstairs taking a shower and readying himself for a congressional dinner that evening, and Michael was standing at the foot of the stairs waiting for him to leave. Estella beckoned to the agent to join her in the living room to get his opinion on a new vase she had purchased for the fireplace mantle. Upon entering the room, she asked him in a very personal voice, "Have you been thinking as much about me as I have about you?"

Michael smiled and said, "More!"

Estella giggled like a schoolgirl and responded, "Music to my ears!"

As they stood admiring her vase, their bodies were so close to each other they were almost touching. She reached down and took his hand and he squeezed hers gently. Estella felt her body shudder in that moment, and then she squeezed his hand in return. He then guided her hand to his lips and kissed each finger. Just that small gesture made her gasp with desire. She leaned into him and she brushed her thigh against his swelling manhood.

At that point, they heard the shower upstairs turn off and they moved to the kitchen table where she poured her secret love a glass of her famous iced tea.

Michael coyly smiled. "Tasty fingers!"

Estella smiled back, "Firm lips. I wonder how they would feel against mine. If that shower were still running, there is no telling where they would have led us!"

He leaned forward and brushed her lips with his. She parted her mouth ever so slightly. The gentle kiss was perfect for the moment.

He mused aloud, "I wonder where you and I will be at the end of the 60's decade, Estella?"

247

She laughed, "You just never know!" Michael looked into her eyes.

"I have a pretty good idea, Love."

Estella stared right back, "I want to be with you too, Michael."

Michael thought to himself, "*This is reckless madness, but I can't stop myself. This must be love.*" Michael had been in relationships but never in love.

They heard Xavier coming down the stairs, and the agent stood up quickly to greet his boss. Xavier told Estella, "Don't stay up for me!"

She coldly assured him, "Don't worry."

Then, the two men were gone.

The phone rang. It was Margret Kahn, "Checking up on my favorite client. How are you doing, Estella?'

"Day-to-day, Dr. Kahn. Up and down."

"I was talking to your mother yesterday. We think it would be good if you took a vacation in June."

"That would be nice; I like that idea!"

"Your mother and I thought we would go with you!"

Estella laughed, "That would even be nicer!"

Her therapist suggested, "I will make all the arrangements. Have you ever been to the Virgin Islands?"

"Never."

"St. John is wonderful. Read up on it. You'll be impressed."

"Marie will be away at camp, so the timing is great. Make it for the second week of June for a week."

Margret laughed, "Nah, let's make it a month!"

Estella smiled, "Can't argue with that. You're the doctor!"

They hung up the phone and Estella murmured aloud, "Exactly what I need!"

When Marie arrived home from school, Estella made her a plate of fresh fruit and sugar-free cookies. They went out on the patio and as her daughter munched away.

Estella asked, "How was your day, baby?"

Marie looked upset, "It was horrible. All the boys laughed at me when we were asked what we were going to be when we grew up and I said President."

"Marie, do you know what women's rights mean?" Estella was now upset too. She would have to talk to Marie's teacher about letting those boys know not to try to be dream-crushers.

"Well," her daughter began, "It is about the rights of women, right?"

Estella nodded, "That is correct, but, do you understand what those rights are?"

Marie thought for a moment and finally said, "The right to do anything as long as its legal?"

"Yes; that is a good answer. Do you know what rights are important to women?"

The little girl blurted out, "A lot of them!"

"Can you tell mommy what the main ones are?"

Marie pursed her lips and racked her brain. Finally, she said, "To be equal to boys?"

"You are getting closer, baby. What does that mean to be equal to boys?"

More silence from Marie; this was not obvious to her. "Ahmm, we should be able to do all the things boys do?"

"Like?"

"Be astronauts, be President and, be respected!"

"That is right. By the time you grow-up, you will be able to be anything you want to be including President, Mommy will see to that." Estella held Marie close galvanized to work even harder on women's rights to make her daughters dreams a possibility.

*****

That night, after her daughter went to bed, Estella spent some time looking up through travel books about St. John and the Virgin Islands. It didn't take her too long to figure out that she loved the idea of going to the remote and secluded Gibney beach. She needed to get a hold of her depression and that seemed a good place to refresh herself.

The island was home to a sandy beach, several shops and restaurants, private beaches and great resorts on the island.

The Queen Beach Hotel.

Estella fell in love with it immediately.

This would be her island paradise!

When Xavier returned home from work, he tried to greet her with a kiss, but she turned her head away and avoided it. This upset him greatly, "What are you mad about now?" he demanded.

Estella just shook her head, "I have no respect for you anymore, Xavier. In fact, I don't even know who you are. Our marriage is an ongoing carousel of lies, secrets, disrespect, and at times, violence. To top it off, I am sickened by your blatant racism that made you abandon your only son in the hospital."

Her husband was annoyed by his wife's assessment of him and their union. And he had some reactions of his own to defend

250

himself.

"I think it is safe to say that there was a question concerning the heredity of the baby that was birthed by you in the hospital. It did not have my skin color nor did it even look like me. It was conceived by you and some guy seven months ago and foisted upon me as his father. You should be ashamed of yourself, Estella!"

That enraged his wife., "How dare you accuse me of cheating, Xavier; especially since that has been your *modus operandi* since we moved to D.C. I'm not the one with lovers, you are!"

He shot back, "I have lovers, yes. But, I never brought a baby into the world and tried to pawn it off as yours!"

"Charles was a *Cyrus*!" She exploded, "No matter what your twisted mind thinks, he was your son as surely as Marie is your daughter!"

Xavier was skeptical, "Then, why is Marie's skin color considerably whiter than that dark boy I saw in your arms in the hospital?"

Estella hurled a glass of cranberry juice at him as she screamed, "You can go to hell!"

Then, she stormed up the stairs while Xavier ran to the sink and tried to clean the red stains out so he could go to a reception, and he was already late. He gave up when the stains would not come out and stripped off his coat, shirt, and tie. "*If only getting divorced from a wife was as easy as stripping off my clothes. In some one of those countries, you just circle your wife three times to divorce, I think,*" he mused to himself.

"Estella, throw down a new set of clothes, I am late." When she ignored him, he became angrier. Standing in the kitchen half-naked and shouted, "Son-of-a-bitch!"

He turned to run up the stairs but was stopped in his tracks by Michael who held him tight in a viselike grip. "Let go of *me!*" Xavier shouted, "This is not your job!"

His Secret Service agent remained cool as he calmly responded, "It is my responsibility to protect you in all situations, both from those who try to attack and from yourself, if need be. If you run up those stairs in the emotional state you're in, someone is liable to get very, very hurt and you may wind up in jail for it. So, just stay put, Congressman Cyrus."

At that point, Xavier had no choice but to remain in Michael Hagar's grasp. He couldn't move an inch if he wanted to. After several minutes, Estella's husband regained his composure, and Hagar led him quietly to the living room and sat him down on the couch.

Xavier took a big sigh and said, "Thank you, Michael. I almost made a huge mistake there. You were right to do as you did."

The agent stared silently back at him. For the next several minutes, Xavier's breathing returned to normal and he admitted, "That woman makes me do crazy things!"

"I need some fresh air, Mr. Hagar. I'll just get some fresh clothes."

Hagar smiled, "No, you will stay here. I will get your clothes. I will also reserve us a hotel room just in case your anger comes back, sir."

Xavier nodded in defeat. His agent knew him well. He still needed more time. Michael went upstairs and knocked on the bedroom door announcing his presence to Estella. She opened the door and handed Hagar a fresh shirt, suit and tie, and then, seeing that Xavier was nowhere to be found, whispered, "Thank you for protecting me, Michael!"

She planted a soft kiss on his cheek and he gently smiled at her.

*****

Alone in the car, Xavier asked the agent; "Do you believe Estella had an affair on me?"

Michael didn't hesitate, "Absolutely not!"

His boss was curious, "How can you be so sure?'

"Estella is not the unfaithful type, sir. You have known her since college; have you ever seen her cheat on you over all those years?"

Xavier put his head down and whispered, "Never. But you saw that baby's skin color; it wasn't White!"

"Neither is Estella, remember?"

Xavier shook his head, "When she told me she was a Negro woman, I didn't believe her. I still don't believe her."

"You are in denial, sir. Your wife is indeed a light-skinned Negro. Sometimes genes skip a generation." Michael tried to calm Xavier and protect Estella.

There was a long silence as Xavier grappled with the truth of Michael's statement. Finally, he admitted, "I'm an asshole."

His agent stated dryly, "Aren't we all, at times?"

*****

When Xavier arrived home the following day, he was carrying two dozen red roses and an envelope. When Estella saw him, her first instinct was to run and hide, but when she saw Michael standing behind her husband, she knew she was safe.

Xavier was full of repentance once again, "I bought you roses, my love, and, I apologize deeply from my heart. Will you forgive me?"

Estella was curt in her response, "I am tired of this roller-coaster ride. Just leave me alone."

Her husband was undeterred, "And, something else! He pulled out two fliers from the large envelope and announced, "You and I are going to PARIS!"

Estella was absolutely stunned. She didn't know what to say. Ever since she was a little girl, her dream was to visit Paris. As she stared at the plane tickets, the reality of her highest hope had just come true.

Why wasn't she happy?

Because the last thing she wanted in the world was to spend a month with the man she respected the least. He was part of the problem she was suffering. Now the goal was for her to endure more suffering?

No chance!

She had to escape the asylum, "Xavier, as much as I appreciate your offer to take me to this beautiful city, I don't think it's a good idea. We will be thousands of miles away from Marie. What if she has an emergency at camp and needs us?"

Xavier countered her fear effortlessly, "We can fly your mother down and she can stay here and be on call in that event, honey!"

Estella's heart sank.

She lamely tried to punch a hole in his plan, "But my mother has just started a new job. She can't afford to leave it and live in Georgetown!"

Xavier laughed, "No problem; I will ask my parents to watch over Marie. They would love to do that for us!"

Estella smiled weakly, "I really am not up to the trip."

Over the next two weeks, Xavier doted on Estella to the point that she felt uncomfortable. There were too many fancy dinners, expensive pieces of jewelry, and mountains of red roses. In her mind, he was overdoing it and she wanted him to stop. Yes, he had been a jerk, but this kind of extravagant flattery was way over the top.

She was also in agony over the trip to Paris. Estella had no interest in traveling to Europe with her sociopathic and volatile husband. She knew she would be constantly on edge the entire time. It would be as relaxing as swimming with a school of piranha.

A whirlwind tour of London, Rome, Athens, Dublin, Barcelona, and Vienna — not to mention Paris — did not sound restful to her. It was a vacation that suited her alpha male husband to a tee; but not her. She ached for the quiet lapping of the waves at sunset on a deserted shoreline. That would have bored Xavier to tears, but it was heaven to her. She did not want to be spoiled; she wished for serenity to heal from the aching pain of losing her baby.

"Let him take his needy mistress," Estella reasoned to herself, "She has never been out of the country. She would love all that crap!"

*****

As Xavier discovered a few nights later, truer words were never spoken. Lying in Mily's arms, he was suddenly confronted by a verbal explosion. Xavier decided it was too much trouble to find a body double to go to the House of D, so he made contact with Mily.

"Europe? You're taking your flaky and ungrateful wench of a wife to all those cities. You are a *son-of-a-bitch*, Xavier Cyrus!"

Xavier enjoyed getting Mily riled up for his entertainment, "Why are you upset, Darling?"

"Because, dumb ass, you should be taking *me*!

Instead of calming his mistress and softening the blow, Xavier turned on the combative jets and amped up the emotional heat. "Tell your husband to take you; that's his job!" he smiled.

"My husband could never afford to spoil me like that! He barely makes enough money to take me to a nice steak house!"

Xavier inappropriately joked, "What... you don't like mac and cheese?"

His now irritated mistress finally reached her boiling point, "Screw you!"

She rolled out of bed and stormed into the bathroom. Suddenly mystified, he shouted at her, "Where are you going?"

"Home!" She screamed back as she violently slammed the door cracking the middle glass insert in the process.

"Why, darling?" He said, as he now stood at the door and tried to reason with her.

"So my mac and cheese won't get cold!" she screamed.

Xavier entered the bathroom and saw tears running down Mily's face. He finally showed her some sensitivity, "Aww, don't be like this! I'm just trying to make peace at home. You're the one I want, you know that!" He lied again.

"No, Xavier; I don't know that! I have hinted numerous times that I want to be your wife and you either laugh it off or ignore my statement. I'm sick of being the other woman in your life. I am fed up with all our secret meetings and pretending to be Estella at your sex club. And, you show your appreciation for me by taking your ungrateful wife — who doesn't love you, by the way — to *Europe*!"

Xavier gently took her by the shoulders and whispered romantically, "Where would you like to go? Just name it!"

Mily had her answer ready, "To *the altar*!"

Xavier couldn't help but laugh.

She put on her coat, grabbed her purse, and exited the room. Her lover watched her leave and had a bemused look on his face as he murmured, "That will never be one of our destinations, my dear Mily; not a chance in hell!"

*****

The voice on the phone said, "Paris?"

Estella fumed, "Yes, Paris with my dysfunctional bully of a husband… for a month!" She added for emphasis. "It will be the worst thirty days of my life! I want that quiet beach with the gentle breeze soothing my soul, Margret. We have to make that happen!"

Her therapist was silent for several seconds; then she asked, "Do you want me to try to talk to Xavier? Because in my medical opinion you need a rest and need to take some time away from him. Honestly, I think you are at a breaking point. I can just hear the trial judge asking you, 'So, you killed your husband because he took you to Paris?'"

"Yes, please call him."

*****

The call ended on that note, just in time for Estella to greet Marie from school. She served her little girl a snack and the two of them sat down at the kitchen table and discussed her daughter's day.

At dinner that night, Marie was all agog at her upcoming summer camp experience, "We're going to ride horses, paddle canoes in the lake, tell scary stories at the campfire, and do a lot of crafts! And cousin Lucy will be there. She is so much fun," she gushed.

Her father was elated for her. "I loved summer camp when I was your age!"

"And there's going to be a talent show and you and Mom can come to watch me play the piano, too!"

"My little girl, I will be at camp with you this summer, but your mom is going away with your grandma. She really needs a break sweetie."

Margret had convinced the ogre. She had escaped the asylum.

She was going to the beach!

Paradise.

*****

"This place is beautiful, but I still can't stop crying at least every hour," confessed Estella to her two vacation mates as she stood barefoot in the warm, blue waters of the Caribbean.

Renee and Margret looked at each other concerned. Their mission to see Estella renew her life was failing. Her healing was stunted. Renee had a suggestion, "Let's hike down the beach and build up an appetite for dinner. Maybe we can find some interesting places worth seeing."

"How is your special friend, Michael the agent?" inquired Margret.

"I didn't get a chance to talk to him alone before we all left yesterday. I miss him already. But we'll be fine."

Her mom added, "Wish he was here, Estella?"

"Of course, I do; that would be a romantic dream – sharing all this beauty with the man I am in love with!"

Margret pointed off in the distance, "What a beautiful lighthouse! Let's explore it."

Off the trio went to get a closer view of the tall, white edifice. While there, they met a native young man and asked him more about the island and for recommendations on places of interest.

"The most beautiful place is Gibney Beach," he informed them. "It is right on the water and a wonderful place for lovers, especially at sunset."

Renee laughed, "What if we don't have lovers; can we rent some?"

The boy laughed, "With three lovely women like you, I doubt you will have any trouble having success in that area!"

Margret winked at him, "So, what happens in St. John stays

in St. John, right?"

He smiled, "That is our island tradition, Ma'am!"

Renee commented, "Interesting; I thought that only applied to Las Vegas!"

The native young man added, "I guess it applies to vacations everywhere!"

Estella asked him, "Is it safe to walk around here at night?"

"Oh, yes!" he assured her. "We are very friendly people. We also love tourists. They allow us to survive financially, so all of us here make certain that is never endangered."

Margret queried, "How do we find the beach?"

The boy pointed west, "Just keep walking. Eventually, you will see a homemade sign announcing its presence. It's so beautiful there!"

The women thanked him and headed towards the setting sun. They were in Paradise and enjoying every scintillating minute of it.

As they reached the beach, the ladies were overwhelmed by its natural beauty and private shoreline. Estella and Margaret sat on a bench overlooking the ocean while Renee went off doing some private scrutiny of the island.

For several minutes, neither woman spoke as they took in the sights and smells of the ocean experience. Finally, Margaret asked Estella, "So, you and the Secret Service agent?"

Her client laughed shyly, "I guess so."

"How serious are you about Michael, Estella?"

"We have beautiful chemistry, Margret. I deeply respect and admire him. He makes me come alive."

Her therapist nodded, "Did you expect this to happen?"

Estella shook her head, "Honestly, no. I was thunderstruck the night I first met him when he was introduced to Xavier and I; but, I had no idea it would turn into an emotional bonding like it has for us. Very little has happened physically between us, but we can feel it coming. With Xavier constantly around, we have been very careful not to go beyond the boundaries of my marriage."

"Are you in love with him, Estella?"

"I believe I am, yes. But we just haven't had enough private moments or extended periods of romance for me to know for sure."

Margret had seen her clients in this position many times before, "At this point, you feel it could go either way between the two of you?"

Estella whispered her answer, "Either way, yes. I am pulling away from Xavier with each passing day. His behaviors, beliefs, and constant abuse have taken me to the point of wishing I were single, with or without Michael. I know, logically, that before I fall in love with another man, I should completely end my marriage to Xavier and be free emotionally, but my heart has a will of its own. I need Michael."

"And Xavier has no inkling that you and Michael —"

Estella cut her off, "Oh, not in the least! If he did, Michael would be fired on the spot. Xavier is a very jealous and possessive man as you know. If he sensed Michael was moving in on me, it could be fatal. I don't know if Michael and I would ever be free to fall in love as long as Xavier is alive, even I were divorced."

Margret smiled at her, "But you would like to experience love with him."

"Yes, I would enjoy that very much. It is an unrealistic fantasy at this point — a very dangerous one — but it often keeps me awake at night, truth be told."

"I admire you, Estella, for your discretion and character. Even though your heart aches for this man, you are doing your best to remain faithful to your wedding vows."

Estella shook her head, "Xavier is making that very difficult. He is an abomination to me. I have no love in my heart for him anymore. I am only staying in the marriage for Marie's sake. I fear losing her in a custody battle. With all his money and his parent's influence; a divorce would force me to say goodbye to her."

"Especially, if that divorce occurred because you were having an affair with his Secret Service agent."

Estella shuddered as she answered, "It would be the most horrific scenario of my life; being shamed in front of all my friends, fighting Xavier in court and eventually losing my daughter!"

"Yet, you and Michael..." Margret summarized.

"I must be crazy to stand on the edge of the cliff with this romantic fantasy. I am playing with fire."

Margret had an insight, "He must be worth the risk for you, Estella."

"He is an amazing man in every way, yes. I know we have something special, realized or not."

At that point, Renee walked up, "There is a quaint little hotel here. It's not as fancy as the one we're in, only six rooms; but it's very romantic and private. A perfect lover's getaway."

Margret looked at Estella with a knowing wink. She was

greeted with a big sigh. They both knew what Estella was thinking about her choice for a romantic getaway here.

It was time for dinner.

That night, Estella had a horrible nightmare. She dreamt that Michael had drowned in the ocean. It was such vivid imagery that even after she awakened it took her several minutes to actually comprehend that it wasn't true. It took her two hours to finally go back to sleep. It had been the most disturbing nightmare she had ever experienced.

It took her two hours to finally go back to sleep. It had been the most disturbing nightmare she had ever experienced.

The dream made her realize how much she loved and needed him. The thought of losing Michael had shaken her to her very core.

Estella spent most of the following day alone walking around the beach. Something about the area resonated with her. She loved the romantic intimacy of it and in a way, it reminded her of Michael's calm that brought her peace. She felt his spirit there with her and wished he was holding her hand strolling along the beach telling her stories that made her laugh to cheer her up. She wondered how he was doing without seeing her every day.

Did he yearn just to hear her voice and hold her hand also?

She sat for hours on the little bench and just stared out at the sea imagining the life her son would have enjoyed had he lived.

She had so many questions in her mind about him, "What would he have looked like?"

"What kind of personality would he have?"

"Would she and him be close?"

"Would he share her political and social passions?"

As the sun disappeared slowly behind the horizon, Estella

suddenly felt sad about the times she could have had with her son and began weeping. She missed her daughter. She ached for Michael.

Maybe this isolated vacation had been a bad idea. She might have been better served to stay busy with the congressional leaders pursuing her passionate causes to keep her mind off of her sorrows.

It was getting dark soon. She headed back to her hotel feeling very much alone.

For the next three days, Estella followed the same pattern, having a buffet breakfast at the Queen Beach Hotel and then going off by herself to the secluded beach where she would spend the entire day alone until sunset, before returning to her room. Her mother and Margret Kahn were more than a little concerned about her and discussed options to help Estella get through her depression.

"You're a therapist, Margret. Is it healthy for my daughter to go off by herself and spend hours alone instead of socializing with us?"

"Every person grieves differently, Renee. What works for someone may not be viable for someone else. Right now, Estella is processing the permanent loss of her baby and the temporary separation from the man she believes she is falling in love with. Those two losses will trump her socialization process with us. If she is healing in her own way; it is healthy, yes. What seems lonely to us may be exactly what she needs the most right now."

Renee was skeptical, "How will we know that her self-imposed isolation is beneficial? She could be recycling her pain and not dealing with it at all?"

Margret remained calm, "We have to trust her and her

process, Renee. All we can do is be available to her if or when she needs to talk to us. Until she feels a need to do that, we have to assume she is happy going off alone every day."

Renee had a question, "Would it be healthy for her if Michael showed up to join her on her vacation?"

Margret was dumbfounded, "Michael, here?"

"Yes."

"Renee, Michael is in D.C. protecting Xavier. How in the world would you be able to arrange for him to come to St. John? He is a Secret Service agent protecting a congressman; not a man available to romance his client's wife in a Caribbean paradise!"

"Well, maybe we could arrange for him to call her for a few minutes to cheer her up? Just being able to talk to him may help."

The therapist thought about that idea for a few seconds and then responded, "Couldn't hurt. But, you would have to figure out a way to get that message to him without her husband finding out, a trick in itself!"

Renee smiled, "I asked him for his home number in case of emergency." Renee called Michael internationally from her hotel room phone when the switchboard connected the call Michael answered. "Hello, may I please speak to Michael Hagar."

"Hello, this is he."

"Hi Michael, this is Renee, Estella's mom. How's D.C.?"

She couldn't believe what she heard next, "I'm not in D.C.; I am taking leave in Arkansas for some personal family time for a couple of weeks!"

Renee was so shocked she almost dropped the phone. "So, you're not with Xavier and Marie?"

"No, Ma'am! They sent another agent to handle protection

for the congressman there. What was your message for me?'

"Michael, is there any way you can get to an airport and fly to St. John?"

There was a stunned silence.

"Michael?"

He responded with prudence, "I'm not sure that's a good idea, Renee."

"Estella needs you, Michael. She is really hurting."

"She is also really married."

Renee corrected him, "You of all people know that isn't true. There is no love there."

"If she gets divorced, I would come to her. But, I'm not a home-wrecker, Renee."

"You won't be wrecking anything, Michael; it's just a week to cheer her up and we will all use discretion."

"Does Estella agree to this?"

Renee laughed, "Not exactly!"

"This is your idea?"

"As her mother, I am concerned about my daughter. She has lost a baby, her marriage is in shambles, and she is lonely, confused, and depressed. You can help her right now. I will send you a plane ticket. Come spend a week with her. We both know how much you two love each other."

More silence. Michael thought to himself, "*I don't feel alive without Estella. I need her no matter the risk or the cost.*"

Renee knew by Michael's labored breathing he was struggling with this decision. She remained silent. It was his turn to speak.

"I can come for eleven days then I have to return to

Washington. I'll pay for my own ticket and room."

"We are staying at the Queen Beach Hotel. See you soon and thank you!"

Renee called the airline and made all the arrangements. She couldn't wait to see the expression on Estella's face when Michael showed up. That would be a moment!

The next morning, as Estella was having breakfast with her two vacation mates, Renee asked about her specific plans for the day.

"I will be visiting my favorite beach and enjoying my thoughts along the water."

Margret interjected, "Enjoying?"

Estella amended the word, "Processing."

The three women laughed; especially Renee. She knew the word, "enjoyment" would become a reality in her daughter's day, for sure.

At 6:00 pm, Renee received a call from the front desk, "You have a visitor in the lobby. His name is Michael Hagar."

Renee almost fell off her chair with excitement, "I'll be right down!"

She collected an astonished Margret and the two of them made their way to the lobby. They encountered a smiling Secret Service agent who was shaking his head in amazement. "This is crazy!"

Renee nodded, "This will mean the world to my daughter, Michael. Thanks for trusting me on this. Why don't you freshen up and meet us back down here in 30 minutes?"

Michael nodded and headed for the elevator. When he returned, he was dressed more casually for a tropical vacation.

The three of them exited the hotel and began the walk down the shoreline.

"You know I could be fired for this, don't you?"

Renee shook her head, "Xavier will never find out. Mum's the word. The risk is worth the reward! I rented you a private bungalow with it's own private beach about a mile walk up from here." Renee handed Michael the keys to the bungalow.

"Renee is right," Michael thought. *"I have never really lived and did not even know that truth until I danced with Estella and she brought love into my life."* The normally level-headed Michael was willing to risk everything for even a moment of true joy.

Finally, they were within fifty yards of a beach umbrella and saw Estella sitting alone on a blanket.

Then, she and Margret waited with hearts pounding as he prepared to give Estella the surprise of her life. Renee whispered to her compatriot, "I hope my daughter finally has the chance to experience the love she deserves even if it is just for eleven days."

The two women watched them gleefully, then headed back to their hotel.

Mission accomplished.

Estella was watching a school of dolphins frolicking happily in the water when she suddenly heard a familiar voice behind her, "Hello, Love. Are you OK?"

Her heart stopped. She said to herself, *"Am I dreaming? This can't be!"* She whirled around just in time to feel herself being picked up in Michael's strong arms and kissed passionately!

Estella had never felt such a jolt of excitement as Michaels tongue slipped inside of her mouth and sensually dueled with her own.

When they pulled back; she couldn't believe her eyes. "You are really here!"

Michael laughed, "You needed me, so I came."

"Thank you, Michael, you are always with me when I need you. And I need you most now."

Michael took Estella's hand, "Let's walk."

They spent the next two hours strolling, talking, kissing, and laughing. Estella felt like she had been romantically born-again. Being with Michael was intimately effortless. It was like they had been together for forever. The best part of it was that they didn't have to hide their affection for each other on their private beach.

They went back to the beach blanket to watch the sunset over the water; kissed and cuddled. The fire was building and they both felt it. When they arrived back at Michael's room, he picked up Estella and carried her over to his bed.

They laid in each other's arms for several minutes until they set about in sensual earnest to enjoy what they both had only imagined until then.

As they kissed even more deeply, Michael undressed his lover slowly and sexily, only stopping after he saw new sensual areas of flesh to run his lips and hands over that were previously covered areas.

As Estella moaned with more intensity as he progressed, he was excitedly pleased with the beauty of her exquisite body. He relished her rounded breasts in his mouth and used his tongue to completely satisfy the ache that had waited for him all these months.

He slid off her floral shorts and ran his lips over her panties, teasing her essence and making it beg for him to completely satisfy her. When he slid her underthings off and began pleasuring her with his mouth, Estella almost came off the bed with desire, arching her back and uncontrollably grinding her lower body relentlessly into his mouth.

She grabbed the strings on his waistline and pulled his shorts down in one motion. Hungry for the manhood, she had teased only a few weeks before by the fireplace. Now, she stroked its massive size and gasped as it grew.

Then, she positioned herself over his member and slowly conquered it inch by inch. Michael leaned back and groaned in wild abandon. She was moving in short and quick spurts, dominating it, teasing it, and exciting it as no other woman had ever done before.

Finally, she could not hold back any longer and began to shudder and moan. He could not hold back any longer either as he exploded violently into her in a simultaneous climax – the strongest either one of them had ever encountered. He was hypnotized by the way Estella continued to squeeze him inside of her rhythmically. Then, she laid back, splayed her legs wide as he rolled on top still inside of her, they fell asleep as one.

They were lovemaking, and it was magic.

They lay there spent, wrapped in each other's arms and after a few minutes, made love again. For the next several hours, they kept exploding each other in the bath, in the shower, in the bed, on the floor and standing up until they were so exhausted; they collapsed satiated just as the sun peeked out in the east.

They slept until noon and woke up deeply in love.

As they lay in bed holding one another, Michael told Estella the story of Zeus separating men and women who were once four-legged and four-armed creatures to make them weak.

"I love you, Estella. I know this is clichéd, but I really feel like you're my other half. I feel my strongest when I am with you."

"I feel the exact same way. My love for you is so deep I feel that we can overcome any obstacle. I was a basket case just yesterday, and today you have given me the strength to keep going."

Estella thought to herself, *"When I am with Xavier, it is an exhausting roller coaster ride, and I just want to jump off the coaster in mid-air. But Michael's calming spirit soothes me and gives me peace."*

*****

As they were about to be seated at the Queen Beach Hotel's restaurant, they were joined by Renee and Margret who had agreed to chaperone since they were in public view. Of course, Estella had a comment for her mother, "There's the Matchmaking Mama now! Thank you so much."

Everyone laughed and Renee rejoined, "Glad to be of service!"

Margret asked the lovebirds, "What are your plans today?"

Estella glanced warmly at Michael and replied, "I am taking him to a special place on the island and surprising him with a delicious treat!"

Michael asked, "What's the treat?" She just winked at him. He said excitedly, "Let's hurry up and finish lunch, then!"

Her therapist noted, "I see you're finally enjoying your vacation, Estella!"

"Michael has brought sunshine to my rainy skies," she smiled as she took his hand and squeezed it.

Renee opined, "Enjoy it while it lasts. You two will have a decision to make when you get back to D.C."

That comment chilled the mood. Estella grimaced as she thought of Xavier and how to deal with him once reality reared its ugly head at home.

Michael spoke up. "One thing at a time, Renee. We just want to enjoy the moment."

After lunch, the couples parted ways and Estella guided her lover past the bench and down the shore for two more miles before steering him into a large cave.

As they made their way into the bowels of the natural formation, they came across a large waterfall framed by a beautiful aqua blue lagoon. Better yet, there was no one else around and in no time; Estella was naked and in the water. Michael roared with approval and joined her!

Like a couple of young honeymooners, the two of them playfully romped in the warm expanse, kissing, hugging, laughing and touching each other intimately.

Soon, they wanted more. It was time to consummate their love, again.

They found a sandbank near the waterfall and laid down on it. They began kissing and touching and soon Michael was on his back and Estella was aggressively mounting him. As she slid her body down over his rock-hard shaft, she moaned with pleasure. Then, she expertly began riding him like a happy cowgirl on her steed.

Up and down, back and forth, Estella moved her entire body from one sexy gyration to the other. Michael moved with her and the two became one for several minutes as Estella climaxed and lay on his chest soaked by the mist of the waterfall that had been their steamy backdrop.

Without warning, Estella shocked them both as she revealed her soul, "I love you, Michael. And I want us to be together forever."

He rolled her over on her back and looked deeply into her eyes and whispered, "I love you, Estella. This is not just a fling for me either. I have never really been in love and didn't know this intensity of feeling before you. I don't ever want to lose this feeling. I need you forever; you're like a drug."

She nodded gently that she felt the same, gazing into his eye with a similar fire. For over a minute, neither of them said a word.

Then, he gently spread her legs and entered her as she lay beneath him. In the most loving and intimate of ways he slowly moved inside her, deeper and deeper until it could go no further and climaxed inside her. When he did, he felt her fingernails digging into his back and heard a wild guttural scream from her lips.

As they lay there panting, the roar of the waterfall expanded the pounding of their hearts and seared that memory into their souls.

Now that their love had been consummated, there was no holding back their passion. They were like an old married couple: no longer shy but tried every position imaginable in their desire to be as close as they could for as long as possible.

It was paradise; a love affair for the ages.

Then, it was time to go home, and Estella felt lost.

Michael had extended his vacation by twelve extra days to be by her side and he would fly from St. John directly back to Washington and prepare to be reunited with Xavier in a few days.

Estella would not enjoy four more days in Paradise, without Michael, until she would make Georgetown her residence again.

As she waited for Michael's cab to take him to the airport and their temporary goodbye, the emotions of the event brought tears to her eyes.

She realized that they were going back to romantic undercover mode once again. It was unbearable for her to think about. He was more realistic in his acceptance of it.

"I'm going to hate pretending again, Michael. I wish we could love each other back home as we have here. Even when I see you now, I'm going to miss you so much and miss the freedom to love each other," she ran her fingers down his face lovingly.

"Just be thankful we had this opportunity, my love. There will be another soon. We'll figure out a way. At least, with my job, I will get to see you every day."

Estella shook her head, "That will make it worse, having you so close and yet so far. It will be torture for me." At this point, she believed that she was the heroine in a Shakespearean tragedy. "I deserve love, peace, happiness, and safety. I don't know how I can go back to Xavier, even though I must."

"It has been torture for me already. Every time Xavier touches you; I have to control my anger to not go to jail. I know you want to stay in the marriage until your daughter grows up, but that is over ten years away. I am going to try my best, but ten years is a long time. I promise to wait for you, my only love."

"I love you forever, Michael."

Then her lips were on his; moist, moving and seducing his mouth with the promise of eternal love.

Finally, it was time for Michael to get in his cab to the airport. As he waved one final time, Estella ran to him and violently hugged him. He returned her firm embrace never wanting to let her go.

She stood at the window and watched the cab drive away, tears streaming down her face. It had been weeks of intense passion and powerful fulfillment, and now she had to be the good wife and pretend it had never happened.

But it had. Estella had a time of serenity, love, and pure joy with her true love that many people have never experienced. It was worth risking their lives to have their moment together; no one could ever take away their memories, even if circumstances dictated that they could never be as one again.

Upon returning home, Estella threw herself into her political passions; women's rights, civil rights, and aerospace.

*****

The first night she arrived, Xavier was anxious to have sex with her and when she refused, he quickly went out for the evening to see his mistress.

The first time she saw Michael again was in her husband's presence, so it was back to the covert romance that Estella and Michael shared, which was very painful for her.

She found two powerful congressmen to propose a new bill on equal pay for women in the workplace, but it failed in the Senate. But it was a good effort on her part, nonetheless. Estella realized when it came to rights for her gender or minorities it would be a long journey to success.

Over the next month, Xavier was getting increasingly frustrated with his wife's reluctance to please him in bed and he began hinting that maybe their marriage would be better served as a divorce. Estella was all for that idea but there was no way she would grant him one for one very important reason:

Marie.

Estella knew she had no realistic chance of keeping her daughter in a custody fight. So, unless Xavier died or until Marie turned 18, he would be her husband for a long time; maybe forever.

Scarily, she was revisited by her nightmare of Michael drowning in the ocean again. It was just as vivid as it had been the first time. She was beginning to believe this was not just a random bad dream but an omen of an actual upcoming event. It terrified her.

Estella's life was set in a predictable routine at this point; raising Marie, fighting off Xavier, living in a sham marriage, secretly pining for Michael and passionately fighting for her trio of causes.

CHAPTER TWENTY-FIVE

The Turbulent '60s

The world was changing as the Eisenhower presidency wound down. The new interstate highway system had revolutionized travel across the country.

Fidel Castro had shocked the world as he announced his allegiance to the Soviet Union, vowing to make Cuba a communist nation.

It was now 1960 and the decade of revolution was upon her in America. There would be nothing routine about the events of the next ten years and no way to prepare for them.

It was springtime and Estella accompanied her husband to a fundraising dinner to hear a renowned voice in the political arena, who had new ideas. His name was Senator John F. Kennedy and he was running for the Democratic nomination for President.

Estella was enthralled by him.

She had never seen a political figure like Kennedy in her lifetime. She had never believed any man could ever be more charismatic than her husband, until now.

The winds of change were beginning to blow throughout the country. Senator Kennedy had challenged voters with the slogan,

"Let's get this country moving again!"

Some believed that the last eight years under President Eisenhower had been slow and sedentary and they wanted to stimulate progress.

Americans responded to his call to action. With the advent of the new interstate highway system and the dawn of much-needed change for social and economic advances, women, Blacks, homosexuals and sexual free thinkers suddenly mobilized and began to raise their voices.

This new environment of volatility was a godsend to Estella who needed radical leaders to promote the causes she had been pushing for years. The women's movement and the civil rights movement now began to march forward in powerful ways. Estella suddenly found herself at the forefront of change and she relished in it!

Xavier was not at all enamored by seeing women or Black people moving up the social ladder. He was horrified, actually. His world was crumbling around him and it was all he could do to maintain the status quo which kept his misogyny and racism intact. The times were changing and sweeping Xavier along with them.

Estella now had a newfound sense of power and opportunity. The new climate of the 1960's had given her a leverage she had never had before. Suddenly, many more legislators were answering her phone calls and meeting with her to see how they could advance the plight of women and minorities. Her little boat had shifted direction from upstream to downstream in a moment's eye!

Unfortunately, Xavier noticed his wife's newfound sense of power. Fortuitously for her; there was nothing he could do about it. Estella was now on the winning side of her causes and if her husband wanted to advance to a higher office; he would have to root for her to help him get there.

It was time for Xavier Cyrus to become the new champion of women and Blacks. It would be the most stellar acting job of his political career.

Of course, his wife wasn't fooled by his act, but she needed his power to propel her passions forward; so, she went with it. The higher Xavier went politically, the more she could rise, as well.

Estella couldn't lose now. The decade had put her in the driver's seat of social and political change.

There was another program that was literally taking off in this era, too. A space program called NASA was gaining momentum and it was revolutionizing space technology and travel like no other administrations before. She began aggressively lobbying for monies and staff to build up this space program and – not surprisingly – she received them.

She now had three viable dreams that were becoming proven realities in her lifetime. Quietly, she and Michael began meeting and planning a collaboration that could effectively and literally change the world around them.

One of her specific goals was to combine two of her dreams into one by funding Black women with mathematical scholarships to further the space program. This way, she would be successful in seeing two of her dreams working together!

Now, when Estella traveled to Capitol Hill, she had an optimism never felt before. Everything she touched was turning to gold. It was nothing short of a political miracle for the indomitable Mrs. Cyrus.

*****

Over a quiet lunch in a secluded restaurant, while Xavier was stuck all day in a committee hearing, Estella and Michael excitedly reviewed their legislative progress. "Those scholarships for your math students were a great coup, Estella! You helped a lot of young ladies. I am proud of you, love," Michael told her.

"It's just the beginning; we have thousands of minorities who have had their potential contributions repressed for decades because of their color. They could have made our country greater had we let them. This is just the tip of the iceberg. In every area of the arts and sciences, we are going to free up young minority students — Blacks, Latinos, Asians, all of them — to help our nation be better."

Michael informed her, "Xavier speaks of you often. He is proud of your accomplishments; not for your sake or for the people you represent, but because he believes it will help win a Senate seat someday soon."

Estella laughed mockingly, "Yeah, that's my Xavier!"

Her lover winced, "I know you are being sarcastic but please don't refer to him in the possessive sense. He is only your husband on paper. He doesn't belong to you, or you to him..."

"I'm sorry, Michael. I am all yours; you know that."

He smiled, "Yes, I know."

"The election is coming up. Will it be Kennedy or Nixon?"

Michael said, "Kennedy. In my opinion, our people are going to support him in droves since he intervened and got Dr. King out of jail and Kennedy has agreed to support civil rights legislation. I believe had he not done that, perhaps Martin would have been murdered in jail. Our community took notice. They will have Kennedy's back at the ballot box next month, even though Blacks have been Republicans since we could vote I think the party is taking us for granted. Thanks again for calling your friend Sargent Nichols."

"However, I can help I will. I believe you're right, Michael."

Michael looked at his watch, "Gotta go, Darling. I need to be in the hallway when that committee ends. Dream of me tonight, okay?"

That last comment sent a shudder through Estella; she didn't want that recurring nightmare of Michael drowning to visit her ever again.

"Of course, I will. You are my love, Michael. Be safe out there."

With that, he was gone, leaving Estella with a heavy heart and only the hope of their next close encounter.

*****

1961 began with a new President. To Michael and Estella's delight, John Fitzgerald Kennedy was inaugurated in January, a Democrat, replacing eight years of Republican rule in the White House. His "New Frontier" promised a set of new challenges for the American people.

Four months later, while Estella was folding clothes in her den, with her daughter. Xavier came home and announced that Kennedy had given a speech to the joint members of Congress.

"Kennedy said we should go to the moon. It seems your wishes are coming true, although I see it as a monumental waste of time and money," Xavier stated dryly.

We should go to the *moon*? The words he used rocked her world.

Estella could barely comprehend those six keywords from

her new President for they encapsulated one of her most fervent passions in life. Her daughter screamed aloud, "Mommy, did you hear what daddy just said!"

Estella's mind was racing, *"Women's rights, civil rights, and space exploration; one of her three passions just got a giant boost from none other than the President!"*

Marie danced around the room shouting, "We're going to the moon! We're going to the moon!" And Estella took her hand and joined her in her moon dance. The decade of the '60s had taken off with a bang, and Estella could not be more excited.

She believed this was going to be the greatest years of her life. At that moment, she had never felt prouder to be an American.

Xavier was still full of compliments for Kennedy: "Although I disagree about the waste of money on space he almost changed my mind, the man has charisma, Estella. Both chambers of Congress sat there in awe at the way he inspired us. He is a great Democrat; I look forward to emulating him when I reach the Oval Office!"

Out of his range of vision, Estella shook her head in disgust at the idea of Xavier becoming President. Michael noticed her expression and broke out laughing. Xavier asked him, "What's so funny?"

His agent just said, "Oh nothing; I just remembered a joke I heard at lunch today!"

Over the next several months, Estella intensified her efforts to see her projects come to fruition. She believed that her dreams of women's rights, civil rights, and space exploration, were not only do-able but on target. She was not only on the right track; she *was* the track!

She saw clearly these goals were the future of America, empowering women, inspiring minorities, and enabling man to discover outer space were worth her efforts in life.

She burned with the desire and drive to lobby, to see women treated equally as men, to give Blacks and Latinos opportunities in education and economics; to aid scientist to unlock the mysteries of the universe. She believed this critical work would lead to success in her lifetime.

Nothing could stop her now. The sky was the limit. But, there were storm clouds on her horizon that were brewing; the likes of which could not only deter her dreams but fatally destroy them.

*****

In late October of 1962, as she was preparing dinner, Xavier rushed in the door with Michael in tow and announced, "We need to get out of here. *Now!*"

Estella gave him a shocked look, followed by a question, "Why?"

Ignoring her, he shouted, *"Where's Marie?"*

"She's in her room, Xavier. What is so urgent?"

Her husband was out of breath and the look on Michael's face confirmed the serious nature of the moment. "We need to pack and go. Move!"

Estella was clueless, "Move where?"

"To an underground bunker. We are on the brink of a nuclear war, Estella; this is no joke! This is being handled on a 'first-come, first-served' basis, Estella. The President, his staff, the Supreme Court and all of Congress are making plans to relocate as I speak. Screw your dinner. Get upstairs and pack and let's get our daughter and leave now!"

Estella looked at Michael for perspective and when she saw him somberly nodding; she knew it was serious. As she hurriedly accompanied her frantic husband up the stairs she blurted out, "What is happening, Xavier? Perhaps we should have invested in a shelter for our family instead of having to go to the first come first serve shelter."

His answer sent a chill through her, "We found nuclear missiles in Cuba, and they are prepared to launch them on the eastern seaboard, specifically D.C. If we survive this situation, then, yes, I will be investing in a shelter like some other families are."

"The Communists?" she asked.

The Soviet Union is preparing for war, Estella. President Kennedy is going on national television within the hour to alert the American people. There's going to be a national panic. You won't want to go near a grocery store!"

She flew into Marie's room and grabbed a suitcase. Her daughter looked quizzically at her and asked, "What are you doing, Mommy?"

"Baby, we have to leave our house for a while. Get your things we need to get out of here!"

Confused, the little girl began crying, "Are we going to die?"

Estella smiled reassuringly, "Oh no, nothing like that!"

Within minutes, the family was packed and ready to roll. At that point; Xavier stopped their departure and turned on the television to listen to the President's speech.

Kennedy appeared calm and cool in the Oval Office as he

addressed American citizens. "Good evening, my fellow citizens. This government, as promised, has maintained the closest surveillance of the Soviet military build-up on the island of Cuba. Within the past week, unmistakable evidence has established the fact that a series of offensive missile sites is now in preparation on that imprisoned island. The purpose of these bases can be none other than to provide a nuclear strike capability against the western hemisphere..."

Marie looked worried. Estella said to her, "Baby, go upstairs. I need to speak to Daddy privately."

As the speech on TV continued, "Our goal is not the victory of might, but the vindication of right, not peace at the expense of freedom, but both peace and freedom, here in this hemisphere, and we hope around the world. God willing, that goal will be achieved."

They watched the follow-up commentary that notified the public that President Kennedy, his cabinet, and the Joint Chiefs of Staff would be working over the next several days; not only to alleviate the situation, but to resolve it.

Xavier then announced, "Time to go!"

Estella just sat on the couch and looked at him. Her husband stared back and said, "Estella, we need to get out of here!"

Her daughter safely upstairs, she turned to her husband, "No, Xavier; I'm not going anywhere... and neither is Marie!"

Xavier gave her a shocked look, "Are you crazy? Do you want to die?"

"I don't get the feeling anyone is going to die tonight."

He frowned at her. "Excuse me? You and your feelings. So, your feelings will tell you when the situation is serious enough to go to the shelter? OK..." Xavier said sarcastically making the ok sign with his fingers.

"President Kennedy looked pretty relaxed to me. There was no panic in his voice, nor was there any suggestion that we needed to relocate to some underground bunker. We are staying here, in our home, until further notice. Understand?"

She glanced at Michael who was smiling at her, confirming that he agreed with her assessment.

"Well, you can stay; but I am taking cover. I will see you and Marie in a few days, *if* you are still around to live through this!"

She just shook her head in disgust, "Xavier, sometimes you have the common sense of a goose. There is no factual evidence or imminent danger to support your wild-eyed ranting. The Soviet Union has no intention of destroying us; they want to use our resources, not obliterate them. If we had evidence or we were told to evacuate or I had any feeling that this was serious I would be the first one out the door."

Her husband had heard enough, "So your feelings are telling you they are bluffing? Let's go, Michael; unless you have a death wish, too!"

His agent suggested, "Well, since you'll be safe; wouldn't you prefer that I stay and protect your family, sir?"

Xavier thought for a second and then announced, "I am taking Marie, my wife doesn't deserve protection!"

Then, he called Marie downstairs who refused to leave without her mom until her dad sternly ordered her to leave with him. They turned and exited the house with Michael dutifully following them.

As Estella sat alone on the couch, she just shook her head in disgust, "And, to think he believes he can lead our country someday!"

Several hours passed, and Estella began to regret not going with Marie to comfort her child, even though her husband was insufferable. She thought, *"There is a slight chance I am wrong, I should have gone. Even though being stuck in a bomb shelter with Xavier would be a fate worse than death; Marie would not be okay without me."*

Estella tried to call Xavier's office, but no one was answering. Then she went into Xavier's study that he annoyingly had decorated to be a replica of the oval office, to try to find additional phone numbers.

Just then, she heard a sound at the study door, turned, and saw Michael. She had given him a spare key in case of an emergency. Her heart that was already beating rapidly, in a panic to find a working phone number, almost burst out of her chest when she saw him. They looked into each other eyes and all the repressed emotions and passions that had built up from not touching each other since their St. John affair exploded as they savagely embraced.

Kissing and caressing each other in wild abandon, Michael picked Estella up and placed her on Xavier's desk on top of his papers. Not bothering to remove all of their clothes, Michael quickly entered her as she moaned, "Yes." The lovers' desire was heightened by the idea that this could be their last time ever to make love; this may be the end of the world.

The couples ecstasy simultaneously spent, Michael, carried Estella to the guest bedroom. He reassured her that Marie was safe in the West Virginia government shelter with Xavier, but explained it was filled to capacity, locked down and officials had turned many families away that had passes.

"The moment I was sure Marie was safely in the bunker, I came back here to be with you. I would never go in the shelter without you, my love, even if I had a pass. Are you second-guessing your decision to stay at home?"

"If it were not for Marie, I would happily die in your arms if it is the end."

They made love for several days as if tomorrow did not matter because if they were wrong, tomorrow did not matter.

As it turned out, Estella and Michael were correct in their assessment of the Cuban Missile Crisis, and America went back to its happy days again; for a year.

*****

But, the turbulence of the '60s was only heating up. Estella was driving home on a crisp November afternoon when she heard the shocking news on her radio.

"Three shots were fired at President Kennedy's motorcade today in downtown Dallas…"

Estella almost went off the road. She gathered herself and was able to find a turnout so she could park her car and listen to updates. As each new one came in, the news became grimmer.

Her eyes misted up with tears as she recalled meeting President Kennedy at a Democratic fundraiser in Washington. Xavier had brought her up to the head table to shake his hand, and she was awestruck by how handsome he was. John F. Kennedy was charismatic and elegant. JFK had a way of making everyone he met feel important, as though he cared about them individually, and what they thought mattered to him greatly.

She had thanked him for his commitment to the space program and he'd smiled shyly and said, "Will you join me in this endeavor?"

Estella vigorously assured him, "Yes, Mr. President, I surely will!"

Now, he was fighting for his life.

Finally, the bulletin made it official; John F. Kennedy was dead, the victim of an unknown sniper. Estella's first thought was, *"America will never be the same again."*

She was right.

The decade had claimed another victim. There would be more over the next six years: Dr. Martin Luther King, Malcolm X, Senator Robert Kennedy, four of the greatest leaders in history, were cut down. Riots in many cities had decimated the Black community burning down many Black-owned businesses. In 1965, the first massive troop deployment signaled the beginning of the civil war in Vietnam that eventually took the lives of over 50,000 American soldiers with thousands more being permanently disabled by Agent Orange and PTSD.

The turbulent '60s were unlike any decade before or since. It was not just a pivotal time of violence; it was the end of innocence in America.

Spree killers, Richard Speck, Charles Whitman, and Charles Manson and his famous family ushered in a new phenomena of mass murder never seen before.

Everything that had been normal in American society was now turned upside down. The movements were powerful and plentiful, women, Blacks, Latinos, gays, and radical counter cultures exploded on the scene.

Drugs entered the mainstream in 1967, including marijuana, LSD, meth, and, heroin. There were flower children and free love, hippies, anti-war protestors, and the loss of absolutes including the identity of God.

It was an America that no one had ever seen before. In fact, no one had ever even suspected there was an America hiding under the one that had existed throughout the first 50 years of the 20th century!

It all happened so fast; Americans were not able to prepare for it or comprehend it.

*****

By 1969, Estella and Michael's love was in full bloom. They still had to be discreet about it, but now they were seriously talking about marriage. It was just a matter of time.

On July 20, they were sipping wine on Estella's couch in front of the television set. Xavier had given Michael the day off to take one of his new mistresses to a Broadway play in New York City. Another agent accompanied them. Estella was thrilled that Michael was sitting next to her during one of the greatest moments of her life; Neil Armstrong was about to descend to the surface of the moon.

As they sat together, they discussed the most outrageous and memorable decade in American history. She asked him, "What stood out to you the past ten years, Michael?

He thought for a moment and then answered, "The March on Washington was my favorite moment and I loved sharing it with you. The assassination of President Kennedy, I will never forget where I was and what I was doing when I heard the news. I don't believe anyone who was alive that day will. I also remember when I heard about the assassination of Dr. King. That was just as shocking and poignant to me as Kennedy. The riots that followed in DC where I almost got killed, trying to get my disabled Aunt out of her burning building. And when LBJ signed the Civil Rights bill in '64. How about you, my love?"

She reminisced, "I heard of President Kennedy's death while I was driving and was so distraught, I had to pull over before I had an accident. When I heard about Martin's death, I was home with Marie. He was my hero, too. We cried all night when we heard the news. I think often of our time together, when we snuck out to go to the *March on Washington* and heard Martin's *I Have a Dream Speech*. I still get chills when I think of that day and how uplifted he made me feel. Sometimes when you get tired of fighting the good fight and you want to give up a leader inspires you to keep pushing forward."

"Yes, the *March on Washington* was one of the best days and I am glad I got to experience it with you." Michael took her hand and kissed her fingertips.

"Robert Kennedy's assassination deeply saddened me also because he fought so hard for minorities, particularly the Latino farmworkers in California. He would have made a great President. And I remember crying for joy one day as I watched a woman's march for equality on TV; I was so proud of them... So many tears this decade."

Michael commented, "Today has to be special for you! I am proud of you and all you accomplished behind the scenes. It upsets me that you can't take any credit."

"In a few minutes, we are going to see the fulfillment of President Kennedy's challenge to land on the moon by the end of this decade. I am happy for any part I played to help the cause." She choked up, "He was such a great man, inspiring us all. He was my hero. I miss him; I will always miss him."

At that moment, they both watched Armstrong making his way down the ladder and finally proclaim, "That's one small step for man, one giant leap for all mankind." Estella began crying,

"I hope President Kennedy is watching this somewhere. If so, he would be so proud!"

She snuggled into Michael's arms and dried her tears on his shirt. He hugged her tightly. The moment brought them together in the closest of ways. The decade of the '60s was ending on a high note. America had taken its heaviest blows and was still standing.

Michael whispered to her, "You still believe in hope?"

Through her tears, she fired back, "You're damn right, I *do*!"

Then they kissed and snuggled together. Michael began to kiss down her neck, undoing her blouse, gently licking and kissing her breasts down to her belly and further still.

Estella knew this was dangerous for them both and wrong, but she didn't, couldn't stop her beloved Michael. For the next several minutes, his tongue destroyed any remaining defenses she had and gratefully, she spread her legs even wider, begging for more.

He momentarily took a break from her quivering thighs and tasted first one nipple and then the other, sending Estella into more sensual histrionics. When her breasts were heaving, she was breathless and her nipples were now hard and distended; he went back to work on her hungry crevice.

"Don't stop, Michael. Please!"

Michael lifted her up in his muscular arms and took her up the stairs to the guest bedroom where he lay Estella softly on the bed. Slowly he removed both of their clothing, as Estella stared at his rippling muscular body which always took her breath away.

He continued his oral seduction, as she moaned waves of pleasure shooting through her body. Michael shifted to a higher plane and replaced his sexy tongue with his sizable shaft and rammed it inside her. It slid in easily thanks to her moist arousal easing the way for his entrance.

Over and over again, he penetrated her with a fierce pounding, knocking her body backward and causing the back of her head to come perilously close to the headboard behind her. Another few inches and she would be in danger of a concussion. He grabbed her legs and pulled her down into the safety of the middle of the bed.

More minutes went by with him not showing any sign of stopping. Estella's body was as limp as a rag doll; she had no ability to resist now nor did she want to resist. In and out, in and out, Michael had his complete way with her. Her entire body was his slave.

He shouted at her, "Do you love me?"

Between gasps, she managed to respond, "Yes, you, Michael!"

"Say it again, Estella!" he ordered.

"Yes, yes, yes!" she cried out.

"Yes, *what*?"

"I love you, Michael Hagar!"

He was finishing her off now. She tensed for his final thrust which sent a high-volume jolt through her. They both collapsed in each others arms and passed out, blissfuly exhausted.

Estella was the first to awaken and she elegantly slid off the bed and went into the bathroom where she prepared a washcloth of warm water and cleaned herself up. Then, she selected a second one and brought it to the bed and gently washed him as he slept.

She returned to the bath and took a hot shower and got

dressed just as he opened his eyes and smiled at her. Then Michael got dressed and went back down to the seating area near where he normally guarded the door.

CHAPTER TWENTY-SIX

Xavier's Big Surprise

When Xavier returned home the following day; he had a surprise for Estella, "I have decided to run for the United States Senate, darling!"

She was shocked, "Really?"

"Yes!" he laughed.

Estella thought to herself, "*Democratic Senator Xavier Cyrus, Texas.*" It seemed so surreal; and, more importantly, so scary. He would be one step away from running for the Presidency.

She gasped to herself.

"Do you realize I will be one step away from being President, Estella?"

"Congratulations, Xavier," she nodded weakly.

Estella realized she would have to help him win the election because as he rose politically, she would rise with him. Her causes were more important than her disgust for him.

Xavier grabbed her, "Let's celebrate this moment, beautiful!"

As he leaned in to kiss her, she pulled away, "I have to start dinner!"

"You don't have to start anything!" he corrected her. We're going out! You're looking at a future Senator here; let's go to *La Maison!*"

"Let me freshen up, Xavier!"

Xavier followed Estella up the stairs, past a frustrated Michael who wanted to punch Xavier in the face and carry Estella out of Xavier's house of horrors.

When they entered the bedroom, Xavier threw Estella on the bed. As she tried to squirm away, he ripped off her pants, slid her panties off and within moments had his long, snaky tongue, deep inside her most intimate area. He quickly pulled off her blouse and unhooked her bra and was rolling her nipples in his fingers, effectively producing wetness between her legs.

"Oh, Xavier!" she whispered, "You are making me crazy, stop it. I will help you win the election but don't touch me again." Rolling off the bed and onto the floor, Estella then ran to the bathroom turning the lock. She had installed a heavy-duty door and lock to the bathroom; it had been her salvation over the years, protecting her from Xavier.

"You're the hottest woman in the world, Estella. My desire for you never wanes, but I will do as you wish; you can't be angry that I tried. I really want to work on our marriage," Xavier cajoled through the door.

She changed the subject by coldly informing him, "Let's go eat. I'm starving."

Xavier had conquered her before and believed he would do so eventually once again during the excitement of the campaign trail. Estella always looked to Xavier for support in large crowds and he believed he could woo and win Estella and the election at the same time. Dominating her sexually and feeling his masculine power over her again was his goal, for it was never about intimacy with him or women; only conquest.

On her part, Estella was struggling on two fronts. First, even though she was going to benefit from her husband's new role as a United States Senator, she did not believe he had the character or the ability to ever be in that position. He had asked for help in winning the seat, but she was reluctant to aid and abet a man that didn't deserve it.

Secondly, she wanted out of her marriage and yearned to become Mrs. Michael Hagar. At best, Xavier had been inconsistent as a husband; at worst, he was a serial abuser that had tortured her consistently over the life of their marriage. She was tired of it. There was no love or respect for him in her heart. Yes, he was a great lover, but he was a soulless one. His technique in bed was superb, but his ability to make her feel loved and wanted was a black hole, and she could never get over the abuse she had suffered at his hands. Even though he had acted better for years now, she was still scarred form his past misdeeds.

"At any moment Xavier can flick and abuse me again I can never let my guard down with him," she thought to herself.

She didn't know how much longer she could put up with him. The only reason Estella was staying in the marriage was because of Marie. A divorce would crush Marie and she did not want her grades to slip in her last year of high school.

Estella was stuck. That is why she did not mind Xavier enjoying the companionship of a mistress. To her, their marriage was on paper only.

There were three aspects of her life that warmed her soul: her daughter, Michael, and her causes — in that order. Being brutally honest with herself, if she divorced Xavier, she would negatively impact two of those aspects: Marie and her causes. Only Michael would be a reality since she would be on the outside looking in, her ability to fight for her political passions would be greatly diminished without Xavier's influence. However once Marie was in college leaving Xavier seemed possible.

As the 1970's beckoned, Estella Cyrus was a very conflicted woman and wife.

*****

Xavier stood in his congressional office, flanked by his wife and daughter as he faced two dozen reporters and squinted into a battery of television lights as they shone down on him.

"Today, I am announcing my candidacy as the United States Senator for the state of Texas. I believe our tough times demand tough leadership, and it is my belief I am made for these times. Any questions?"

A reporter asked him, "You are facing a Texas political legend, Senator James Bridges, who has been in Congress for over 30 years. What makes you think you can win?"

Xavier smiled, "He's been there a long time; youth must be served!"

Everyone laughed. Another reporter had a question, "What will be your campaign themes, Congressman?"

Xavier looked over at Estella and spoke clearly into his microphone. "Lower taxes, women's rights, civil rights, and space technology. I believe in the empowerment of people and the unlimited promise of tomorrow."

His wife silently gagged when she heard the hypocrisy pouring out of his mouth.

"You want to champion the rights of women and minorities?"

Xavier nodded vigorously, "Absolutely! Over half of our population are women and they have long needed a voice to be heard, especially in the areas of equal pay, unlimited opportunities, and the respect of Americans everywhere. Blacks and Hispanics, too! I am all for following in the footsteps of the late, great Robert Kennedy and JFK, my heroes, who began great work uplifting the downtrodden and social underdogs to give them hope! Their work was cut short in their prime I hope to pick up the baton."

It was everything Estella could do to not burst out laughing at her husband's misleading agenda. She thought to herself, *"He is making all this up on the spot; he doesn't believe any of this!"*

Another reporter asked him, "Who are those two lovely ladies standing next to you, sir?

"I apologize for the oversight; these two beautiful women are my wife, Estella and my daughter, Marie. Without them, I am nothing."

Amidst a nice round of applause, Estella and Marie waved to the crowd as his wife muttered, *"He is earning his Academy Award!"*

Xavier finished the press conference with a challenge to his constituents, "Let's get Texas moving again!"

Estella laughed to herself, *"He doesn't have one original thought in his body. Now, he believes he is John F. Kennedy!"*

The press conference was over. Now, Xavier Cyrus had a primary battle to win against one of the most powerful men in the Lone Star State to qualify for the general election in November for the Senate.

As they rode with Michael in the limo back to Georgetown,

Xavier asked his wife, "What do you think, sweetie?"

Estella didn't pull any punches, "Women's rights, civil rights, and space technology? Have you no shame, Xavier?"

He feigned ignorance, "What do you mean, Estella?"

"Since when did you start caring about women and minorities? You are a classic misogynist, who has used women all your life, and, an avowed racist; especially towards Black people!"

Xavier slyly smiled, "A man can change, honey. Maybe I have seen the light!"

She shot back, "The only light you have seen is the one that shines down from the Senate ceiling in Congress!"

"I believe it time for me to start giving hope to those constituents that need me. And, I want to thank you, my dear wife, for showing me the way here. Your passions have become my passions. You should be very proud of that!"

"Xavier, you are the biggest phony I have ever met. There is not a sincere bone in your body!"

He grabbed Estella by the wrist and twisted it painfully, "Take that statement back or I will break it in half!"

Suddenly, he felt Michael's grip on his own wrist with a warning, "Let go of her, sir!"

Xavier snarled at him, "You work for me, Hagar; not her!"

His agent firmly said, "I am working for you right now. If you want her to help you win your election, then let go of her!"

Xavier pulled his hand away, giving Estella relief from the excruciating pain.

"I'm sorry, Estella. Michael was right. I was acting inappropriately. I'm wound up after the earlier events of today.

Will you accept my apology, honey?"

Estella ignored him. She wanted to kill him.

They finally arrived at their home in Georgetown and Estella quickly exited the car. Xavier turned to Michael and said, "Thanks, Michael. I do love her, honestly."

His agent responded, "Then show it more. We need her help in Texas, right?"

"Yeah, I got it," Xavier said sullenly.

A week later, Xavier, Estella, and Michael flew to Dallas for a kickoff campaign rally. It was well attended with over 2,000 excited constituents.

Estella spoke first, introducing her husband and when this beautiful woman reached the dais and began her address, a hush fell over the crowd as they beheld her presence.

She spoke their language, "I'm just a regular girl raised by a poor Texas family who is bursting with pride to be back home!"

The crowd erupted in thunderous applause. She was one of them!

"I honestly don't know about all this political stuff; I just believe that no matter how much money you make or what color you are, male or female, you deserve the same rights as anyone on this Good Earth!"

More applause. She had these Lone Star citizens in the palm of her hand.

"Seems to me that the less talking we do and the more action we take, well, that's what good folks want, am I right?"

Shouts of, "Yeah, you're right!" and, "preach it, honey!" were heard as the applause continued.

"Husbands aren't perfect; all wives can agree with me on that idea! But I've seen Xavier work hard for all of you here in North

Dallas County and I know you're right proud of him. Well, so am I! He was really good as a Congressman and he's gonna be *great* as your Senator!"

The crowd was roaring now.

"If you women out there want equal pay, more respect, better jobs, and the attention of Washington D.C. then, give my man a chance!"

Women were screaming his name, "Xavier, Xavier, *Xavier*!"

"And, if you are a member of the minority race, be it Black, Hispanic, Asian, Native American or any other color, and are sick and tired of losing out to the rich and powerful, vote Xavier Cyrus and my husband will take good care of you!"

The sound was deafening in its intensity.

"I'm just a country girl from the greatest state in the Union, and I believe Texans not only need to be proud of their state but be even prouder of their Senator; not just because he has been in office a *long* time; but, because he is vibrant, has fresh ideas and is ready to take all of us to the stars! Make me proud, y'all... Let me welcome your new Senator and my man, Xavier Cyrus!"

It took Xavier over five minutes to wait for the crowd to quiet down so he could speak. Estella had been magic!

Xavier spoke for 30 minutes on his themes for election and after following his dynamic wife, he could have read out of a phone book and the crowd would have gone nuts.

The local girl was the star of the show. The campaign had begun and over the next several months leading up to the primary, the incumbent; the honorable James Bridges, knew he was in a fight for his political life.

Thanks to Estella Cyrus.

Xavier blew through James Bridges like a Texas tornado.

The primary wasn't even close as he won with 66% of the vote. The general election was even more of a landslide in the heavily Democratic state.

Everywhere Estella went, she lit up the adoring crowds that couldn't get enough of her. She was not only Xavier's wife, but had evolved into one of the most powerful female speakers in American political history. Estella had grown from the shy, stuttering girl she once was into the woman she was meant to be with a lot of therapy from Margret and support from Renee.

There was no way Xavier could have won without her and no way he could have lost with her, her down-home Texas style of talking worked wonders with rural folks, while her sophisticated D.C. persona wowed the social crowd, And when she engaged her favorite demographic, the minorities, she gave every black and Hispanic citizen hope that they counted; that they were the real future of not only the Democratic Party, but the nation, as well.

Xavier said it best on election night when he told her, "I'm just lucky I didn't have to run against you!"

He was not joking.

Estella felt appreciated by her husband for one of the few times in her marriage. She thought to herself that perhaps she had made the right decision in sticking it out with him. since as the wife of a United States Senator, her future as a political mover and shaker was going to be paying major dividends.

It was late at night when Xavier returned home. He was so exhausted that he didn't even bother to close the front door or say goodnight to his wife. He just stumbled up the stairs and collapsed on the bed in the guest room.

When Estella walked to the foyer to close the front door, she saw Michael standing on the front steps smoking a cigarette and looking irritated.

She addressed him, "Are you coming in? I made up the bed in your room, Michael?"

He was upset about something, "I'll be in shortly," he said curtly. The agent for the next shift was already inside to relieve him for the evening, but he often slept in the spare bedroom if it was late.

Estella heard an edge in his voice. "Something wrong?"

"With me, no. With us, yeah!"

She closed the front door and walked outside, "Are you upset with me, Michael?"

He was sarcastic, "Why should I be upset with you? You're a happily married woman with no intention in ever leaving your husband."

Estella immediately grasped the problem, "You're upset with me because I have decided to stay with Xavier instead of divorcing him to be with you, is that it?"

"You're no dummy, Estella. You catch on real fast!"

"Michael, you have to trust me. I am doing my best to hold on to my daughter and preserve my standing in Congress. If I leave Xavier, I lose both!"

He shook his head exasperated, "You want my pity, is that it?"

"No, Michael; just your understanding." She whispered to him, "I love you; but this is not the right time to act upon it. Don't you see?"

The agent cut her to the quick, "If you did not leave him when he was a congressman; you sure as hell won't leave him now that he is a Senator!"

"Why are you pushing me away, Michael?"

"Because I no longer trust you. You're all talk when it comes to us, Estella! Your priorities are Marie and your precious projects. Please forgive me if I don't take advantage of your hospitality tonight. I have to go!"

He walked down the driveway and jumped in the car and said to the driver, "Take me to the nearest hotel."

Estella stood there stunned as she watched the car and the man she deeply loved, drive away.

CHAPTER TWENTY-SEVEN

A No-Win Situation

With her husband now a U.S. Senator along with the passage of the Civil Rights bill of 1964, the moon landing in 1969, and the women's movement in full force, Estella now had more power to affect legislation for her causes than ever before. In addition, Xavier's continued involvement in the House of D had afforded assistance in getting the green light on some of her requests as long as they were in the members' power and not in conflict with their own interests.

She and Xavier were sleeping in separate bedrooms and Marie was beginning college at Vale, so, Estella had all her dreams in high gear.

Except one.

She had lost her beloved Michael.

It was a very expensive, but necessary trade-off for her. He had told her it was him or her daughter and all her dreams. It was an easy, but painful decision for her to make. Losing Marie and her lifelong passions were far too important for her in lieu of choosing Michael. No matter how much she loved him, and she did, no man was worth the price she had to pay to keep him.

But, as the days went by, she ached for him. He was her emotional life. Her soul had been denied its most important sustenance. Every time he showed up at the house or she saw him in public guarding her husband, the memories of what they had shared together kept flooding her consciousness.

She wracked her brain to figure out a way to continue their relationship, but his mandate had prevented negotiation or compromise. As far as he was concerned, it was all or nothing, and she had ultimately chosen the latter.

One day, her husband came home with a different Secret Service agent, when it was Michael's shift to be on duty.. She casually asked him, "Where's Michael?"

Xavier replied, "He's taking some time off to go to the Caribbean for a vacation. He has evidently fallen in love with some woman and wants to be with her."

Estella made her way upstairs and vomited in the bathroom. Ever since she had turned Michael away, she had dreaded this moment. She didn't blame him for moving on with his life without her. But, the reality of him with another lover had absolutely crushed her.

She cleaned up and returned to the living room where she found Xavier relaxing in front of the television set. She asked him unemotionally, "Well, I am very happy for Michael. Do you know anything about his new love?"

Xavier answered her question without taking his eyes off the screen, "She works as a legislative aide for one of the Senators; quite a beauty. Black, of course. I believe her name is Shonda or something like that. What's for dinner?"

Estella walked into the kitchen and held on to the counter for support. Her legs felt like jelly. She imagined Shonda in St. John, with the man she loved. She wondered if Michael would take her to the Cove and the waterfall and make passionate love to her there.

She screamed inwardly, *"Calm down, Estella; you had a chance to keep him and you refused. Let him get on with his life. He deserves that!"*

It was easier said than done.

Two weeks went by, and finally, Michael returned to his position of protecting Xavier. When he showed up at the house, Estella had just baked his favorite snack, chocolate brownies. She put several on a plate and served them with milk to him. He thanked her and sat down at the kitchen table and happily munched away.

Xavier confiscated a few brownies and went upstairs to shower and change clothes, then left for the evening to go to the House of D.

As soon as Xavier walked out of the door, Estella pounced, "How was the beach, Michael?"

He looked up at her between bites and calmly replied, "Fine."

She couldn't resist, "Did you take her to our waterfall?"

He shook his head, "We didn't go to St. John, Estella. I took her to the Bahamas."

Her voice dripping with sarcasm, she shot back, "How gracious of you!"

Michael frowned at her, "What did you expect me to do, Estella? Sit around and wait indefinitely for you to free yourself up for me?"

She grabbed the plate of brownies and threw it in the sink, shattering the plate. "These are too good for you! Why don't you wait outside?"

He stood up and put his arms around her, "Look, I'm sorry. But, I didn't cause this separation between us."

"I still love you, Michael. You put me in an impossible position, one that I had no ability to resolve."

Michael shook his head, "Wrong, Estella; you're the one that killed us by wanting your cake and eating it, too!"

Her face turned red and her heart was shattered., "Go to h*ell*!" Even though logically she knew she was being the unreasonable one in this situation, her pain made her illogical.

Estella stormed out to the backyard.

Michael sighed and after a brief pause of indecision; followed her there.

He began to explain, "Estella, you know how I feel about us."

She cut him off, "Are you falling in love with this woman?"

There was a long pause. Finally, Michael replied, "Yes and no."

Estella shook her head, "You're full of shit, Michael. Just tell me!"

"I love her as a person, and I am trying to fall in love with her."

"Is that what you want?"

"Honestly, I want you, Estella. But, not part-time; I want to be married and raise a family with someone that is available, that's all!"

"Then, marry her, Michael, and leave me *alone*!"

She locked her bedroom door and sobbed uncontrollably for over an hour.

The next several times she saw Michael were laden with tension. Neither one of them spoke to each other. Finally, at an event for the new Senators, Michael brought his girlfriend and introduced her to Estella.

"Nice to meet you, Mrs. Cyrus; I've heard so many great things about your husband. Michael loves working with him."

Estella was equally gracious, "You are very blessed to be with Michael; we love him as a family member!"

When Michael's lady friend turned her back, she glared at him with a hurt expression on her face and then walked away leaving him at a loss for words.

Then, three months later, Xavier informed her, "We're invited to Michael's wedding. Pick out a gift, Estella!"

On the day of the wedding as Xavier presented a sterling silver tea set to the newly-weds. He apologized for his wife's absence, "Estella sends her regards and is very sorry she was not able to make it; she has a vicious virus and chose not to put others at risk."

Michael remarked, "Totally understandable; what an unselfish gesture!"

Of course, he wasn't buying her excuse in the least.

The wedding was a lavish affair due to the hundreds of government employees, other Secret Service agents and the dozens of legislators that came out to support Michael.

Upon returning home, Xavier found his wife buried under the covers with the lights off. When he turned them on; he realized she had been crying. "Are you okay, sweetie? Are you in a lot of pain?"

She was, but not in the physical sense, of course.

All through the following week, Estella buried herself in her work, lobbying fervently to progress her causes, trying not to think about the final loss of her lover to another woman.

When Michael came back from his honeymoon, he was informed by his Deputy Director that he had been given a healthy raise due to a strong recommendation from Xavier Cyrus. When he thanked the Senator, Xavier told him, "Well, now you have two mouths to feed, so I wanted to provide for that!"

Estella had a different take on Michael when he walked into her home wearing his new gold wedding ring. That was not one of the happier moments in her life.

For the next two years, Estella and Michael only spoke to each other a handful of times. She did her best to avoid him whenever he showed up at her house. It was just too painful for her to engage him after all the love they had shared.

There was one other major development; a leading candidate for the Democratic Presidential nominee, George Bivens, was very impressed with Xavier and he and his wife paid a visit to the Senator from Texas at his home in Georgetown.

The four of them had a nice dinner together and then sat down in the Cyrus living room for a chat. It was there that Bivens asked Xavier, "Would you be interested in being on the ticket with me as my Vice President, if I win the nomination?"

Xavier was elated while Estella almost coughed up her coffee. Her husband beamed, "I would be very interested in serving you as your Vice President , George. I believe we would make a winning team that would greatly benefit the American people!"

Bivens turned to Estella and asked her, "Am I making the right choice here, Mrs. Cyrus? You know Xavier better than anyone else. Your opinion is one I would highly regard!"

Estella, as usual, was in a quandary over his question. As the

Vice President , Xavier would give her even more power, but he would only be a heartbeat away from the presidency; he was far from suited for the position.

She carefully couched her answer. "My husband has always flourished in any endeavor he has been involved in, Mr. Bivens."

Bivens smiled at her, "That's a good enough endorsement for me from a wife who knows him!"

Estella felt sick to her stomach, but she had done her best when put on the spot.

Xavier sighed in relief. He knew that Estella had lost all respect for him and was not looking forward to her response. Thankfully, she had come through for him.

But Estella was not going to help her husband win this election; far from it. Being a Senator was one thing, but being one step away from the Oval Office was quite another.

If Xavier thought his wife would work her magic to help him become the Vice President of the United States, he was more than delusional.

CHAPTER TWENTY-EIGHT

Major Developments

Marie was doing very well at Vale and keeping Estella informed about everything on their weekly Friday call, including her love life. She had brought her boyfriend and now fiancé home to Georgetown on a few occasions and he had passed the test with her parents.

David was a nice young man who had aspirations of becoming a medical doctor in Africa to treat Third World patients that could not afford quality medical care. It was a noble vocation charted by Marie's boyfriend. Estella was proud of him and was happy about his impending marriage to her daughter.

However, Marie was not convinced that David was the man she was looking for although she had agreed to marry him when he surprised her with a proposal in front of all of his friends and family last Christmas. He was, "a nice guy," but the feisty daughter of Estella and Xavier wanted someone with a more fiery disposition, like hers, and there were no sparks in the bedroom.

Marie chalked up the bland experience to their both being virgins, but after a few months, it did not improve. Marie was getting cold feet about marrying in a year as planned.

Still, all her friends liked him; he came from a good family and her parents approved of him. David was well-connected and a member of the prestigious and secretive Skeleton Society at Vale,

317

so Xavier especially liked him and encouraged the relationship.

He was a safe choice in a husband.

*****

Meanwhile, Xavier began campaigning to aid George Bivens win the Democratic Primary and was more than a little surprised when Estella declined to help him.

He asked her, "You know how important this is to me; I am depending on you to do your part in getting me elected. I think you are the greatest female campaigner in the country. You can make the difference between George and me winning this thing!"

His wife shook her head. "You're on your own. Xavier. I just can't keep pretending any longer. You're not qualified to be Vice President : you lack the character and the abilities to represent our country. I don't even know why I am still married to you. We lost our love and respect for each other years ago!"

Xavier shot back, "Then, maybe after we win the election, it will be time for a divorce!"

Estella smiled. "Fine with me."

She not only wouldn't support the Democratic ticket if Xavier was on it but she actually began using her mesmerization skills to deter people from voting for Bivens since he promised Xavier that he would be his running mate.. And, whenever she was in the vicinity of Xavier's campaign speeches for Bivens, she partially disabled his thought processes to make his oratory ineffective, just as she had done to his opponents in his first campaign as a congressman in Texas many years ago.

He never noticed what she was doing to him because he assumed he was just exhausted from the grueling schedule.

As the Primary election neared, Bivens was five points down to the new leader in the Primary polls. It would take almost a miracle for them to win.

They came up short. Xavier's career had taken a considerable hit and was now floundering in political waters. He had not only lost the chance to run for the Vice-Presidency; he was now no longer a Senator, having relinquished his office to team up with George Bivens and campaign all over the country for him. A victim of hubris, Xavier had such a strong belief that he would become the Vice President, he gambled his Senate seat to spend all his time campaigning for Bivens and lost.

Realizing that her marriage was over and that Xavier would no longer be able to pave the way for her, she sat down with him at their kitchen table to have "The Talk."

"Xavier, I have been in Stockholm Syndrome love with you since college. We have had a roller coaster ride of ridiculous proportions. As the years have passed, we have drawn farther and farther apart. We began as husband and wife, and now we are straying husband and roommate. I'm sorry, but it's time to face the facts."

Xavier rolled his eyes when she mentioned Stockholm Syndrome referring to a psychological response made famous by 1973 hostages who developed a bond with their captures. He interrupted her, "Don't say what I think you are about to say, Estella. We belong together."

She shook her head, "We did once, yes. But that ended years ago. I have stayed in this sham of a relationship waiting for our daughter to grow up and be on her own. That is a reality now. It is time for us to face the other reality, Xavier."

With a tortured look in his eyes he confessed,"I can't live

without you, Estella. In all honesty, I have only ever loved you. You are my wife and first love, don't leave me."

Now, it was her turn to interrupt him. "Stop it, Xavier. I've seen this act before. You can live without me because you have been doing it for years! You have a career, national acclaim, millions of dollars, adoring parents, powerful friends, and a mistress. You don't need me. It's time we went on our separate ways."

He began begging her, "Estella, just tell me what I need to do to keep you! I can change. There is nothing in my life I want or need more than you, I swear. I will give you all my money — I will fight for all your projects, I'll dump my mistress, I will..."

She cut him off, "This isn't a negotiation, Xavier. It's over. Accept it. We had a good run for the most part. I grew up with you. We will always have a daughter together."

Xavier tried to rationalize his actions, but Estella was having none of it. "Xavier leave me alone, this marriage is finally over."

As her soon to be husband left the kitchen, Estella turned out the lights and sat in the dark.

Sobbing.

*****

Estella was on the phone with Renee, "Yes, this time I am really going to do it, mother!"

"Cutting him loose will severely limit your passionate programs, Estella!"

"It will also give me peace of mind. I need to be able to smile when I look into the mirror again. I need to get Estella back," she vowed.

"You know he's not going to give up without a fight. He's addicted to you."

Estella was adamant. "He can fight all he wants; I am no longer his, Mama!"

"What about Marie? Why not wait until after her wedding?"

"I just can't tolerate Xavier another day now that Marie is about to graduate and is marrying into a good family. This is not like the past. They are not going to call off the wedding because of the scandal of my divorce. Everyone is getting divorced nowadays. My daughter will be fine; she has a good head on her shoulders. She is intelligent, rational, and grounded; and she would want me to be happy."

*****

Mily was aghast, "Divorce?"

Xavier nodded, "After all we've been through. Can you believe it!"

His mistress was ecstatic, of course, "I cannot only believe it; I hope it happens. I have waited for this moment for ten years. I'm in love with you, Xavier."

He was more cautious, "Well, it's not official by any means. There's a long way to go. Don't get your hopes up!"

"From what I know about your wife, I think she is going to follow through on this. When she says things, she means them."

Xavier was in emotional agony as he lay naked with the needy Mily. "We shall see."

His lover was already making plans, "The day it's final, let's go somewhere, like Hawaii. It will give you a chance to start over. If you'll have me, I will be a great wife for you."

Xavier repeated himself, "Long way to go!" He was treading water. He had no intention of marrying Mily; she was not worthy of being his wife, in his opinion. He had only used her to fill in the sexual gaps in his life.

"Do you think you could love me, Xavier; I mean really love me?"

He hedged his answer. He didn't want to tell her the truth, "Time will tell. Just give me a little space to work all this through, okay?"

She cuddled against him, "Will do!"

Mily had no idea that her dream of becoming Mrs. Xavier Cyrus was never going to happen.

"*Never. Not this lifetime,*" Xavier mused to himself.

*****

As Xavier drove home, he was plotting a way to keep Estella in the marriage. All options were on the table in his mind.

Xavier was back at the kitchen table again for Round Two of the divorce wars. Estella was ready for him.

"Just tell me, Estella: what I need to do to keep you and I will abide by your request. I promise."

She responded with no emotion in her voice, "There is nothing you can do. I don't love you any longer, Xavier."

Her husband pleaded, "I want to die in your arms, Estella. I cannot imagine us ever being apart!"

"You should have thought of that before all your lies and abusive behavior, Xavier. You've been a terrible husband. I refuse to tolerate you one moment longer."

"I can change, Estella. Just give me one more chance…"

She stood up and began washing dishes. He rose and put his arms around her from behind.

Estella called out, "Michael!"

The Secret Service agent immediately appeared from the foyer, "Yes, Ma'am?"

"Will you remove my soon to be ex-husband from the house before I call the police?"

The much larger Michael glared at Xavier. Even though he knew he could be fired, he no longer cared. He had only remained in the job all these years to be near Estella.

"Mr. Cyrus, it is not worth the negative publicity to have the police involved," Michael rationalized to an irrational Xavier.

"I'm going, Estella. But this isn't over!" he threatened.

"Goodbye, Xavier. It's finally over."

*****

Later that night, following her confrontation with Xavier, Estella heard the doorbell ring.

It was Michael.

"May I come in?" he asked her.

Estella nodded and they retreated to the living room with the fireplace. A scene of their many romantic trysts.

"I want to tell you something, Estella."

She waited for his words.

"I'm still in love with you."

His former lover gently rejoined, "You're a married man, Michael. You need to stick to your vows."

323

He smiled at her, "*You* didn't."

Estella blushed and whispered, "You are married to a good woman; I was married to a monster."

Michael nodded, "True, but cheating is cheating. And, we were in love, so you broke your vows for me."

"I won't help you break your vows with your wife, Michael. I can't do that. I'm sorry."

He stared into her eyes, "Look at me and tell me you no longer love me!"

Estella looked away and said, "I no longer love you."

"Look at me and say it!" he demanded.

"I think you should go now," she suggested. She stood up and began walking to the front door. Michael quickly followed her and grabbed her arm, spinning her around, "Look into my eyes, Estella! There is not a day that passes that I do not think about you your laugh, your smile the way you bite your lip when you're nervous. There is not a night that passes that I don't reminisce about our lovemaking when I felt our bodies and souls were one. I can't be without you, and I know you can't be without me so don't do this to us."

Tears filled her eyes, "You know my heart, Michael. Don't make me say it. Just go. Please!"

He moved his lips to the edge of hers and then stopped. Her eyes were closed. She was ready to kiss him; she could feel his warm breath on her lips making them tingle for only his mouth.

Then, he let go of her arm and quickly strode out the door and drove away. Estella staggered to the couch and collapsed on it.

In one day, she had lost the two most important men in her

life. She lay there devastated until the wee hours of the morning.

She had the same nightmare of Michael drowning. It felt so real that she woke up crying from the pain of losing him. The dream was her wakeup call; she was not doing Shonda any favors by advocating her staying in a loveless marriage with no young children and wasting more years.

Life was too short; she needed to be with her only love and Shonda would eventually find her true match once she was free of Michael. She awoke around noon the next day and staggered upstairs and into the bathroom. She took a leisurely shower and spent the rest of the afternoon on the patio reflecting on her life.

*****

That night, she received a disturbing call from Marie's boyfriend, David.

"Marie is missing, Mrs. Cyrus. I'm very concerned!" He informed her.

Estella was immediately concerned, "When is the last time you saw her, David?"

"At a party near the campus four nights ago;" was his response. "We had an argument and she didn't come home, and for the next few days, I assumed Marie was still angry and just telling Lucy to say she ran off with some guy to torture me. But after speaking with most of her friends this week, they have not heard from her, so I'm really worried now!"

Estella tried to calm him down although her own heart was pounding, "There's probably a good reason for her disappearance. Let me handle this, and I will get back to you, okay? Marie is a very resourceful individual who can take care of herself. I'm sure there is a reasonable explanation for all of this."

She hung up the phone and immediately called Xavier and asked him to come to the house.

Within thirty minutes, he and Michael appeared, and Estella sat down with them at the kitchen table. She steeled herself and broke the news to them, "Marie is missing. Her boyfriend has not heard from her in four days."

Xavier's face turned ashen and he mumbled, "Oh, dear God!"

Michael was upset but still approached it from a practical perspective: "Have you checked all the hospitals and every close friend of hers? Have you contacted the local police? Have you gotten a list of all the people she was with at the party? Have you called all the funeral parlors within fifty miles of her last location?"

His last sentence sent a chill through Estella. It was then that the reality of what possibly happened to her beloved daughter smacked her right in the face.

Phone calls were quickly made to find answers to all of Michael's questions and trickles of information began revealing possible solutions to the girl's disappearance.

One of the partygoers remembers Marie leaving the night of the party with a "really good-looking Black guy," but, she did not know his identity.

No hospitals or funeral homes confirmed her presence and two detectives were assigned to her case and began working on the list of the partygoers. The FBI was called in at Xavier's behest and her credit card activity was scrutinized.

But the card she used showed no purchases over the last four days, which alarmed everyone further.

Estella called Renee who flew down and joined the family in Georgetown, as did Sr. and Catherine from Texas.

An APB was issued for several states in and around Connecticut and New England.

There were still no solid leads and the tension in the Cyrus household became unbearable.

Estella was beside herself with grief.

Where was Marie?

*****

Vale University, 4 nights earlier

"Look what I've got." Lucy smiled mischievously jiggling a bag of marijuana to her friends during the end of spring semester party. Even though Lucy would have to attend summer session to make up for a class she had failed, she still felt like celebrating. Tossing her waist-length straight blond hair, she twirled around singing her name and jiggling her diamond-clad wrist, "Oh, they are playing my song."

Marie, who had recently returned from a two-year church mission in South Africa, declined. "You know I have never tried weed and I am not going to start now."

"You do know those brownies you just ate next to the punch bowl had weed in them?" Lucy laughed.

"Lucy, you knew and didn't say anything? I had three," Marie stated, annoyed with her assigned dorm roommate, Lucy Cyrus, who was also her third cousin.

"Oh well," Lucy shrugged her indifference.

Still sitting on the comfy couch with Lucy and her friends, Marie looked around for David, Marie's fiancé, who she had met in her freshmen year in college, was across the room catching up with his Skeleton Society brothers.

"Damien's here, and he brought a friend. Let's go over and

ask him for a light. I need some of his fire," Lucy giggled, referring to the record playing. Both roommates had a crush on Damien, but Marie's was secret. Marie told no one about her attraction to Damien because of her fiancé David, and especially not Lucy, who had a one-night stand with Damien.

Tall, caramel complexioned Damien, whose intense amber gaze seemed to be able to burn a hole in one's soul, was not just a handsome face, but a scholar and activist on campus. His deep voice resonated in Marie's ears and touched her spirit when she heard his fiery unforgettable speeches. Although he was only a freshman at Vale and she a senior, robbing the cradle was not an issue since he was already eighteen. She felt he had an old soul because of the depth of his oratories. But Marie decided to ignore her attraction and take the safe route by trying to work on her relationship with David.

"You are such a stalker, Lucy. The only reason you came here tonight is because you overheard Damien saying he was coming to this party," Marie knowingly commented.

"Right, Damien is hot I can't get him off of my mind no matter how many other guys I date. Huge I tell you, huge, and the motion — no words. I have been with other Black guys and thought the rumor was not true, but the rumor is very true about Damien." Lucy put up her hands to provide a measure of Damien's manhood.

"I thought you were getting serious with Scott." Disgusted and a little jealous Marie reminded Lucy of her commitment to Scott, a star tennis player and heir to a shipping dynasty.

"I know, but he is like Dull as Death David," Lucy pouted prettily. Marie hated David's nickname that Lucy had coined for him and others on campus had begun to call him behind his back.

"Scott is for marriage, Damien is for fun and f-ing, unless of course Damien suddenly wins the gazillion dollar lottery, and then still probably *not* since I have my own money," giggled Lucy.

Even though times were changing, they were not changing enough for Lucy to lower her social status to marry a Black man unless she was desperate for his money.

"I am going outside to get some fresh air." Disgusted with her shallow mean girl roommate, Marie got up from the couch and was quickly replaced by one of Lucy's girlfriends.

"Whatever, goody-goody Marie Magdalene," said Lucy coining a nickname for Marie, making fun of her Christianity while taking a drag on her marijuana blunt.

"Later Loose Lucy." Marie defensively created an offensive nickname for Lucy referring to the fact that most guys had one-night stands with Lucy then said they would call later but never did.

"Stop trying to slut-shame me, prude. I am a rich bitch. I don't care what anyone thinks I am doing whatever I feel like, free love style." An unabashed Lucy kept giggling passing the blunt to her friend.

Lucy was a little bit of an outcast in the family because of her bad reputation and vulgarity. The Cyrus family had hoped this was just a phase, that Lucy was just following popular culture and that Marie would rub off on Lucy by asking the school to assign them as roommates.

*****

"Can I bum a cigarette?"

Marie looked up at the handsome young man smiling down on her. It was Damien. Her heart began to race. "I don't smoke; but when my fiancé comes back, you can have one of his!"

The attractive college student shook his head, "I don't want to meet your fiancé; I want to meet you!"

"Sorry," Marie laughed, "We come as a package!"

"I thought Vale fostered more independence in its women!"

She gave him a quizzical look, "How'd you know I go to Vale?"

I've seen you around, but you were always with the guy who I assume is your fiancé." He grinned.

Marie smiled back, "You're pretty sure of yourself, aren't you?"

"Life's too short to be indecisive," he countered. "Do you prefer bland men you can dominate?"

"For a while, yes;" Marie agreed, "After that, they bore me!"

"How about your boy? Does he bore you?"

She smirked, "Sometimes!"

Damien cockily proclaimed, "I would never bore you. Take my hand, you'll see!"

"Nah, I'm the faithful type. I don't stray!" She looked around the gathering, "I'm sure there are a lot of women here that would be enthralled by you, though!"

He looked right into her eyes, "I don't want a lot of women; I want you!"

Marie felt a jolt go through her body, "Now, how do you know it is me you want. You know nothing about me!"

The young man laughed, "Because you're cute and honest

and sexy!"

"That's all you want in a woman?" she grimaced.

"Of course not," he shot back, "But, it's a helluva start!"

"I told you; I have a *man*!" Marie corrected Damien calling David a boy earlier.

"Then, he should never leave you alone at a party!"

Marie's eyes flashed, "I'm not the kind of girl that wears a leash."

"If you were my girl, you would. I would never let you out of my sight!"

"This conversation is over. Have a nice night, whoever you are!" She glared at Damien, pretending not to know of him.

As the young man sauntered off, Marie laughed to herself, "*That was interesting!*"

When her fiancé walked up with her drink, he asked, "Well, what did Damien want?"

"A cigarette," she replied.

David fumed, "You sure talked with him a long time about a cigarette!"

Marie confronted him, "You were watching us?"

"I was curious, yeah!"

She shook her head, "Why didn't you come over and find out for yourself?"

"I wanted to see how long you two would talk, okay?"

Marie reasoned, "David, this is a party. People come here to meet and mingle. That is the purpose of a social occasion!"

He corrected her, "You're taken, Marie. You don't engage single guys!"

"All the more reason you should have come over to us!"

"I just wanted to see how faithful you were with other men."

Marie was now irritated, "Did I pass your test?"

"Are you still with me?" he asked her.

"Honestly, I'm not sure, David. Your jealousy is a turnoff!"

He stood there glaring at her. Finally, he said, "Let's go back to my apartment!"

Marie stood her ground, "Why?"

"Because we need to re-establish our love."

"Every time you open your mouth, you remind me how shallow our love is, David!"

He grabbed her arm, "Are you coming or *not*?"

Marie pulled her arm away, "Not!"

He uttered, "Goodnight, then!" and stormed off.

"Unbelievable!" She muttered under her breath.

*****

To clear her thoughts, Marie wandered out on the expansive terrace of the mansion which overlooked the carefully tended lawn, while everyone else partied inside. The dim lighting still revealed the six-figure landscaping work that made it as stunning during the night as it had been in the daylight.

As Marie stood alone sipping her wine, behind her, she smelt Damien's intoxicating scent. She whirled around and he was only an inch away, before he could speak, she touched her fingers to his lips. His tongue darted out, firmly stroking her finger back and forth, as she melted at the thought of his tongue doing the same motion between her thighs. Although she knew she should not, she leaned into his body giving him access. He passionately devoured her lips his incredibly long tongue thrusting into her mouth mimicking the movements that Lucy had bragged he made. Marie's head spinning with desire, she reluctantly pushed Damien back thinking of him with Lucy and also of her relationship with David.

"I still don't see your fiancé. Are you sure you are not making up a relationship to keep me at arm's length?"

She laughed, "No, David is really my fiancé, but we had a fight, so he went home."

That perked up the spirits of the cocky suitor, "Oh? I love a damsel in distress! I can take you home. I promise I won't do you any harm."

"Relax, I am not in any distress. I am getting ready to leave so I can join him and make up."

"I don't think that's a good idea, fair maiden!" he chortled.

Marie asked him, "Oh, you have a better idea?'

"Actually, I do!"

"Pray tell, my knight in shining armor," she sarcastically giggled.

"Let's elope. Tonight. Right now!"

Marie had to laugh aloud at that suggestion. Now, she knew the guy was certifiably nuts!

"I don't know you well enough, Sir Galahad."

"Damien at your service, Guinevere. I am bold and dashing and very dangerous! I will answer any questions you have."

She shook her head. Marie decided to test him, "So, you're a bad boy? How bad are you?"

"I have mainly plundered and looted several villages and

broken the hearts of damsels all over the kingdom."

"Why should I run away with you, then?"

"Because I have a feeling you will force me to change my ways, My Lady!"

Marie played along; she thought him wildly entertaining. "And, how can I count on that, Camelot Knight Sir Damien?

Without warning, her new friend stepped up, took her face into his hands, and kissed her again passionately.

When they finally parted, Marie was stunned to her core and burning with a desire that she had never felt before. She was so shocked she had no words. As she stood there speechless, Damien stepped up and kissed her again!

Finally, Marie pushed him away, saying more to herself than to Damien, "I can't do this I am getting married in eight months."

His amber eyes drilled into her blue ones, "You can do whatever you want."

Marie exclaimed, "You're maddening!"

"Faint heart never won fair maiden," he quoted Cervantes.

"So, you will elope with me?"

She shook her head, "Not in a million years!"

"Do you like dinosaurs?"

Marie smiled, "As a matter of fact, I have loved them since I was a child."

"Then, think of me as a lovable Brontosaurus!"

"That's my favorite!" she gushed, a little startled. *"How could he possibly know about my love for Brontosaurus, is he psychic or a psycho stalker,"* her inner voice warned.

"Let me get you another glass of wine!"

She demurred, "I really need to get going; my fiancé is

waiting for me!"

Damien looked Marie straight in the eye, "Yeah, but are you truly excited to see him?"

She hesitated and then lamely answered, "Yeah, sure."

He pounced with his piercing amber eyes, "I don't believe you. I think you are ready for a new adventure! Don't marry him, marry me. I have never felt this way before and neither have you." Somehow Damien knew it was now or never.

"What are your goals in life, Damien?"

"To change the world and have as much fun as I can while doing it!"

He proudly stated. "How about you?"

"To become the President," she replied soberly.

He looked at her quizzically. "The President of what?"

"The United States."

He stared at her to see if she was putting him on and after he realized that Marie was stone-cold serious, he gasped, "You believe you will be our President someday...really?"

"Why not?" she reasoned, "Someone has to."

He laughed, "Can't argue with that logic! Can I be First Gentleman?"

She shook her head, "Maybe if you play your cards right."

"Then, let's get started! Do you have a car?"

Marie nodded, "Of course, I have a car. Don't you?"

"I did until I totaled it. Let's take yours!"

She was puzzled. "To where?"

"Let's drive to Vegas and get married."

Marie started laughing, "You're crazy!"

He shot back, "Exactly what you're looking for Madame President!"

*****

"This is all happening too fast. I can't believe I am driving us to Vegas to get married!" Marie exclaimed.

"I don't even know you! Is this the weed and the wine making me think I want to rush to marry my crush?" thought Marie.

Damien laughed, "I love pleasure, I drink and smoke too much, I'm a rebel who believes the masses have their head up their ass and I ad-lib my way through life, but my words come from my heart and soul. The first time I looked into your eyes... I knew that I loved you. Now, you know me!"

Marie just shook her head. *"This is crazy!"* she thought to herself. "No I don't really know you. You could be a kidnapper, serial killer or a rapist and I just let you into my car, so I must be crazier than you are."

"Don't worry; beyond anything else, I am loyal. I will never cheat on you and I will always be on your side and have your back. Just get ready for a wild ride through the rest of your life!"

*****

As Estella was at home, worriedly trying to contact Marie to no avail.

Her daughter was driving through the night to Vegas.

To get married.

As they were driving, Damien suggested, "Pull over for a

336

minute!"

Marie eased her car off the highway and onto the shoulder near a small grove of trees. She turned off the engine and looked at him,

"Well?"

He smiled at her, "Well, *this*!"

Taking her face into his hands, he kissed her passionately for several minutes. She fervently returned his kiss and they began groping each other.

"Damien. You make me so wild," whispered a breathless Marie.

He kept nuzzling her neck with his lips, "The next motel we see, pull into its parking lot."

Marie quickly started up the engine and planned to do just that.

Two days later, they were in Vegas deciding in which chapel they should wed.

Marie, as it turned out, was as crazy as he was!

*****

"I now pronounce you husband and wife; you may kiss the bride!"

Damien had no trouble obeying that request. Then he carried Marie down the aisle, out of the little church and into her car.

"Where do you want to go next, my beautiful bride?"

"Georgetown. I want you to meet my parents. I want to see the look on their faces when they see their responsible daughter with her new husband!"

"What will they think of me?' he asked her.

"My dad will sneer at you because he secretly hates Black people, but my mom will adore you!"

Damien shouted, "Hey, one out of two ain't bad!" realizing that the feeling of now or never he had was well-founded. Marie's dad would never have let them get married or even date. However, now that the deed was already done, he felt he had a chance of keeping his wife versus having no chance at all with Marie if he had not rushed the marriage.

The impulsive newlyweds hit the highway to Washington, D.C.

******

Finally, around noon on the seventh day, as everyone was emotionally wrung out with worry, a funny thing happened. Marie called on the day she always called, Friday.

"Mom, I just married a fellow student who is an activist. I love him and we have a lot in common. I know this is crazy, but please support me. I am on my way home from Vegas. Don't tell anyone else I'm married," she announced. She decided the best approach was to tell her mother everything and to gain her reaction. She was having second thoughts about bringing her husband home to meet her racist dad.

"We were so worried about you we thought you were kidnapped."

"I told Lucy where I was going. I didn't tell you because I didn't want anyone to talk me out of what I wanted to do."

"Ah Lucy," Catherine had always called Lucy a *wackadoodle*, and Estella thought that she might have been right. "I sort of understand considering how your dad and his side of the family would react to your marrying a man so quickly, and I am guessing not someone of whom they would approve. Okay, I will just tell them you are on your way and nothing else. But this is cruel to do this to David. He really loved you, Marie."

"I know, that is why I couldn't face him. I felt a little cowardly just leaving a message with Lucy, but I didn't want to see the hurt look in David's eyes. I love him, in a way but nothing in comparison to how I feel with Damien. The fire that David lights in my heart could be lit by a match, while Damien's is like a blow torch. But one other thing: Damien is Black and Daddy is racist. What do you think I should do?"

Warning sirens went off in Estella's head. This poor man did not know the type of danger he had stepped into. "Why don't you take a honeymoon and a few months to see how you feel before you announce your marriage, it may just be an infatuation. You really don't know if you can get along with him on a day to day basis for any length of time."

Estella reminded her daughter, "Also, you have wanted to be President all your life do you want to give up that dream and create a new one? The chances of you becoming President with a Black husband is nil the way things are now. You may always resent him if you give up your dream."

"You too, Mom? I would have thought you of all people would understand that is why I called you first," an intuitive Marie replied. Marie was disappointed that she did not have an enthusiastic ally in her mother, who she recently sensed was in love with Michael.

"If you really love him, I understand and will support you in any of your decisions. But you have wanted to be President since you were a child."

"Yes, I want to be President, but I prefer to be happy.

However, I will take your advice and wait a few months to see how things are going, before I announce the marriage. I will go on a honeymoon with him and we'll live together off campus, before the fall session begins."

"What would the Cyrus family do to Damien if they found out about this marriage? They could harm him as they did Adrien," Estella thought as she shuddered in fear.

She started making phone calls letting every concerned party know that Marie was okay and everyone was relieved and happy.

*****

Renee was in and out of the hospital, fighting high blood pressure. With the added stress of Marie's disappearance, she passed out and saw the blue star once again.

"Auset, come to me! Your family will perish if you do not. There is an asteroid that will endanger them," Ausir's deep voice pleaded.

When Renee awoke, she remembered the dream clearly and now recognized the blue star as Sirius, due to the pictures provided by the new telescope that Estella had lobbied for all those years ago.

When Estella and Marie visited her, she relayed this information and they were shocked. They both agreed to do whatever they could to lobby to have a probe sent to investigate Sirius.

CHAPTER TWENTY-NINE

Estella and Michael

Xavier was out. He had been hanging by a marital thread, anyway, but his threats, stalking and harassment since Estella kicked him out of the house, was easily the final straw for Estella. She completely ended their dysfunctional union. Ironically Estella had helped by lobbying over the years to create and strengthen the laws that aided her in gaining a fair divorce settlement from Xavier; protecting her legally from him.

Xavier had now lost his wife, the respect of his daughter and his political career. He was bitter and angry at several people and carefully plotted his revenge at the ones who had hurt him the most, namely Michael.

Estella was still in love with Michael.

During the divorce proceedings Xavier sensed it, the way Michael and Estella had looked at each other when Michael ousted him from his home at Estella's behest had planted a seed in his mind. That seed grew until he was convinced with no actual evidence they were having an affair. He began looking into ways he could prevent his ex-wife and the agent from finding love together. He also had designs to remarry Estella, as he continued to believe he was the only one for her.

For years his class conscious arrogance blinded him to the

idea that Estella would cheat on him with a man that had no power and no wealth. He had thought fleetingly that she was having an affair with one of the Black caucus members, they were at least members of congress with some power. It never dawned on him that she would have an affair with an agent. He mused, *"They could be award winning actors if they hid their feeling all this time."*All it took for him to put two and two together was their mask dropping just that one second in front of him, that one look of longing between them, for Xavier to realize what was going on under his nose.

Xavier having a memory like a steel trap sifted through the years for clues and came to the conclusion that he was being cuckolded and disrespected in his own home for at least over a decade. He vowed he would have his revenge against his former trusted ally, Michael.

*****

Estella heard the news that Michael had gotten a quick divorce in Mexico where he had legally married Shonda. He was free to remarry. After all these years, he and Estella could enjoy a public relationship.

But would they?

Since Xavier was no longer a Senator, he had lost his need for protection from a government agent. Michael was reassigned two week after the day that Marie had reappeared following the scare of her disappearance.

Estella and Michael ran into each other at an appreciation dinner for past and present Secret Service agents at the Bilton Hotel. She saw Michael standing at the bar with some of his fellow agents and she approached him. She had no idea how he would react to her. It was their first meeting since his divorce.

"Hello, Michael. I was sorry to hear about your divorce. How are you doing?"

He turned and smiled warmly at her, "I'm fine, Estella, thank you. How about yourself? How is Marie? I am so glad she was okay. Has she been home yet?"

She nodded and smiled, "In the immortal words of Dr. King, 'Free at last, free at last, Thank God almighty I'm free at *last*!' Marie is fine, she will be going to school in the fall for senior year and will visit me next week with her new man." Not ready to share that Marie was secretly married since she had not made a final decision to stay married or pursue her career goal to become President.

They both chuckled.

He asked her, "Are you still pursuing your political passions, Estella?"

"More than ever! It's a never-ending battle. Are you still an agent?"

He said, "For now, yes. I love this kind of work."

She suggested, "Maybe we can meet for a drink sometime?"

Michael beamed, "I would like that!"

"You know where to find me; I'm still at the same house and same phone number!"

As she walked away, she felt her heart pounding and her mind filled with possibilities. Estella and Michael after all these years?

Why not?

She had never lost respect for him. Estella always believed that it was circumstances beyond their control that had kept them apart.

Those scenarios no longer existed.

He called her the following night, "How about dinner?"

They met at a quiet Italian place in McClean, Virginia. The food was terrific, the atmosphere was romantic, and their feelings for each other had not dimmed in the least.

Estella and Michael were on again.

"Why did you and your wife divorce, Michael?" she asked him.

"I couldn't live a lie any longer," he confessed. "I was in love with another woman."

Estella was curious, "What was her name?"

"Estella Cyrus," he admitted without reservation.

She gasped: "You got divorced because of me?"

Michael nodded in assent, "Yes, love. Because of you!"

"Does your wife hate me now?"

He shook his head, "I never mentioned your name. I kept the other woman anonymous. I didn't want future complications involving you and us."

"If we get married, don't you think she will figure it out?"

Michael stared at her, "Are we getting married, Estella?"

That question gave her pause, "I don't know, Michael, are we?"

"If I asked you, would you say yes?"

She coyly responded, "I guess you'll have to take that chance, huh?"

He leaned into her and kissed her passionately. When they broke apart, he smiled and said, "Based on your sexy kiss, I like the odds!" He reached into his pocket and pulled out a box inside was a beautiful emerald cut engagement ring.

"Yes, Michael! Yes!" Estella cried out full of joy as they embraced.

Coming Soon:
Memoirs of the Senators Wife II
Excerpts

Lucy's Revenge

"I knew something was up between you and Damien because every time I mentioned his name, you would blush. So, you are going on a trip with Damien, and you'll be back in a few days? Whatever..." Lucy commented, dryly. She was attempting to seem like she didn't care over the phone to Marie while trying to control her inner anger. She hung up the phone with a click but then quickly threw it against the wall. The big rotary phone left a dent in the plaster.

"Ugh! that bitch stole my man," Lucy took a swig directly from the thousand-dollar bottle of champagne she was holding.

"Your man? You mean one of the guys you slept with one time. You know the rules, you can only pick one main guy on campus that is off-limits, and yours is Scott, remember? If you had dibs on all the guys on campus you ever screwed over the past three years, then there would be no good-looking guys for anyone else in our sorority to date," reminded Cathy. Cathy was Lucy's best friend and line sister, who pledged Gamma Alpha the same year, thus making her a "line" sister.

"So, you are going to take her side, bestie? She knew how much I liked him." Lucy tried to win Cathy's agreement so that she could have an ally in the revenge plot was forming in her mind against Marie.

"Marie is my line sister, too, and what is fair is fair. Marie is also your cousin. We have all been friends from summer camp since we were six years old. Give Marie a break." Cathy knew how Lucy's mind worked. Even though she loved Lucy's friendship because she was wild fun and popular, Cathy wanted no part of a vengeance plan against Marie.

An ally and helper in her revenge would be nice. But Lucy didn't care if she had one, she was determined to plan and execute her revenge and get her "man" back. Lucy thought to herself, *"I am going to get that prissy little man thief. She is so dry she'll never be able to keep Damien's interest; he'll probably dump her on the car ride home."*

Circle of Auset's Ceremony to Resurrect the Dead

"Please, Aunt Sharon, please help me with the resurrection ceremony, that Renee told me that you know," cried Estella.

"You will have to do what your grandma and Renee refused, which is to join The Circle of Auset. You need three invitations from members, that will not be a problem since I am not only a member but the bloodline leader. I will get the invitations for you." Sharon explained that as the first granddaughter of the former leader of The Circle, Sharon inherited the leadership of the organization so she could easily help her niece to join.

Estella, hesitant even though in great pain, through her tears, she croaked, "Is there any way that you can give me the details without my joining?"

"No, you must be a member. Once you join, I will go over

348

the ceremony in detail. Don't worry; we are all Christians."

"Yes, I will join," Estella said shakily – but now hopeful.

Xavier Suffers Horribly

When Xavier's soul reached the bowels of hell, it was terrified by Satan's presence. The sense of pure and powerful evil emitted everywhere from him accompanied by a musky odor that Xavier's sensed as burning flesh. There was wailing and shrieking among the never-ending fires that tormented other souls without relief. The burning sensation began to set in on Xavier, and as the oppressive heat grew more intense. He quickly understood the loud gnashing of teeth around him. It was the excruciating pain that all the eternally doomed inhabitants were feeling and what he was soon destined to feel forever.

He begged Lucifer, "Please have mercy on my soul; I cannot survive this!"

The devil laughed and replied in a mocking voice, "You don't have to survive anything, Xavier. You're already dead! However, I can send you back as a junior demon. But we'll talk about that after we have a little fun first."

The pain now intensified with a heat Xavier had never imagined before. And, it was only going to get worse without relief.

The Honeymoon

On a secluded beach on the island of St. John, two lovers

were enjoying each other next to a waterfall. It was a poignant reunion for Michael and Estella as they relived their first passion years earlier. She softly rubbed her body against him, feeling his member rising to the occasion.

She whispered, "I have to make sure we are always together, my Michael. We can't ever waste our waterfall!"

"It is our heartbeat, Estella my wife; a reminder that our love is always present." He relished the words, *my wife*.

With that, she guided his now hard manhood inside her and began moaning. As he entered her they intimately rocked together, in the lotus position, as one.

They were home. Michael and Estella. Finally.

Made in the USA
Coppell, TX
11 February 2020